LEILA:

THE BEGINNING

GW00541590

By

Keith Holroyd

Cover Design by Karen Davies

I dedicate this book

to my two sons

Daniel and Dean,

and to their mother

Patricia Anne.

In Memory

One very sad day in March 2012 we lost one of the Golfin

Crew our friend Johnny 'Malonie' Malone.

The following Crew; Honey Monster, Pete the Fish, Malco

Mick, Eddie, Lonsdale and the Author will always remember

'Malonie' as a dear friend both on and off the Golf Course.

We affectionately remember the day when 'Malonie' was ju

starting his so called Golf Swing, when a well known sound

the countryside came from the adjacent field

"Baa"   "Baa"

This sound 'allegedly' caused 'Malonie' to hit his golf ball in

the very same field.

We will always remember 'Malonie's' now legendary respons

"Those ******* Sheep"

R.I.P 'Malonie'

ABOUT THE AUTHOR

orn in Leeds in 1946, Keith Holroyd remains a very proud Yorkshireman. He has two sons and one granddaughter.

Most of his working life was in Industrial Engineering and Production Management working throughout the United Kingdom.

He also spent 2 years in Zambia, Managing Planned Maintenance in the Copper Mines and 5 years in South Africa, Managing Distribution and Warehousing.

He is a keen sportsman, but describes his participation in tennis, football, bowls and golf as 'mediocre'.
He is now satisfied to be an 'armchair' sports participant, spoiled only by the occasional dally on the golf course.

INTRODUCTION

As this story starts it concerns a small group of friends enjoy
bouts of general 'mickey taking' as they work as a team wit
the Warehouse and Distribution environment.
However, events soon turn nasty, when one of the team beco
involved with a mysterious and beautiful woman, which lead
a violent ending to his life.
Further strange and horrendous murders follow that are baffl
to all, especially the various investigating Police Officers.
These Officers don't seem able to conclude the investigatio
until, unknown to them they are assisted by the existence of
'visiting' force.

The story then changes significantly, when one of the Polic
Officers realises that he has inherited special powers, with
regard to Body Transit and the subsequent Materialisation.
The Officer uses these powers to benefit his Police work, and
occasions, to assist with problems within his personal life.
His main Police activities concern the investigation of a numt
of murders that may involve a group of lesbians, and variou
known criminals that could be involved in child prostitution
His new abilities are paramount in successful conclusions to
most of these investigations. However, can his new abilities
become a problem?

CHAPTER ONE

Gary sat staring at the newspaper advertisement,
"What should I do? Is it really me?" he mused.
"Bollocks" he shouted,
"I'm goner do it"
He read the advert again, scrutinising every word.
Sugar Daddy required by a sexy 22 year old exotic lady, please reply to Box No. 222, Evening News.
"Yes, that young lady is going to have my undivided attention, lucky bugger", he murmured.
Gary rose from the bed and walked across the room glancing at his watch as he walked.
"Good God Look at the time" he exclaimed.
"I'd better get my arse into gear or I'll be late for work again"
"Now where's the bloody envelopes" he muttered, as he sorted through some miscellaneous papers on the table.
"Ah, this will do"
He separated a small white envelope and a partly used writing pad from the mass of papers.
"Pen, pen, come on pen" he shouted, as he looked around the immediate area of the table.
Gary spotted the pen on one of the chairs, where it had obviously just fallen as he had sorted through the papers on the table.
He sat down on his one and only, so called easy chair and started to write;

'Dear Miss Exotic Lady, I would like to respond to your invitation for a Sugar Daddy, rest assured you will be treated like a Perfect Lady, by a Perfect Gentleman'.
'Please reply to telephone number 563896'.
Gary signed the letter and placed it in the envelope.
"There you are the start of another perfect working day" he said to himself.
"Now what's next, shit!"
"It's twenty to six, time to go".
He grabbed the letter, pulled his coat from over the chair and disappeared into the cool autumn night.
Gary works for West's Supermarket as a 'General Dogs Body', or given its technical term Warehouse Supervisor.
He is responsible for the unloading of delivered stock, its movement to the despatch area, and then onto the relevant Supermarket vehicle.
Gary is the leader of a team of four that works permanent nights; 1800 hours to 0600 hours Monday to Friday.
The other team members are;
        Roddy – better known as 'Mansell', drives the Fork lift Truck, the youngest at 21 years, perhaps the worst driver ever, but doesn't know it.
        Billy – also known as 'Bantam', the oldest at 34 years, very fit and cocky, a bit of a comic.
        Stuart – 23 years unsure of himself, a tendency to stutter.
        Last but not least, we have 32 years old Gary, a loner living in a single bedroom flat near to the University.
He thinks that he is 'Gods gift to women' and can't understand why they don't think the same, A bit of a dreamer.

It was just before six that evening when Gary ran into the locker room area.

"Hey Gary, have you seen this"

"Just a minute Roddy, I have to clock in" Gary replied, as he sprinted through the room and down through the warehouse.

He turned the corner close to the loading bays, grabbed his card from one of the racks, and clocked in.

"Bloody Hell, Made it, right on the button" he exclaimed.

The card was replaced in the rack and Gary walked back to the locker room, eager to find out what Roddy was so excited about. Roddy was holding a copy of the Daily Journal against the wall, with half a dozen other guys staring at the main story on the front page.

"What's the big deal?" Gary asked, as he approached the group, "Has Lord Lucan has been found driving a bus on the moon?"

"Did I or did I not, tell you that the Ripper has returned as a woman", crowed Roddy.

He handed the paper to Gary; the headlines were describing the grisly find of the mutilated corpse of a young man, the fourth such find in the last two months!

"Ripper my arse, those poor buggers will have been the work of some sort of Drugs War, if a female ripper was at work, she would have chopped their bollocks off!"

With that earthy statement, Gary folded the paper, returned it to Roddy and walked into the Despatch office.

Stan, the Grocery Manager, handed Gary the shift working schedule and told him not to let Mansell knock hell out of the new racking that had just been erected within the receiving area.

Gary smiled and walked through an adjoining door to the mess room, closing the door behind him.

"How's it Rat Bag" cried out Billy.

"Good to see you managed to prise your hand off your prick to join us today"

"Bantam, you, Stuart and Mansell, start unloading the tinned fruit, before the same hand plays with your head"

"I'm just going to sort out these deliveries and then I'll be along".

Billy mumbled something and left the mess room to locate the other two.

Apart from the usual bout of 'Mickey Taking', they all worked well as a team, in fact, they were looked upon as the best team at the West's Warehouse, but no one was going to say that.

As the shift moved towards a conclusion, they all returned to the mess area.

"What's on for the weekend, 'Rat Bag'?" queried Billy.

"I thought that I would give that new Disco down at the Queens another go, last week I almost made it with that 'Long Legged Christine'" replied Gary.

"Long Legged Christine" chipped in Roddy, "she's a bloody Lesbian!"

He continued,

"If it doesn't take a battery, it won't be poking around in that bird"

"Anyway that's where I'm going, and that young girl will definitely get to play with my 'action pack'" Gary confirmed.

"I d-don't kknow what y-you see in disco's, y-you never ccan hear w-what people are saying, a-and its s-so dark" said Stuart.

"That's the whole point, you stupid pillock"

"Where else do you need to be breathing down their cleavage, in order to communicate, it makes for 'close encounters of the body'" Roddy retorted.

"Fuck off, y-you f-fucking p-prat" said Stuart.

"Leave him alone Mansell" interrupted Gary.

"It's time we weren't here, let's get this place tidied and let's get gone".

He motioned with his hand towards the miscellaneous papers and personal items that were strewn around the mess.

A few choice comments were made, but not too loudly and the instructions were carried out, leaving the room presentable for the next shift.

It was Saturday evening, the football results were on the television and Gary was putting the finishing touches to a cheese and pickle sandwich.

The phone rang.

Gary threw the knife into the sink and picked up the phone.

"Hello, City Morgue!"

The voice on the other end of the line seemed surprised.

"Oh I'm sorry I must have the wrong…."

"It's only my little joke"

"I'm sorry if I startled you" Gary replied.

He had recognised the voice of a woman on the phone.

"You sound full of life, my name is Leila you answered my advertisement, to be my Sugar Daddy"

Gary's heart missed a beat, he could feel his manhood rising, so he tried to compose himself and think of a glib reply.

Eventually his brain clicked into gear, but the mouth didn't connect and the reply suffered accordingly.

"Y-yes" he stuttered.

"Do people call you Gary? Or do you prefer Gareth?" asked Leila.

"Come on, chat the bird" Gary whispered to himself.

He continued talking to himself, stressing.

"Come on Gary, make a bloody impression!"

"Well actually, It's Gareth, yours is a nice name", he replied, rather meekly

"Thank you, I think Leila and Gareth sound good together, don't you?"

By this time Gary had recovered his composure, and started to talk normally.

"We should meet, where would you like to go?" he asked.

"I like eating out, could we meet for a meal? And then, maybe we could get to know each other" pouted Leila.

Gary's manhood started to rise again, causing his imagination to run wild.

He then tried again to 'act the part'.

"I know just the place, a nice little restaurant on the outskirts of town, 'Toni's', the best service and Italian food in the area" he suggested

Although, if the truth was known, he had never been there, it was well outside his pocket.

"That sounds lovely" said Leila.

"That's a date then, where do you want to meet?" asked Gary.

Leila had been decidedly coy on her personal circumstances, and stated that she would leave her car at home and catch the train.

They decided that would meet at the Railway Station at seven that night, and Gary would book a table for half past eight, thus allowing time for a drink on the way to the Restaurant.

As Gary put the receiver down, he started to jump around the room, shouting "'Eureka', 'Eureka, you lucky buggar, you've cracked it"

"You've bloody cracked it!"

He still had a 'silly smirk' on his face as he walked into the bathroom, to prepare for his date.

He finished showering and, clutching a towel, he walked over to the bed.

"Now let's get this body smelling of roses" he muttered.

Standing on a carefully placed mat, he proceeded to smear his torso with 'Mate' body lotion.

With the body well and truly primed, he walked to the wardrobe, where he removed his one and only grey suit, a blue pin striped shirt with a buttoned collar and a navy blue tie.

When dressed, he checked himself in the mirror.

He then placed the mirror onto a chair, and studied himself from another angle.

"Gary, you are ready, 'Ready to Rock and Roll'" he shouted.

He picked up his wallet and checked the contents, slid the wallet into his pocket, picked up his car keys and disappeared into the street.

Gary drove a 1986 Blue Ford Cortina Mark.IV, although not mechanically minded he kept it in prime condition and was proud of the car's appearance.

As Gary approached the Railway Station parking area, he wondered how he should introduce himself.

His first idea was to be the cocky 'lady killer' that he certainly believed he was, but he decided to play along with Leila's request, for a Sugar Daddy and be 'Mr Nice Guy'.

They were to meet opposite the ticket office at the side of the first telephone booth, and as he approached, he rekindled the description she had given him;

I am five feet five inches tall, slimly built with large brown eyes and long black hair. My father's family originate from the Middle East and my mother is English.

This means that I have a slightly 'sun tanned tinge' to my skin, and coupled with a radiant smile, I am sure you will like what you see.

The very thought of Leila's description had the unintended effect between his legs, so much so, that he had to make a concerted effort to redirect his thoughts, as it was becoming increasingly difficult to hide his aroused state from the gathering crowd within the Station complex.

He must have been about fifty metres from the booth, when he realised that she was waiting there.

Could he be dreaming, or was the heavenly nymph at the appointed place, really his Leila?

She waved as he approached Gary just smiled and tried to be cool, although at 'boiling point'!

He greeted her casually.

"Hi, you must be Leila? I'm Gareth, and I am very pleased to meet you".

"Hi Gareth, you look very smart, I hope you like the way I look?" She answered coyly.

His heart started to beat at an incredible rate, and it felt like it would burst from his chest at any moment!
He also felt the momentum almost disappear from his knees, this gave him the impression that they might buckle, at any minute.
But to his credit he kept his cool.
"Leila, you are very beautiful, and I feel honoured to be your date tonight".
He continued.
"Right then, let's get going, I'm parked in the Station car park".
He reached out an arm to direct her towards the car park, when she stopped him and looked into his eyes.
"I hope you don't mind Gareth, but I decided to travel in my own car after all, and as luck would have it, I am also parked in the same area".
"I thought it the best thing to do in the circumstances, I'm sure you understand?"
She put her hands on his shoulders and whispered in a very sexy manner.
"Anyway, I thought that we could get something to eat and go back to your place, it'll be more 'intimate' Gareth"
The Choir started singing 'Jerusalem' in his mind, and he kept thinking "Thanks God", over and over.
He then remembered that he had booked a table at Toni's.
"Oh bugger it" he mused.
'Shock Horror' then took over; he had left his sweaty socks on the bed!
"You bloody idiot Gary" he said to himself, when will you bloody learn to be prepared if she gets a whiff of them, you're a non-starter!

He then cleared his throat and answered her request with a question.

"What would Madam like to drink with her meal?"

"I'm rather partial to Southern Comfort and Babysham, with a sprinkling of Crushed Ice, What's your 'poison' Gareth?" she queried.

"Whatever you desire, I desire, come, let's go to the ball" he cavalierly answered.

They then linked arms and picked their way through the crowd, on their way to the car parking area.

"That's my car, where's yours?" Gary asked.

"Mines over there Gareth, the Blue Beetle, next to the Astra, It looks a little dirty, but it's a lovely car".

For such a 'Divine Bird', she certainly doesn't drive much of a car he thought, as he started to give her some sort of directions.

"We will be heading through the city centre, and then on to the ring road, but don't worry, I'll make sure that you don't lose me".

Gary pulled out of the car park and headed towards his flat. He glanced through his rear mirror on numerous occasions during the journey, often wondering what he would do, if he lost her in the traffic.

"Shoot my bloody Self!" was his conclusion.

They stopped at the Wine Supermarket to buy the Southern Comfort etc. and then to the Pizza Palace, for a 'Deep Pan Southern Quest'.

Once they were parked opposite to Gary's flat, Gary quickly walked ahead; he opened the door to his flat, placed the drinks on the table, waltzed through to the bedroom, and threw the dirty socks out of the window.

Returning to the open flat door, just as Leila appeared from the street!

"Shall we start with a drink?" she purred.

"You make yourself comfortable, while I crush some ice, I'll be with you in a moment" answered Gary.

He closed the door and disappeared into the kitchen area.

Leila started to survey Gary's flat.

It consisted of two rooms, the living quarters that contained a single bed, and the kitchen. Where Gary was making a noise like a 'Love Crazed Tom Cat' that he obviously passed off, as singing.

"Here we are".

Gary returned holding two wine glasses, full to the brim with the drink that Leila had requested, and of course, topped with crushed ice.

"That looks lovely" commented Leila, as she removed her coat, and sat on the edge of the bed.

"Right then, I'll just get a couple of plates for the Pizza, and we can eat before it get's cold".

He then picked up the coat from the bed and put it over the chair arm, on his way to back to the kitchen to fetch the plates.

When he returned, Leila had moved up to the top of the bed, and was making herself comfortable.

Gary noticed that her shoes were off and that she had finished her drink.

"I can see that you enjoyed the drink, would you like another?"
"Yes please Gareth".
Gary set off to replenish her drink, but he was not prepared for what he saw when he returned to the bedroom.
Leila was sat on the bed in an upright pose; Gary could see that her nipples were enticingly exposed through the transparency of the material of her blouse and that she was not wearing a Bra!
Gary just stood there, his mouth slightly open, he felt the glass in his hand starting to shake.
"I can see that you are glad to see me like this Gareth"
Her eyes pointing to his manhood that had become uncontrollable and was climbing up his stomach.
To the point, where it was almost peering out above the waistband of his pants!
"Err yes, I'm glad to see you like that" he muttered.
"Then bring yourself over here, and prove it" Leila ordered.
That was the signal for 'All Hell' to break loose, and Gary was about to prove that above all else, he was Not Valentino.
He rather clumsily gave Leila her drink and fell on her, all in one clumsy movement.
"No silly, take your coat off Gareth, you're a bit over dressed at the moment" she laughed.
Gary realised that he was acting a bit like a 'Bull in a China Shop' and deliberately slowed down his movements, to try and hide the fact that his body was in Overdrive!
He removed his jacket and his shoes and casually returned to the bed.

But Leila was moving too fast for him.

She had bared her breasts and held out her arms, to welcome him to her.

Once in her arms, his control disappeared completely!

He was pulling and tugging at her clothes and getting absolutely nowhere.

Leila calmed him down; she removed Gary's clothes slowly and deliberately, she then invited Gary to remove her clothing in the same manner.

This he did, garment by garment, as she enticingly guided him through the task, thus ensuring that they both enjoyed every moment.

Once they were both completely naked, the lovemaking began and they enjoyed each other's bodies with unrelenting passion.

They kissed and stroked one another with obvious delight, until a very enjoyable and vigorous climax by both, was achieved.

Once spent, they both fell into a deep contented sleep, entwined in each other's arms.

Gary's eyes opened slowly, things were a little blurred, and he blinked and rubbed his eyes until they began to focus.

He scratched between his legs and yawned, he then turned to where Leila lay, but the bed was empty!

He sprang from the bed and looked around the room.

The unopened Pizza was still on the coffee table, the empty wine glasses were still on the bedside table, and his clothes were still laying where they were discarded, but no Leila.

He walked over to the window and looked out, his car was still there, but there was no Beetle.

Did she exist? Or had he been dreaming?

Gary wandered around the flat in the nude talking to himself, trying to unscramble his mind, and trying to come to terms with the past events.

He wandered over to the mirror, and as he checked on his bedraggled reflection, he ran his fingers through his hair.

But something was wrong, Very wrong.

Gary slowly pulled his left hand from his hair, and as he observed the hand he cried out with Horror.

The little finger was missing!

CHAPTER TWO

Gary returned to his bed, and, holding his left wrist with his right hand, he slowly sat on the bed and leaned against the wall. After a while he lifted his left hand closer, so that he could inspect the damage.

The finger was missing from its base, with the skin of the hand neatly welded, as he started to prod the affected area, there was no soreness or pain whatsoever.

He mumbled to himself.

"What the fuck has happened to me?"

Gary then turned his attention to his bed he removed the duvet and checked the mattress and sheet.

He couldn't really believe what he was seeing, as there wasn't any sign of any bleeding.

He returned to his 'so called' kitchen area, where he half filled a cup with cold water, which he drank slowly as he pondered on his next move.

Gary's mind, understandably, was in a state of confusion, he decided to return to his bedroom, where he covered himself with the duvet, closed his eyes and very easily returned into 'sleep mode'.

It was dark when he lifted his head from the bed and walked over to the sink, where he splashed cold water over his face.

He then stretched his limbs, yawned and decided to get dressed. The clothes that were lying on the floor, were straightened and placed in the wardrobe, he slipped into a pair of jeans and a long sleeved jumper.

A glance at his watch confirmed that he had slept all day as it was now ten minutes past seven in the evening.

It wasn't until he started to tie the laces of his shoes that the nightmare of the 'missing finger' resurfaced, causing him to again 'mull' the problem over in his mind.

"I'll leave the Police out of it at the moment, I'll go and seek out the lads at the pub, maybe they will be able to come up with something" he mused.

Gary knew that the Police should be informed, but he needed time to get his head together.

With this in mind, he picked up his car keys from the bedside table, locked the flat door and set off to find Roddy at the pub.

As he entered the Queens Public House, he could hear the chatter of the Disc Jockey above the early evening introductory tunes.

He walked into the saloon bar that was situated to the rear of the pub, adjacent to the car park and the toilets.

The room was tastefully decorated, with the walls littered with framed photographs of the Landlord's past sporting endeavours; namely, an International Rugby Player.

Billy and Roddy were playing pool and they both looked up as Gary approached.

"Well look at this, is it Animal? Mineral? Or Vegetable? No, it's 'Fuckerman'!

Was the expected greeting from Billy.

"Where the hell were you last night?" queried Roddy.

"You were supposed to be coming down here, you wanker" he added.

"Listen Mansell, I never said that I would definitely be here, I just mentioned that I MAY BE" retorted Gary.

"Anyway, forget about it, I've a more pressing problem, let's talk"

Gary motioned to them both to follow him, as he left the room and made his way to the Gents toilet.

Once inside the toilet, Gary lent against the sink opposite the urinals and waited for Billy and Roddy.

He rubbed his left hand and stared at the joint where his little finger used to be.

"O.K Rat Bag, what's the big deal?" queried Billy, as he entered the room.

"Why all the cloak and dagger stuff?"

"Bantam, Mansell, before you say anything else, take a look at this" requested Gary, as he lifted up his left hand, and spread out his fingers.

Roddy was the first to react.

"What the fuck!"

He grabbed hold of Gary's arm and brought the hand closer to his face, he then prodded the area of the missing digit.

"How did you manage it?"

"Where are the stitches?"

Billy also pulled the hand closer.

"What have you been doing?"

"What was her name? Razerpuss!"

Gary pulled his hand from Billy's grasp he took a deep breath, cleared his throat and started to relate the events of the previous evening.

Apart from the occasional visit to the urinals by the other pub customers, the story was told and received without interruption.

Only when Gary explained the total absence of pain or blood, did Roddy respond.

"Bloody incredible, this is bloody incredible, that bloody bird must be a bloody vampire"

"Don't talk a load of bollocks!" snapped Billy.

"Vampire my arse, she's just some kind of bleeding pervert" Billy continued.

"Hey, she may have something to do with those bloody mutilated bodies that have been appearing all over the place?"

"Listen you two never mine about mutilated bloody bodies" interrupted Gary.

"I don't think you have really understood the reality of it all" He started to outline the facts; I spent the night with a woman, who disappears into thin air, I wake up without my fucking finger without any pain, without spilling blood, without a single stitch, without fuck all!"

"Don't talk to me about fucking perverts, or vampires, or even mutilated bodies this woman is more than that, she is bloody MORE than that!"

The arguments continued as they wandered from the toilets and back through into the lounge of the pub.

Here the Disco was beginning to 'warm up' and the air was heavy with anticipation.

Gary was becoming more and more insecure with the situation, and he was beginning to wish that he had gone straight to the Police.

"That's it, that's the bloody answer" exclaimed Billy.

"It's simple, all we have to do is go to the newspaper and find out the address of the bird that you met last night, surely that can't be difficult?"

"Difficult"

"Difficult"

"Are you completely cuckoo?" Gary shouted.

"There is such a thing as integrity, the paper can't band names and addresses about, 'Willy nilly'"

"Get real for Christ's sake" he added.

"Listen you two, cool it, let's have a drink, it's my shout" said Roddy, as he pushed between them on his way to the bar.

They decided to let the subject drop for a while, and try to enjoy peering at the local talent, while downing a few pints of best bitter.

It didn't take too long before their attentions were directed towards the centre of the dance floor where two so called 'prick teasers' were gyrating to the music.

"Come on Gary; let's give those two the works"

"We can sort out the other problem tomorrow" suggested Roddy.

"Yeah, I agree, you two go for it" said Billy,

"I'm not staying much longer, the missus wants an early night, so I had better not get too drunk"

The music, or the drink, or both, must have got to Gary, for he didn't go through his usual routine of circumspection in every detail, before agreeing, he just shrugged his shoulders, and said "OK"

Roddy and to a lesser extent Gary, approached their 'quarry' like a couple of 'inebriated tigers' brushing the other dancers from side to side as if they were just clumps of elephant grass! Roddy was the first to pounce.

"What brings a couple of classy gals like you two, to a place like this?" he asked.

He then continued,

"Don't tell me, you heard that we would be here, No need to say anything, just fall into my arms and let's dance."

Without further ado, he grabbed the nearest of the two women and led her away, in a sort of 'quick step, cum rumba, cum half nelson'!

Gary and the other woman just looked at one another in amazement.

"I'm Gary it appears that your friend has gone missing, so we may as well dance, Shall we?"

Gary held out his hand, the second woman smiled, clasped his hand and they started to 'Bop',

Gary normally 'Bopped', rather badly and this occasion was no exception!

There followed a period of general chatting, her name was Janet and her friends name was Gail.

They usually went to the cinema on a Sunday evening, but they had decided to have a change and so the visit to the Queens.

Gary really went to town in the 'Billy Liar' stakes; he spun the tale, that she first attracted his attention, because of her uncanny resemblance to Bridget Bardot in her younger days.

Whether Janet believed this was irrelevant, she smiled and giggled, just enough, to convince Gary that he had 'cracked it'.

Meanwhile, Roddy had moved at 'twice the speed of sound'.

He had his tongue so far down Gail's throat, that to quote a pun; 'he could wipe her arse'!

The night moved on, and the love birds were getting on famously, and as time progressed, they were all dancing in a foursome with their arms intertwined above their heads as they circled the dance area.

As the last record ended, they all disengaged and sat at a table near to the bar, where the girls had left their coats.

"Shall we go for a curry, or something?" queried Gary.

"Yeah, there's a great one just round the corner from here" said Roddy, very enthusiastically.

"We can have a nightcap at our house, my parents are in Spain and won't be back until next week" said Janet, casually.

In fact she spoke so casually, that Gary began to wonder if nightcaps at her house were a regular event.

"What a great idea"

"We could get some booze from Ken before we leave" stated Roddy, trying desperately to act pleasantly surprised, while he was just, desperate!

They all agreed; the girls went to powder their noses, while Gary and Roddy organised a bottle of Vodka, a bottle of Gin, and a bottle of Tonic Water from the Landlord Ken.

Roddy's eyes opened slowly, the room was in darkness, and he could feel the warmth of the body next to his.

He excitedly moved his hand slowly towards the rather warm buttocks. Moving in slow circular movements, he began to caress the back of the legs and then moved eagerly between them.

"I'll give you two seconds to move"

"You stupid pillock"

"What the fuck" exclaimed Roddy, as he jumped from the bed. Fumbling towards the window, he pulled open the curtains, and gazed at the bed occupant.

Gary's head appeared from under the sheets.

"Fancy a sixty nine?"

"Or will you settle for a hand job?" he said sarcastically.

"This is your flat" countered Roddy".

He then added.

"What the hell are we doing here?"

"What am I doing here?"

"What happened to Janet and Gail? What…."

"For Christ's sake"

"Put a sock in it!"

"Go and make some coffee, make yourself useful, and be quiet, I'm tired and pissed off! Gary interrupted.

"I'm making naff all until you tell me why we are here"

"And why I am sleeping with you?" Roddy asked.

"You are sleeping with me, in my flat"

"Because you are a wanker of the first order, that's why"

"You really excelled yourself last night, you really did, shall I tell you, you useless twat!"

"What you did"

Roddy tried to interrupt, but Gary was at full speed ahead, and he waved his protests aside as he continued.

"Not only did you drink half a bottle of vodka in the car, but you lost the rest, when you dropped the bottle outside poor Janet's house!"

"Not only did you wake up half the neighbourhood, swearing and pissing on her doorstep"

"Not only were you utterly and hopelessly drunk"

"But to cap it all"

"Yes to cap it all"

"You were sick"

"And I MEAN SICK!"

"Covering the poor bloody cat from head to toe"

"Needless to say, we were told to piss off!"

"Now go and make the coffee, before I remember that you lost me a good shag last night"

A few more choice words were exchanged, before Roddy left the room to carry out the assigned task, as he was by now, feeling a bit like a 'pillock' for spoiling the night.

As soon as Roddy disappeared through the doorway, Gary sprang from the bed and began to sort through his loose change, and more importantly, the remaining contents within the pockets of his jeans.

He eventually sorted out a small piece of paper and placed it under the mattress.

"What are we doing today then?" Roddy queried, as he returned, carrying a couple of mugs containing a liquid, which could only loosely be termed 'black and wet'.

"I have to spend some time working on the car" replied Gary. He then added.

"Roddy, I've been thinking, why don't you go down to the Newspaper Offices, and see if you can find out something about that bird that pinched my finger"

"Really, and what did your last slave die of?"

"I may have been drunk last night, but I seem to remember that you said going to the newspaper was a waste of fucking time".

"Yes, I did think that last night, but as I just said, I've been thinking again about it, and with your direct charm, you could just find out something" said Gary, trying desperately to sound convincing.

They both then drank the 'Black and Wet Liquid' in silence, before Roddy stood up, stating.

"Well, there's no point wasting time in this bloody Morgue!"

He got dressed, picked up his crumpled coat from the chair, and as he gave it a quick brush with his hand, he then turned to Gary as he opened the door.

"Right, 'shit face' I'll see you at work tonight, see if you can be on time, you never know, I may have some information for you"

"I'll be there, I really appreciate your help Mansell I really do".

The door closed, and Gary watched through the window as Roddy strode off.

Gary continued to peer from the window until Roddy rounded the corner of the street and out of sight.

He then dived on to the bed and reached under the mattress, pulling out the piece of paper that he had placed there a few minutes earlier.

He picked up the phone and dialled the number contained on the paper.

It rang a couple of times.

"Hello, 983956" was the answer.

"Hello, this is Gary, is that Janet?"

"Oh hello Gary, this is Gail, Janet's in the bath, are you still coming round today?"

"Sure, I'll be there directly, unfortunately Roddy can't make it, he's had to go into work".

"That's a pity, but never mind, I'm sure we can still enjoy ourselves", said Gail invitingly.

The truth of the matter was simple; Roddy had not acted foolishly by pissing on the doorstep and spilling the contents of his stomach on the cat!

He hadn't even set foot on Janet's doorstep.

What he did achieve, was to become very drunk, and fall asleep on the back seat of Gary's car.

When they arrived at Janet's house, her brother was unexpectedly at home, and the party had been put on hold.

Gary took a very selfish attitude to the situation, and he had decided to 'fill his boots' so to speak, or as he put it 'shagging two birds are better than shagging just the one'.

Gary stared at himself in the mirror, and muttered.

"You handsome bastard"

"You bloody handsome bastard"

Smiling to himself, he continued to get dressed, making a special effort to ensure that his body was well scented and prepared.

He then searched the cutlery drawer in the kitchen.

"Ah, there you are, I knew you would come in handy one day"

He picked the small packet from amongst the cutlery and read
the literature.
'Erotically ribbed condoms, Banana flavour'.

When Gary pressed the doorbell, he was full of the 'Joys of
Spring', so as he waited for the reply from inside the house, he
used the delay to straighten his tie and to check out his posture
after all, he had to look the part.
"Coming, coming" said Janet as she approached the door.
Once she opened the door, Gary could see that her hair was still
slightly damp and she was dressed in a pale yellow dressing
gown.
"Hello again, sorry to hear about Roddy, but I'm glad that you
could make it Gary"
"You look absolutely fantastic" was Gary's 'over the top' reply.
They entered the house and Janet closed the door.
She reached forward to kiss Gary on the cheek and Gary's
reaction was swift and decisive.
His arms encircled her waist and he pulled her body firmly
against his.
Although a little startled, Janet did not pull away, in fact she
welcomed the contact and moved her body even closer to
Gary's.
With their lips totally engaged they kissed passionately, Gary's
hands started at her bottom and worked their way up along her
body, which he fondled tenderly.
Her dressing gown fell to the floor and this was the signal for
Janet to lead him up the stairs and through to the bedroom,
where they kissed again as she undressed him, and when Gary
was also naked, they fell on to the bed.

"So Janet, you won't need this dressing gown?"

Was the sarcastic comment from Gail as she walked into the bedroom, having picked up the discarded garment from the floor adjacent to the front door entrance area.

Gail then allowed the towel that she had wrapped around her own damp body, to drop to the floor, and she too joined in the activities.

Gary Had Found Heaven!

As Gary was driving back to his abode, he couldn't help but smile to himself as he remembered the very pleasurable activities he had just experienced with Janet and Gail.

He parked his car in the parking space opposite his flat, he then locked the car door and walked across the street to the flat, it was dark and the rain was falling steadily.

Gary whistled, very badly, and although completely knackered, he almost floated, his feet hardly touching the ground.

When experiencing such a state of euphoria, it was hardly surprising, that Gary didn't notice the movement from behind.

All he heard was a slight hissing sound, as he first felt the razor sharp tongue coiling around his neck.

Unfortunately for Gary, he didn't get the chance to lift his hands, there was a sickening cracking of bone and sinew, as his head was viciously, but efficiently, removed from the rest of his body!

His torso fell to the ground, with his legs kicking wildly, and the blood pumping from the neck area of his dying torso.

Something moved silently and quickly from the scene, treasuring its grisly prize.

CHAPTER THREE

The coffee soaked biscuit fell from his opened mouth and stained the blue striped tie, as it passed on its way into a gooey heap on the desk.

"Oh bollocks" shouted Detective Inspector Preece, as he quickly wiped his tie, hoping that this swift action would avoid a stain.

He then wiped the biscuit mess from his desk and threw it to the waste bin, just as his phone rang.

He continued to wipe the partly stained tie with his handkerchief and picked up the receiver.

"Detective Inspector Preece"

"Yes, yes, Oh God"

"Not another one"

"Give me the address, right, same procedure 'under cover' I'll be there in five minutes".

The term 'under cover' was instigated by the Detective Inspector, to cover up the fact that the recent mutilated murders were in fact 'Headless'!

This fact was something that the Police, at this stage of the investigation, did not want the general public to know about.

The significant part of 'under cover' was that all the victims were single, and this meant that the Police had less pressure put on them to inform their immediate families.

In fact, all of the bodies were still in the control of the Police at the Station Morgue, with the official line being;

The victims have not been identified!

Sergeant Mick Cooney was talking to a group of onlookers, as Jim Preece's car pulled up.

"Right Sergeant, where's the new club member?" was Preece's tainted comment.

"He's over here Inspector" replied the Sergeant.

They walked towards the covered body at the opposite side of the street.

"Has the body the same problem with the left hand?" Preece queried.

"Exactly Inspector, it's the same 'dicko' no doubt about it" confirmed Cooney.

Preece then pulled the sheet to one side in order to inspect the victim.

"Shine your torch Sergeant".

He surveyed the torso, paying particular attention to the missing finger of the left hand, and the clean and clinical severance of the head.

"Any witnesses?"

"Not a one Inspector, not a bloody sound was heard by anyone". Cooney replied.

"How does the prat do it Sergeant?

How does he cut off some poor sods head, so quietly and so bloody cleanly?"

"I don't know Inspector, but there's something bloody strange with these cases, that's for sure".

Preece replaced the sheet and stroked the back of his neck with his hand

"What's the poor sods name?" he asked.

"Gary Sinclair, he lives at number seven" Confirmed Cooney.

As he pointed to Gary's flat, not more than twenty metres away.

"Have you looked inside yet?" asked Preece.

"No Inspector, we're waiting for the landlord to arrive, apparently, similar to the other victims, Gary was a single lad, living alone".

"Sod that" stressed Preece.

"Get one of the uniformed guys and force the door".

Sergeant Cooney shouted to PC Walker and they both set off in the direction of Gary's flat to carry out the Detective Inspector's request.

When Sergeant Cooney and PC Walker arrived at the flat door, they noticed that a side window had been left open.

"Right PC Walker, get yourself through the window and let me in we might as well save the council a bill for a new door".

After conducting a thorough search, they left the premises no wiser, and returned to the murder scene.

Detective Inspector Preece had been talking to Forensics and to some of the neighbours, but without any worthwhile information forthcoming.

So he was feeling a little 'cheesed off' when Sergeant Cooney walked up.

"Well we have searched the flat Inspector, but unfortunately nothing seems to be out of place, so the search has proved fruitless" said Cooney.

"Right then Sergeant, continue with the neighbours, and stress the importance of any strangers seen in the street recently, in particular, anyone seen with the victim. I'll see you back at the Station tomorrow, it looks like we need to have a rethink concerning this bloody business"

After that remark, the Inspector returned to his car and sped from the scene.

Detective Inspector Preece opened the door of his office and threw the morning paper on his desk. He placed his overcoat on the stand in the corner and then sat down at his desk.

As he closed his eyes and leant back in his chair, his thoughts returned to the recent headless victim.

Detective Inspector Preece was known as a no 'nonsense copper', although he was well liked by his fellow officers, they all would agree that he could be a 'little bossy'.

After a couple of minutes, there was a knock on the door and Sergeant Cooney walked in.

"Morning Inspector"

Preece mumbled a reply and opened his eyes, he gave them a quick rub jumped off the chair and motioned to Cooney to follow him to the 'case board' that was on the wall behind his desk, asking the Sergeant.

"What did you find out regarding our latest victim"?

"Sod all" was the terse reply,"

"It's like all the others, not a bloody thing"

"Right Sergeant, update the board and let's get to grips with this enquiry"

Sergeant Cooney added the information regarding the murder of Gary to the case board and stood back next to the Detective Inspector as they both began to check the information.

Preece picked up the marker pen and started to write the facts of each case.

"Right then Sergeant, last night was the fifth murder within the last five weeks. Right"

"Right" answered Cooney.

"All the bloody victims were single blokes, Right"

"Right" answered Cooney.

"All were murdered by the removal of their heads, Right"
"Right" answered Cooney.
"All had the little finger of their left hand missing, Right"
"Right" answered Cooney.
"Stop saying bloody 'Right'" Preece shouted.
"Right, Err, I Mean, Right, No, Right!
Sorry Inspector" Stuttered Cooney.
The Detective Inspector's phone rang.
Just in time to stop Preece from ramming the marker pen where
the sun don't shine, thought Cooney.
Preece answered the phone.
"Yes, Detective Inspector Preece"
"Who? Where? OK".
Preece turned to Cooney.
"We have some guys in Reception, who may have some
information, go and get them Sergeant"
Cooney left the office, Preece sat in his chair with the marker
pen in his mouth, still pondering on the information contained
on the case board.
There was a knock on the door and Sergeant Cooney entered
with Roddy, Stuart and Billy.
"Grab a seat chaps, Oh, we only have two, well one of you lot
will have to stand"
Preece then waited patiently while they all played a game of
pass the parcel with the chairs.
"Come on, sit down, we don't have all bloody day" demanded
Sergeant Cooney.
They all eventually settled, with Billy and Roddy seated and
Stuart standing, Cooney was stood next to the Detective
Inspector, leaning against the wall behind the desk.

Roddy spoke first.

"We all work at West's Supermarket Warehouse with Gary".

"Used to" interrupted Billy.

"Yeah" continued Roddy.

"Anyway, we were out with Gary the other night"

"Which night?" asked Cooney.

"Sunday night" answered Roddy.

"N-not M-me" muttered Stuart.

"Keep bleeding quiet" Billy shouted to Stuart.

"Right lads, stop bloody pissing about and let's get to grips with what you all bloody know" the Detective Inspector growled.

"Roddy, would you like to continue" said Cooney, as he motioned with both hands.

Roddy continued and repeated the story that Gary had relayed to him and Billy in the Queens.

He expanded it further, outlining his visit to the Newspaper Offices and the subsequent non-compliance with his request for the address of the main subject, Leila.

"Just a minute" interrupted Preece.

"Are you seriously trying to say that this 'Leila' is a serial killer?"

Billy answered as only Billy could.

"There is definitely something bleeding queer about the bird, don't you think?"

"She was the last one to see Gary before he lost his fucking finger!"

"Calm down lad" Cooney interrupted.

"Y-yeah, C-calm down S-silly B-bloody Billy" retorted Stuart.

The Detective Inspector decided that the interview period with Gary's mates had run its course, so he decided to bring an end to the proceedings.

"Right lads, like all the information that we gather on this matter, we will have to check out your story".

He continued.

"The Sergeant and I will check out what you all have just said, and we will be in touch".

"Give your addresses to the Sergeant on the front desk and thanks for coming".

With this statement he motioned to Sergeant Cooney to usher them out of his office and sat back in his chair, a worried frown upon his face.

Sergeant Cooney left the office with Gary's mates on his way to the Station Reception.

When Sergeant Cooney returned to the office, he had a real silly smirk, cum smile on his face.

"What's the bloody joke? Sergeant" said Preece.

"Well what a load of bollocks that was".

This caused the Detective Inspector to forcefully spell out the Sergeants next move.

"Bollocks it maybe, but you are going to the bloody evening news and you WILL get the address of this Leila bird, and you WILL eliminate her from our bloody enquiries, WON'T YOU" Shouted Preece as he started to manipulate the marker pen menacingly.

"Yes Inspector, I'll go straight away Inspector, you'll have the answer tomorrow". And with that comment Sergeant Cooney left the office before the marker pen found its 'intended target'.

Detective Inspector Preece had just had a nice warm bath and he intended to have a nice quiet and relaxing night, to this end, he had just poured a glass of his favourite wine, Tempranillo Valencia, when the phone rang.

"Yes, it had better be good, what? What!"

"Bleeding Hell"

"Right, first thing tomorrow, no wait, go to the Station and get all the CCTV tapes from the area where Gary and this 'Leila bird' first met".

"My office 0700 hours tomorrow" shouted Detective Inspector Preece, as he slammed down the phone.

Sergeant Cooney had just informed Preece that the 'Leila bird' had paid the newspaper in cash at the Evening News Offices and furthermore, a check on the address she gave to the newspaper, showed it was false!

As arranged, the Sergeant and Preece met in the Detective Inspectors office at 0700 hours and the conversation went as follows:

Preece: "Did the newspaper have any idea of the names of the 'Tossers' that replied to the adverts?"

Cooney: "No Inspector, Helen said that the newspaper likes to stay neutral in these matters".

"Helen, who the 'bollocks' is Helen?" Preece retorted.

"Sorry Inspector, Helen is the girl who controls the 'Find your ideal partner' section of the newspaper" replied Cooney.

"Right Sergeant, we need to take control of this situation, we need to lead and not be led, I have just had a Bloody Great idea Sergeant and it gives you the chance to be a Bloody Hero, take a look at the 'case board'".

Preece motioned to Cooney to follow him to the board and pointed out the salient facts

"All the buggers were single, they were all male, and they were all looking for a good shag!"

"Doe's that remind you of anybody Sergeant?"

"No, not really" answered Cooney.

"It's you!"

"You, you tosser" countered Preece.

"It fits you like a Bloody Glove" he suggested.

"Come on Inspector, I get stuck into loads of lucky ladies" Cooney meekly replied.

"Loads of LUCKY LADIES my arse"

"Now this is what we, sorry, what you Sergeant are going to do".

The Detective Inspector outlined the spur of the moment plan he had devised;

They needed to get Sergeant Cooney to answer the advertisement for a 'Sugar Daddy' and to meet this 'Leila bird'. For his part, the Detective Inspector would arrange through the Technical Section, to have Cooney's flat fully fitted with the appropriate cameras etc.

Once Cooney had enticed the bird into the flat, all the information required would be collected to catch the 'bugger'.

"What do you think of that" asked Preece

"Do I get to shag the bird? And could I shag *off* camera?" asked Cooney politely.

"How the fuck can you? We are collecting information on a bloody murder enquiry you shit" retorted Preece.

The Detective Inspector continued.

"Now, I'll get your place sorted, you reply to the advert".

With this statement Preece picked up the newspaper, threw it on the desk and left the office.

Cooney picked up the newspaper and sifted through the pages until he found the 'Find your ideal partner' section.

Much to his delight, the advert for a 'Sugar Daddy' still appeared in the section, so he made a note of the contact telephone number.

After a slight hesitation while he cleared his throat, Sergeant Cooney picked up the phone and rang the number.

"Oh hello, this is Cooney, Err, No, this is your Suuggaar Daaddie"

"You sound like a real dishy bird. Err, I mean, a real dishy lady, my name is Maurice, we need to meet, here's my number".

Cooney relayed his phone number into the message and replaced the phone to the desk.

"This bird doesn't know how lucky she is going to be" he mused.

The phone rang.

"Detective Inspector Preece's office"

"What!"

"No he's not here, yes I will tell him, don't worry we will be there directly".

Cooney replaced the phone and stared out of the window.

"What the Fucks Going On" he shouted.

"The Fucking Bird has struck Again!"

CHAPTER FOUR

Sergeant Cooney phoned Detective Inspector Preece, who was on his way to the Sergeants flat, and informed him of the phone message he had just received.

"Oh Bollocks" was the Detective Inspectors initial response.

He then thought for a moment and continued.

"Right Sergeant, give me the address"

Sergeant Cooney relayed the address to Preece, and they agreed that they should meet at the murder scene.

Detective Inspector Preece was stood over the body talking to a member of the Forensics' team, as Sergeant Cooney arrived. The Sergeant parked his car and approached the Detective Inspector at the scene.

"What do you think Inspector?"

"It's a bloody nightmare Sergeant" was the reply from Preece.

"It's like all the others, but funnily, I seem to recognise those bloody socks"

Sergeant Cooney took a closer look at the headless body and in particular the socks as pointed out by the Detective Inspector.

"It sounds silly, but I agree with you Inspector, they could be of the same silly pattern, that was worn by one of the 'dick heads', that came to see us the other day when that Gary was a victim" confirmed Cooney.

"You're right Sergeant go and see the stupid buggers at that bloody West's Warehouse, I'll get the identity of this poor sod and I'll see you back at the Station"

"OK Inspector" said Cooney.

Sergeant Cooney headed to his car, leaving the Detective Inspector to continue talking to Forensics and the guy that had found the body.

At this moment within the investigation, Detective Inspector Preece was concerned that he was losing control of the case; consequently, he was desperate for someone to come forward with any kind of information that would ease his heart-felt vulnerability.

When Detective Inspector Preece returned to his office, he closed the door and he sat at his desk. After a few quiet moments, he started to swear out loud.

"You are a fucking plonker Preece, You are a plonker" he shouted.

"Why the fuck did you not see this coming, you stupid prat!"

There was a knock on the door.

"Yes, get lost!"

"Excuse me Detective Inspector, but Sergeant Cooney has been trying to get in touch" was the reply.

"Oh bollocks" muttered Preece.

"OK, I'll sort it" he countered, "Thanks for the information" he said, without even taking the trouble to see who was on the other side of the door.

Detective Inspector Preece had left his mobile at his home and, with his handling of the so called 'Leila murders' was feeling a little inadequate.

He picked up the phone.

"Sergeant, where the fuck, are you?"

Cooney answered.

"I am at West's Supermarket Warehouse, where you sent me Inspector".

The Detective Inspector's mind was in such turmoil, that he had totally forgotten his last instruction to the Sergeant.

"So, what's the deal" asked Preece.

"This is the bloody deal Inspector, the dick head with the 'crazy socks' has gone missing, and what is more, the other two dicks say that he was going to try to contact that Leila bird"

"He made contact alright" stated Preece, he then continued.

"Stay where you are Sergeant, keep hold of the two 'dick heads', I'm coming over".

"O.K Inspector I'll see you soon"

Detective Inspector Preece left the Station on his way to West's Supermarket Warehouse, still muttering to himself.

"What a fucking plonker you are, you so called Detective Inspector"

Detective Inspector Preece arrived at West's Warehouse, having decided during the journey, to try and get to grips with the situation, especially with the 'dick heads' he was there to meet. Once in Reception he was directed to the conference room by the receptionist, where Sergeant Cooney, Billy and Stuart were waiting.

As he entered the room, he was just in time to encounter an argument between Billy and Stuart.

"Y-y-you F-fucking W-wanker" blurted Stuart, "Y-you f-fucking k-knew he was g-going"

"I told him not to do it, you stuttering idiot" retorted Billy.

"OK, be quiet" said Sergeant Cooney as he intervened.

"Both of you sit down, the Inspector needs to talk to both of you"

"Right lads, settle down, we need to talk" insisted Detective Inspector Preece.

"WE need to TALK" he repeated, in a more pronounced tone.

"It sounds silly to tell you this, because I fear that you both have your suspicions, but the latest victim, yes, the latest victim, was a Mr Roddick Temple, your workmate, I'm very sorry to say".

Billy jumped up and Stuart simultaneously smacked him on the jaw with a left hook that Henry Cooper would have been proud of!

Cooney grabbed Stuart and threw him to the floor, he helped Billy to his feet and, turning to Stuart, he told him to sit down or he would spend a night in the cells.

"Right, we will all spend a night in the cells, if we act like this" shouted Preece.

"Billy, did you know that Roddy was trying to contact Leila" he asked.

"I said that I would do it" answered Billy, his voice almost at breaking point.

"So, what happened?" asked Cooney.

"He said that he should do it, because he was single"

"Y-you d-didn't t-take m-much c-convincing, d-did y-you", said Stuart.

"Keep quiet Stuart, let's try and be positive" countered Preece. He then continued with the questioning.

"Did you not think to go with him, or even try to follow him?"

"I did follow him, but he left his car on the Bus Station car park and he got into her car".

"I tried to follow, but I lost them in the traffic, and when I eventually got to Mansell's flat, he wasn't there, I waited, but he never came back, I waited for two hours, but he never came back!" Billy answered, as tears started to flow.

Preece beckoned to Cooney.

They stood in the corner of the room and whispered to one another.

Preece stated:

"Roddy was found outside his flat right"

"Right" said Cooney,

"His car was parked outside the flat, right"

"Right" said Cooney.

"So we have to assume that he was alive when he left this Leila bird, because he obviously drove his car back to his flat, right".

"Right" said Cooney.

Preece turned to Billy and Stuart.

"O.K lads, I'm sorry that we should meet again under these circumstances, but I have to be very clear;

UNDER NO CIRCUMSTANCES DO YOU TWO TRY TO CONTACT THIS LEILA, JUST GO HOME AND LET COONEY AND ME SORT THINGS, RIGHT?"

Billy and Stuart nodded their heads in unison.

"Right, Sergeant, make sure our two gents are returned to their department, I'm going for a piss!

And then to the Station, I'll see you there Sergeant".

With that rather curt remark, the Detective Inspector left the room.

When Detective Inspector Preece arrived back in his office, he sat back in his chair, and again started to re-evaluate the situation in his mind.

He picked up his mobile phone.

"Sergeant Cooney, where are you?"

"I'm half way to the office Inspector" was the reply.

"Well go to your flat and I'll meet you there" Preece instructed.

"OK Inspector" replied Cooney.

With that, the Detective Inspector left the office and headed for Sergeant Cooney's flat.

Preece walked from room to room in Cooney's flat, with the Sergeant walking respectfully behind him.

"Did you respond to the advert?" asked Preece.

"Yes Inspector"

"I hope you tried to impress in your reply" said Preece sarcastically.

"I always impress the ladies Inspector" countered Cooney.

The Detective Inspector then beckoned Sergeant Cooney to sit beside him on the single bed, as he had finished with his visual inspection of the room.

He then suggested that the Sergeant should also survey the bedroom; One single bed, one rather old fashioned wardrobe, one modern chest of drawers and one chair.

"Not exactly the bloody Ritz" commented Preece.

"No Inspector, but it performs the function" was Cooney's smug reply.

"How many birds have you…..Never mind"

"How do you think we should play this Sergeant?"

"You're in charge Inspector, how do you intend to proceed?" asked Cooney.

The Detective Inspector answered the Sergeant with a question, obviously unsure of the direction of the investigation.

"Do you think we are in with a chance of nailing this 'Leila bird', if in fact, it is her, and her alone, that is involved with these murders?"

"Well Inspector, if I can get the lady into this place, we need to make it like 'Fort Knox', before I also lose my bollocks" answered a slightly perturbed Sergeant Cooney.

"You'll lose your finger, and then your bloody head Sergeant with this bird it appears that your bollocks are safe!" Preece joked.

"Ha Ha, but how do we get the evidence, or any evidence, before she chops off the mentioned body parts?" asked Cooney.

"Fucked if I know" answered Preece with unusual honesty.

The Detective Inspector then walked to the window and looked out into the street.

The bedroom overlooked a well-lit main road, all the parking and the entrances to the flats were to the rear of the building.

"You will obviously park at the rear, where there's no lighting, apart from the single light above your door" Preece stated

"We will have to get a good camera angle of her entry to the flat with you Sergeant Cooney".

"Make sure you get her looking in the direction of the camera and hold hands, the camera must get both of you"

"Both of you" he stressed.

"Easy Inspector" countered Sergeant Cooney.

"Nothing in this investigation is bloody easy" Preece stressed.

"I'll get the Tech Guys to position four cameras in this bedroom we must make sure that nothing is missed, especially the decanting of your bollocks" he joked.

"Very funny Inspector" was Cooney's uneasy reply.

Detective Inspector Preece then grabbed the Sergeant by the elbow and led him to the flat entrance.

"Let's go over the plan again" he said,

They walked through the flat door to the parking area outside.

The Detective Inspector then continued with the devised plan.

"You both get out of the car; you grab her by the hand and lead her to the flat door, making sure that she his facing the camera that will be located there". Pointing to the proposed camera location

"You both enter the flat and close the door behind you"

"DO NOT LOCK THE BLOODY DOOR, whatever you do, get to the bedroom as quickly as possible".

"Inspector" Cooney interrupted.

"I have entertained a lady before and I have no intension of hanging around making bloody tea"

"Yes Sergeant, but remember, if you want to stay alive, concentrate on the matter in hand and forget about her bloody body! You are in this to catch a bloody murderer, not to arse around"

They then discussed the basic plot:

Cooney was to enter the flat, the camera would photograph both on entry, and the flat door would be closed but not locked.

The back-up team would be hidden close to the flat parking area and they would be in possession of a duplicate of the door key, just in case.

Cooney would entice the lady into the bedroom as soon as possible and……..

That's where the plan stopped!

As they both agreed, they did not know what to expect, they hoped that she would try to cut off his finger in some way and not his head!

The Detective Inspector concluded

"Right Sergeant, are we clear on what's required?"

"Yes sir. Clear as mud" was the answer.

"OK then, the beers are on me".

And with the Detective Inspector's last remark, they left the flat and headed for the nearest pub.

THREE DAYS PASSED

Thursday night, Sergeant Cooney was opening the door to his flat, when he heard the phone ringing.

He rushed to pick up the receiver

"Hello"

"Hello, are you my Sugar Daddy?" was the sexy reply.

"Y-yer err" Cooney's voice had deserted him.

"Y-yes yes this is he. Are you my dishy lady?" he eventually replied, trying to sound like a real 'cool dude'.

"Yes, this is Leila you sound like my kind of man".

"It's Leila, its fucking Leila!" Cooney muttered to himself.

He kept repeating this to himself, as he started to shake.

Cooney had lost his line of thought for a moment, as he continued to talk to himself.

He resorted to a swift 'smack' to the side of his face, as he tried desperately to concentrate his mind and to regain his composure.

"Leila is a very nice name, where have you been all of my life" he answered.

Cooney was now in control, well almost.

"That would be telling" replied Leila.

"We need to meet, I'm a great cook, we could meet for a drink and I will cook us both a meal to die for" he requested.

Hoping that she would not take this remark, too much to heart!

"That sounds nice, I'm available on Saturday, is that OK with you?" asked Leila.

"Saturday's fine with me Leila"

"What is your favourite food and what do you like to drink when you are eating?" asked Cooney.

"I'm rather partial to Partridge, and I absolutely love Champagne" was Leila's answer.

Cooney almost dropped the phone.

"She wants Partridge and Champagne! Does she think I'm a bloody millionaire?" he mused.

"I always like to please a lady, you shall have the food and drink you have requested" was Cooney's reply, hoping that M&S would be able to accommodate her wishes.

Sergeant Cooney informed Leila of his address with specific instructions on the best route to the flat.

"Are you clear on those directions?" he asked.

Leila didn't seem to be listening she just asked

"Shall we go for a drink before we eat?"

"If that's your wish my Dishy Lady, then that's what we shall do" answered Cooney, as he tried to think of somewhere cheap. He then realised that he knew just the place.

"We can go to the Golden Cock Public House, it's not too far from the Bus Station, and we can meet there"

Leila agreed to Cooney's proposal. She was less than enthusiastic, but she did agree, and they set the meeting time for 1830 hours.
She then rather abruptly ended the conversation, saying.
"That's OK I'll see you Saturday, Maurice".

CHAPTER FIVE

It was Friday morning, just after seven thirty, when Sergeant Cooney knocked on the Detective Inspector's door and entered the office.

"Morning Inspector" he said joyfully.

Detective Inspector Preece looked up from his position at his desk.

"What makes you so bloody happy? Wipe that stupid grin from your face it makes me want to be sick"

"Happy, happy, I'm shagging tomorrow Inspector, I'm shagging tomorrow" joked the Sergeant.

Detective Inspector Preece quickly stood up.

"The bloody bird has called! What did you say? What did you say?" he queried impatiently.

"I gave her the old Cooney charm and she agreed to meet me tomorrow, that's all" was Cooney's triumphant answer.

The Sergeant then struck a more serious note.

"However, I'll need an advance on my expenses Inspector she's a very expensive bird"

Detective Inspector Preece paced around the room with his hands tucked into his pockets.

He turned to the Sergeant and answered in a cautionary manner.

"Right, we have to be very careful, very careful Sergeant, very careful".

He then asked

"What time are you meeting tomorrow?"

"What about the money advance Inspector?" Cooney reiterated.

"Never mind the bloody money Sergeant, I'll sort it, now, what bloody time are you meeting?"

"We were to meet at my flat, but we decided to have a drink first, so we are meeting at the Bus Station kiosk at 1830 hours"

"From there we are going to the Golden Cock for a drink and then to my flat...."

Preece interrupted

"Golden Cock eh, well that won't be you! Do you understand?"

"Yes Inspector, I totally understand, but don't stop me from dreaming." Cooney pleaded.

"As long as it remains a dream Sergeant, dream on"

Preece continued

"I will arrange for Ted Draper, Head of Forensics, and his boys to be at your flat at 0800 hours on Saturday morning to install the cameras. Don't sleep in Sergeant, or it'll be me doing the shagging, now where is this Golden Cock?"

"It's just off the main street in High Town, King Lane Inspector"

"Right, I'll get a couple of uniforms to go there for a drink".

"Just to keep an eye open, you never know" Preece stated cautiously.

The phone rang and Preece walked over to his desk and picked up the receiver.

"Hello, Detective Inspector Preece"

"Yes Mr Bantam, err, sorry, Billy, what can I do for you?"

Billy asked the Detective Inspector if he had made any progress regarding the investigation and Preece told him that he may have some more news for him after the weekend.

Then Billy said that he had been making some enquiries himself, and he also may have some more news after the weekend.

This comment didn't go well with the Detective Inspector and he shouted down the phone

"Don't you do anything on your own Mr Bantam, err bloody hell, Billy, anyway, what are these enquiries?"

The Detective Inspector suddenly changed this question to a more forceful instruction.

"Forget what I just said, just stay out of it leave it to the Police, DO YOU UNDERSTAND!"

Billy answered "You got it Detective Inspector, sorry"

Billy put down the phone and muttered,

"I'll show that dick!"

Preece put down the receiver and turning to Sergeant Cooney stressed.

"This investigation has to be handled very carefully, we are entering a difficult phase and it could easily go 'tits up' if we're not very careful, we have to keep people like this Billy 'Bantam Guy', well away from any involvement"

Back at West's Warehouse.

Billy replaced the phone and walked back to the loading bay where Stuart was completing the paperwork for the trailer that they had just unloaded.

"That 'toss pot' Detective Inspector and his 'prick' of a Sergeant are getting nowhere regarding this Leila bird"

"B-bantam, w-what do y-you expect th-them to do?" was Stuart's quizzical answer.

"More than they are doing, pissing about in the bloody Police Station"

He then stated.

"Come here Stuart baby I have a plan".

Billy beckoned Stuart to join him in the off-loading bay office. They both then sat down at the office desk and Billy started to lay out his plan, to a totally startled Stuart.

"I have already contacted this 'Leila tart' I answered the advert, just like Gary".

"The D-detective Inspector t-told you n-not to, y-you w-wanker" retorted Stuart.

"Be quiet tosser and listen"

Billy then told Stuart how he had answered the advert and the Leila bird had rung him.

They decided to meet near the Abbey at noon on Saturday and they would go for a light lunch at Leila's apartment at the side of the river, adjacent to the Abbey.

"B-Bantam, you c-can't, you c-can't" Stuart shouted.

"Will you shut your fucking mouth and listen" Billy insisted. And then he continued.

"You are going to be my bodyguard, you are going to follow us to her apartment and help me conduct a citizen's arrest."

"A-a citizens' arrest, A-a c-citizens' arrest, y-you are f-fucking d-daft, y-you're lliving in f-fucking c-cuckoo land"

"Why? How else are we going to avenge Gary's death, you prick, we have to do something" insisted Billy.

He then continued with his plan.

"Look",

He pulled a set of handcuffs from his jacket pocket.

"You will have these! And at the appropriate moment, you will cuff the bloody bird and 'Bob's your Auntie' we've got the bitch"

After this statement, there followed a heated debate regarding the pros and cons of such a plan, with the uneasy conclusion that it could work.

Or as Stuart mused; a plan conceived by an idiot, carried out by two fucking idiots!'

They continued to finely tune the anticipated sequence of events and the specific role that Stuart would be taking.

"S-so l-lets get th-this right, I b-bust int-to L-leila's flat aand just h-handcuff her?"

"No, you wanker" Billy retorted,

"You wait for my signal, the bloody whistle, you dick"

Billy continued.

"How many times do I have to tell you, I leave the door unlocked and you enter when you hear the bloody whistle, is that simple enough for a plonker like you?"

"B-Bantam, you are the b-bloody p-plonker, and I'm a b-bloody p-plonker for agreeing to th-this crap p-plan" was Stuart's final comment.

They both agreed that they would carry out the plan, but they continued with the arguments until they parted company at the clocking out machine at the end of the shift.

Billy's parting comment to Stuart was.

"See you at twelve, dick head"

Countered by Stuart, shouting

"W-wanker"

It was Friday evening Sergeant Cooney parked his car and walked towards the door of his flat, as he mumbled to himself "Tomorrow you will be a Super Hero Cooney my boy, a bloody Super Hero".

It was getting dark and he fumbled in his coat pocket for the flat door keys.

"Hello Sugar Daddy"

"Leil…..

There was a sickening thud, as the severed head fell to the ground!

Unperturbed, Leila took a small globe from her pocket.

She then spoke softly into the globe.

"My Love, It is done"

The answer came thro' the globe

"My Darling, the time has arrived; we need to be ready to leave this planet"

Leila then moved quickly from the scene, followed by a large hunched figure, carrying the head of the unsuspecting Sergeant.

CHAPTER SIX

Saturday morning, just after 0730 hours Detective Inspector Preece had just entered his office, when his mobile phone rang.
"Hello Detective Inspector Preece"
"Hello Ted, have you got the lazy bugger out of his bed?"
"What? What the fucking hell are you saying?"
"Are you sure?"
The news that he had just been told, really had the Detective Inspector's head in a spin and he still didn't believe it.
He countered forcefully.
"If this is some sort of fucking joke, if it is, I'll have your arse!"
He then changed the tone of his voice and started to plead with Ted Draper.
"PLEASE SAY YOU'RE KIDDING"
"PLEASE TED, SAY YOU ARE KIDDING!"
There was a deathly silence, as the Detective Inspector listened to the reply.
Preece then ended the call when he threw his mobile phone to the floor, as he stood up from his desk.
He paced up and down the office muttering to himself, before he eventually regained some of his composure.
He then casually picked up his mobile phone and placed it into his pocket, straightened his clothing and slowly sat down at his desk, asking.
"What am I going to tell Mick's Mother? Poor Christine, what am I going to tell her?" he kept asking himself.
After a few minutes of mind searching, he made his decision.
"Right, first things first, let's get to the flat" he shouted to himself as he stood and walked to the office door.

Detective Inspector Preece left his office and travelled across the City to Sergeant Cooney's flat, still feeling numbed by the news that he had just received.

Ted Draper and his Forensics team had secured the area and had conducted a thorough search of the scene for any evidence, regarding the Sergeants demise.

They had Sergeant Cooney's body bagged and ready for transportation to the Station, when Detective Inspector Preece entered the flat.

"Where's the Sergeant, Ted?"

"He's in the front room Detective Inspector" was Ted's solemn reply.

Preece went into the front room; the bagged headless body of the Sergeant had been placed on the sofa.

Preece kneeled down next to the sofa as he opened the body bag, in order to view the lifeless body of his Sergeant.

He bowed his head and stayed silent for a few seconds, before closing the body bag.

He then stood up and returned to the car parking area, to find Ted Draper.

"Right Ted, what have we found" he enquired.

"Absolutely nothing Detective Inspector we have found absolutely nothing" was Ted's reply.

Preece was not surprised, in fact he expected it, as it was the same at all the other crime scenes;

No evidence at all had been found at any of the previous murders.

"OK Ted, I have to go and see someone, I'll meet you back at the Station, do your best, try and find something that we can act on"

And with that hopeful comment, the Detective Inspector left the scene and returned to his car.

Preece knew that he had to make the most painful journey of his life, to Sergeant Cooney's mother's home and to inform her of the awful news.

When the Detective Inspector arrived outside Christine Cooney's house, he just sat in the car for a few moments, taking the opportunity to clear his mind. He was still sitting in the car when Christine walked past, glanced round, recognised the Detective Inspector and returned to the parked car.

"Detective Inspector Preece, how nice to see you, where's that 'so and so' of a son of mine?"

Preece opened the car door and slowly stood next to Christine, he then tried to put a sensible sentence together as he started to offer some sort of explanation regarding her son's death.

But it did not work!

Christine just fell to the ground with the Detective Inspector following, both weeping uncontrollably as they hugged each other.

After a while, Preece wiped his eyes, helped Christine to her feet and with his arms supporting, he led her to the house, where they both disappeared inside.

Once inside the house, Preece led Christine to the sofa, where they both sat.

"Has my Michael suffered the same as the others?" was Christine's immediate question.

"I'm afraid so Christine, and yes, we will have to keep Mick for a while", as he placed his arms around her again, trying desperately to lessen the pain she was obviously feeling.

Christine just sobbed and sobbed.

Billy kept looking at his watch.

"It's Bloody ten past, where is the Bloody 'Leila tart'" he muttered.

He kept looking up the road towards Stuart, who was stood in Boots Chemist's doorway.

Suddenly, Leila appeared on the opposite side of the road.

She crossed the road and walked up to Billy.

"You must be 'Billy the Kid'?"

Billy turned and stared at Leila.

"What a Fucking Beauty" he muttered silently to himself.

"Yes I am, and you must be the lovely Leila" he countered.

"You are more mature than I expected" said Leila.

"Mature and fit to go" was Billy's silly answer.

"OK 'Billy the Kid' lets go and dine"

Leila linked her arm with his and led him down the road towards the river that ran adjacent to the Abbey.

Stuart left Boots Chemist doorway, and keeping a respectable distance, followed the couple towards the river.

"I hope you have plenty of wine Leila" Billy enquired.

"I have plenty of everything, I'm sure I can keep you entertained 'Billy the Kid'"

Billy's mind ran wild.

"I'm sure you bloody can" he murmured.

Billy tried to make sensible conversation, but only ended up sounding more and more immature with each and every comment.

They crossed the road and walked along the riverside to the rear of the Abbey.

"This is my abode, 'Billy the Kid'"

Billy was looking at a row of about six Maisonette type flats, which overlooked the river. Leila pointed to the end flat that had a small garden and a balcony that overlooked the river.

She then unlocked her arm from Billy's as she led him to the front door.

"This looks very nice Leila, how long have you lived here?" Billy enquired.

This was Billy trying to be the ultimate Detective!

"Oh not too long, but long enough to meet you 'Billy the Kid'"

Billy then started to feel a little uneasy, was she just 'taking the piss' or was she genuinely glad to see him.

Leila opened the door to the Maisonette and they both walked inside.

Billy then closed the door and left it unlocked as planned, however, when he turned to face Leila, he had to shield his eyes.

"Wow Leila, it's bloody bright in here!" he shouted.

Just then, Stuart entered the flat.

As Billy noticed his entry, he turned to Stuart and shouted.

"Not now you dick head!"

"You are supposed to wait for the fucking whist……

The knife entered Billy's chest and continued straight through the Rib Cage into his heart!

Billy fell to the floor with an expression of total amazement etched on his face, as blood pumped from the wound.

Leila then greeted Stuart.

"My Love"

Stuart answered.

"My Darling, we are finished here, we have to go, but first the Follower must be hibernated".

CHAPTER SEVEN

The death of his Sergeant and close friend had been the most harrowing and heartbreaking experience in the life of Detective Inspector Jim Preece.

However, he realised that he had to move on, not only for his own sanity, but as far as he was concerned, to bring the perpetrators of Mick Cooney's death to justice.

It was ten days after the death of Sergeant Cooney, and Detective Inspector Preece was sitting at his desk, trying to re-evaluate the murder enquiry.

He had cleared his desk of all the usual items, phone, computer etc., and had replaced them with all the relevant information regarding the investigation, in some 'sort of chronological' order.

As he sifted through the information, the phone rang.

"Hello, Detective Inspector Preece, Morning Commander, Yes sir, 1300 hrs, I'll see you there sir, Bye"

Commander Steele had just invited the Detective Inspector to a meeting at Police Headquarters, Preece knew that the 'Chiefs' were not happy and that there could be repercussions.

He re-focused on the information on his desk and started to turn over the most recent events in his mind;

Sergeant Cooney is murdered; his head is removed, but not his finger.

This Billy character, is murdered, no finger or head removed.

And to cap it all, Stuttering Stuart has disappeared!

There was a knock on the door.

"Yes, come in" shouted Preece, without even looking up from the material on his desk.

The door opened and Detective Sergeant Peter Morgan walked into the office, politely closing the door behind him.

Detective Inspector Preece looked up.

"Oh, I wondered when you would turn up, pull up a chair and let's know what you have learned about the Leila investigation" Preece ordered.

31 year old Blonde-haired Detective Sergeant Peter Morgan had been assigned to the 'Leila Case', much to the disgust of the Detective Inspector.

Preece thought that Morgan was a little young to be a Detective Sergeant, but he was good at his job, and in some ways, very much out of the same 'mould' as his new Detective Inspector, Jim Preece.

"I hope you are well Detective Inspector" said Sergeant Morgan, rather meekly.

"Never mind the pleasantries" grumbled Preece, "Just sit down and give me what you have found out."

Detective Sergeant Morgan pulled up a chair and began;

"Ted and his Forensics team gave me the technical assistance regarding Sergeant Cooney's flat and the Maisonette rented by the Leila Lady"

"Lady, bloody lady, take it from me Morgan, that bloody 'tart' is no lady" Preece shouted.

He then composed himself and respectfully continued.

"Right, Detective Sergeant, I'm sorry for the interruption, please carry on"

"Yes Detective Inspector, anyway, Forensics didn't find any clues at Sergeant Cooney's flat and as for the Leila flat, well it was very strange"

"In what way did you find it strange, Detective Sergeant?" Preece enquired.

"Well Detective Inspector that 'Leila bird' had rented the flat from HNT Associates for three months, but there was no sign that anybody ever lived there"

"Explain Detective Sergeant" asked Preece.

"Yes Detective Inspector, there was no food anywhere, no clothes, no utensils, no bedding and the fridge wasn't even plugged in!"

"As for Mr Stuart Taylor his parents are both dead, he has a married sister called Margaret living in Manchester and she stated that apart from a few phone calls from his mate Billy, she had not seen, or heard, from Stuart for more than a year"

"The flat, Morgan, what about the flat?" stressed Preece.

"Yes Detective Inspector."

"Stop saying bloody 'yes Detective Inspector', just call me Inspector and tell me about the bloody flat"

"Yes, err, OK Inspector, the flat was rented to Mr Taylor by the owner of the local paper shop, a Mr Quarmby, who stated that Mr Taylor had paid him six months rent, three months ago".

"About the same time that the 'Leila tart' rented her apartment" Preece replied.

"Yes, and again the state of the flat, well, it looked like it had not been lived in for a good few months"

"Exactly, Detective Sergeant Morgan, this case is coming together" Preece said excitedly.

"The bloody 'Leila bird' and Stuttering Stuart are a team.

"You mark my words Detective Sergeant Morgan these two are a bloody team!"

The Detective Inspector then jumped up from his chair and started to pace round his office with his hands in his pockets, staring at the floor.

"Right, Detective Sergeant Morgan, this is what we do, I have a plan"

"Let's not bother too much with the earlier murders when fingers and heads were removed, we need to find the 'Leila tart' and that Bloody Stuart"

The Detective Inspector continued.

"Sergeant Cooney 'bless him' did not have his finger removed and that Billy 'Bantam' character was just stabbed"

"It looks very much like there was a panic situation, yes a panic situation".

"Detective Sergeant Morgan, we have to find out where they are, before they skip the country" was Preece's rather desperate plea.

"Shall I contact the Ports and Airports Inspector?" asked a slightly perturbed Morgan.

"Right, Detective Sergeant Morgan, that's exactly what we do, but do it quietly, just say we suspect them of passport fraud or something" said Detective Inspector Preece mischievously.

"Inspector, our press officer has a meeting with the media tomorrow, should I inform him about Leila and Stuart?"

"No, no, no, let's not tell him anything, just yet, we don't want to get the public too excited" stressed Preece.

"The public have only been told that the murders were of an unusual nature, we don't want to go into too much detail, not just yet"

Detective Inspector Preece continued.

"Now for my plan"

Preece sat down at his desk and started to outline 'the plan' to Morgan.

"Tomorrow, you will go to the 'Leila tart's' Maisonette and tear the bloody place apart, there has to be something there that will give us a lead, something that will generate a path to follow"

"Likewise, I will spend tomorrow morning at Stuttering Stuart's flat, also looking for something that will help us locate him, I

….

The phone rang.

"Hello Detective Inspector Preece. Yes, Commander, What now? O.K I'll be there directly"

Preece put down the phone and looked up at Detective Sergeant Morgan.

"I have to go and see the Commander he's turned up at the bloody Station"

"Talk to the Airports etc. and get to the bloody 'tart's' flat, we'll meet in my office at 0800 hrs tomorrow"

"Yes Inspector, I'll see you tomorrow Inspector" answered Morgan.

They both left the office with Detective Inspector Preece on his way to the Station Superintendant's Office and Detective Sergeant Morgan to arrange his visit to Leila's Maisonette.

Detective Inspector Preece knocked on the Superintendent's door and entered the office.

The Superintendant and the Commander were sitting adjacent to the circular meeting table at one corner of the office as he entered.

"Sit down Detective Inspector" said the Superintendant as he motioned towards a chair next to the table.

Preece walked to the chair, sat down and folded his arms, expecting the worst.

The Commander spoke first.

"Now Detective Inspector, how would you say the Leila investigation was going?" he enquired.

"We are following a number of positive leads sir" answered Preece.

"What do you consider to be positive!" queried the Superintendant.

"Well Superintendant, we are concerned regarding the whereabouts of the mentioned Leila and a Mr Stuart Taylor, we are concerned that they may have been acting as a team, and…

The Commander leant forward and peered at the Detective Inspector across the table.

"Concerned, concerned Detective Inspector"

"Don't you think we are all concerned?"

"The truth is Detective Inspector Preece we are all bloody concerned regarding your handling of this investigation!"

He leaned further forward and, stressing even more, he stated "The Superintendant and I, think that we need a change of direction"

He then leaned back in his chair.

"It's with great regret, that we are taking you off the case"

This statement hit Detector Inspector Preece like a punch to the heart!

He tried to explain.

"Sir I……"

The Commander interrupted his intended answer.

"The time for excuses Detective Inspector has expired!"

He continued,

"I'm Sorry Detective Inspector, but you are suspended until further notice, this meeting is concluded"

"Thank you Detective Inspector, close the door after you, thank you again Detective Inspector Preece"

"Sir I think I should have an explanation" Preece pleaded.

"In time Detective Inspector, in time" retorted the Commander.

And with that final comment, the Commander left the table, walked over to the Superintendant's desk and started to make a phone call.

Detective Inspector Preece stood up, stared in the direction of the Commander, who was having a conversation on the phone, and muttered "twat", turned, and left the office, leaving the door wide open.

Detective Sergeant Morgan had arranged for a representative of HNT Associates to meet him at the Maisonette apartments adjacent to the river.

As he walked along the side of the river, he could see a young woman waiting outside the row of the Maisonettes.

"Morning, you must be from HNT" he enquired as he offered his hand.

The woman shook him by the hand.

"Yes, my name his Susan, it's nice to meet you Sergeant".

"O.K Susan, let's go inside"

The Sergeant walked behind Susan as they entered the flat.

"I hope that this will be the end of the matter, we need to get this property back on the market" Susan stressed.

"I'm sure it will be" answered Morgan

The Maisonette had a kitchen, dining room and living room on the ground floor level, and one bedroom with a balcony and bathroom/toilet on the upper level.

Sergeant Morgan wandered from room to room aimlessly, just generally looking in all the corners, not really knowing what he was looking for, but trying to act professionally.

"What do you think?" asked Susan.

"It's obvious that this place has not been lived in" he stated.

He continued

"It's spotless!"

He then walked into the kitchen.

The floor was tiled, so Morgan, trying to look interested, took a closer look at the tiles in the far corner of the kitchen.

So he had a look of total surprise, when, turning to Susan, he asked

"Do these tiles look a little odd to you Susan?"

Susan took a closer look at the mentioned area of the floor. "They do look a little new, don't they" she answered.

This encouraged Sergeant Morgan to bend down onto one knee and with his finger followed along the outline of what looked like new grouting between some of the tiles.

He stood up and with his hands on his waist, turned to Susan. "That area is about a metre and a half square, just a minute Susan, wait here, I'll go and get my wheel brace"

Detective Sergeant Morgan went to his car, returning shortly afterwards with the wheel brace.

He knelt down at the side of the tiles in question, pushed the flat end of the wheel brace into one end of the 'new grout' area and exerted leverage to one side.

He wasn't surprised when a section of the floor lifted, so he placed his hands under the tiles and slide the section to one side.

"There" he exclaimed

They were both looking at stairs that led into a cellar, approx two metres deep.

"Susan, do you have a torch?"

"Yes, it's in my car" she answered.

"Go get it, Susan".

Susan left the Maisonette to get her torch from her car.

She returned moments later with the torch and they both entered the cellar, rather gingerly at first, but then with more than a little bravado!

It looked like the cellar had been cut into solid rock as Detective Sergeant Morgan shone the torch along the walls and on the floor.

"What's that? Susan queried, as she pointed into one of the corners of the cellar.

The Detective Sergeant shone the torch in the direction that she was pointing.

They were looking at some sort of giant chest, and at first glance it appeared to be made of ice!

They both walked towards the chest.

Susan then touched it.

"Christ! It's warm" she said.

Detective Sergeant Morgan touched the top of the chest with his finger, and then he continued to feel the rest of the chest with the palms of his hands.

"It's bloody warm alright, yet it doe's looks like ice!" he confirmed.

He then started to feel a little uncomfortable.

"I think we had better get the guys from the Station down here, I'll give Detective Inspector Preece a call"

Detective Sergeant Morgan took his mobile phone from his pocket and attempted to phone the Detective Inspector.

"Shit, no signal"

"Wait here Susan, I'll go and make the call from upstairs, here's the torch, don't touch anything"

"OK" answered Susan.

Detective Sergeant Morgan then climbed the stairs into the kitchen area to make the phone call.

Susan initially just stared at the chest, but perhaps to her peril, and against Morgan's request, she again started to feel the chest.

And against all expectations, and much to Susan's surprise, it started to glow!

With a gasp!

Susan jumped away from the chest and turned to shout to the Detective Sergeant who was in the kitchen area, trying to inform him of this startling development.

"Sergeant Morgan it has started …

You could hardly hear the Crack as her head was removed from her body allowing her lifeless torso to fall to the ground!

CHAPTER EIGHT

Detective Sergeant Morgan was on the phone to the Station, and
he was standing just outside the cellar opening.

"Yes Constable, tell the Detective Inspector to get down to the
Leila apartment"

"What?"

"He's been suspended!"

"You are saying that Detective Inspector Preece has been
suspended?"

"Who?"

"Davy?"

"Well, OK, you had better inform him"

His call was interrupted by the sound of Susan shouting to him.

"Yes Susan"

"Susan"

"I have to go Constable don't forget to inform Detective
Inspector Davy"

Detective Sergeant Morgan then walked to the entrance of the
cellar in order to answer Susan's call, peering down into the
gloom.

"Susan"

"Susan, what's happened?"

"Where are you?"

Morgan continued to peer into the darkness as he was more than
a little concerned, with the deathly silence.

He then started to descend the stairs, but not able to see, he took
his lighter from his pocket and tried to make sense of the
darkness with the use of the flickering light.

As his eyes became more accustomed to the gloom, he could just make out a hunched figure on the floor some four paces to his right.

He moved towards the figure and although the lighter flame did not offer much light, it became apparent that the figure was, in fact, Susan, slumped on the floor.

Detective Sergeant Morgan's heart started to beat at an astronomical rate and almost jumped from his chest!

As further inspection of Susan's body indicated that it was headless!

"Jesus Christ" he shouted.

And with that, he turned on his heels and in a state of panic he flew up the cellar stairs like an Olympic sprinter.

Detective Sergeant Morgan carried on running through the open door of the flat and without stopping, along the river to where his car was parked, a good half a mile.

He then stood at the side of his car, totally out of breath, spread his arms open wide and leaned against the car, laying face down on the roof.

Morgan stood there until his heart started to beat normally, before he reached inside his coat, located his mobile phone and phoned the Station,

The Desk Sergeant answered his call.

"Hi Sergeant, this is Detective Sergeant Morgan, you had better send the Morgue van down to 37 The Mews, we have the same situation that Detective Inspector Preece called 'under cover'"

"OK Sergeant, speak to you later" Detective Sergeant Morgan replaced the phone in his jacket pocket.

He then started to wonder what he should do, should he wait, or should he return to the crime scene.

The decision was made for him.

Detective Inspector Paul Davy's car pulled up alongside Detective Sergeant Morgan's.

"Well, well, fancy meeting Detective Sergeant Morgan here" was Detective Inspector Davy's sarcastic comment.

Morgan did not like Davy, he knew he was a womaniser, full of his own importance, and was shagging the Commander's wife Wendy.

"Hello Detective Inspector Davy" answered Morgan.

"What's the problem Detective Sergeant?" asked Davy.

Morgan started to describe the events to the Detective Inspector, but was rudely interrupted.

"Look at the 'Lumps on that'" exclaimed Detective Inspector Davy.

This untimely interruption annoyed Sergeant Morgan, so he stressed.

"Detective Inspector, we have a bloody murder scene here!" as he tugged at the Detective Inspector's arm, to turn him away from the young girls on the opposite side of the road.

Detective Sergeant Morgan insisted that he finished outlining the horrendous events that had just occurred.

"OK, carry on Detective Sergeant, I'm sorry for the interruption" apologised Davy.

Morgan completed the sorry tale that ended with the demise of the unfortunate Susan.

"Have you called the Morgue Guys" asked the Detective Inspector.

"Yes Inspector"

"Have you been back to the apartment?"

"No Inspector, I don't have a torch"

"You don't have a torch"

"You don't have a bloody torch"

"Now that's not the best excuse, coming from a member of the constabulary, IS IT Detective Sergeant Morgan!"

"Sorry Detective Inspector" answered Morgan, feeling rather stupid.

Detective Inspector Davy grabbed his torch from his car and they both headed back to the Maisonette.

As they approached the door to the apartment, the Detective Inspector turned to Morgan.

"Lead the way Detective Sergeant" as he handed Morgan the torch.

Morgan led them both to the cellar opening and then hesitated.

"Go on Detective Sergeant, go down, I'm right behind you" said Davy as he prodded Morgan in the back, almost pushing him head first down the stairs.

Morgan rather reluctantly led the Detective Inspector down the stairs and towards the headless corpse of Susan.

Detective Sergeant Morgan then shone the torch on the lifeless body of Susan.

"There Detective Inspector, what did I tell you" he stated.

"Yes Detective Sergeant, I can see, what would 'suspended' Detective Inspector Preece do in this situation?"

"He would let the Morgue team remove the body and place it 'under cover', we would then keep the scene secure, especially from the media" Morgan answered.

Detective Sergeant Morgan continued to use the torch to survey the rest of the cellar he then walked over to the chest and stroked it with his hand.

"It's bleeding cold" he exclaimed.

Detective Inspector Davy walked over and stroked it with his hand.

"Course its cold, wouldn't you be cold in this bloody place, and it looks like a bloody tomb to me Detective Sergeant"

"But it was hot when Susan and I touched it earlier" Morgan stressed.

"Course it was, maybe it was the 'Susan effect'" was Davy's glib reply.

"I'm not like you Detective Inspector".

There was movement above the cellar in the kitchen area.

"Hello, are you down there Detective Inspector?" enquired a uniformed police officer.

Detective Inspector Davy answered the call and both he and Sergeant Morgan left the cellar and moved into the kitchen area. Two uniformed officers had turned up, along with two members of the Morgue team.

Detective Inspector Davy instructed the officers regarding the sensitivity of the situation and informed the Morgue team likewise, he then walked out into the garden area and beckoned the Detective Sergeant to follow him.

"Now Sergeant, lets get this right, You find the poor sod Susan minus her lovely head and run like the 'clappers'"

"I couldn't see and who ever did it could still have been down there" answered Morgan meekly.

"Yes Detective Sergeant and if he had still been down there, because of your action, he bloody well isn't down there now, is he!"

The Detective Inspector started to prod his finger into the Sergeant's chest.

"Not only have you let the poor women come a cropper, you've also let the 'Toss Pot' that did it, get away!"

"I didn't think Detective Inspector. I just didn't think"

"No Detective Sergeant, you bloody panicked, you arsole, further…"

The Detective Inspector's phone rang.

"Yes, Hi love, what now? OK"

The call to Detective Inspector Davy was from Wendy, she needed some attention!

Davy then turned to Morgan.

"Detective Sergeant, you have a chance to redeem yourself, make sure all the guys secure the scene and the body is removed properly, arrange for the removal of that bloody tomb and, last but not least, contact HNT Associates for Susan's next of kin".

"You'll need to inform the Station Sergeant and he'll send the relevant neighbourhood team to speak to them, I'll meet you in my office tomorrow, nine sharp".

"Where is your office Detective Inspector?"

"I am using that 'useless bugger's' office, Suspended DI Preece".

"OK Detective Sergeant, I'll see you tomorrow" was Davy's final comment as he turned and walked to his car.

Sergeant Morgan returned to the crime scene to assist the other officers, feeling a little inadequate following his earlier rather clumsy actions.

Next morning, DS Morgan arrived at the Station at 0730 hrs and went straight to DI Preece's office.

He updated the case information on the wall chart, adding the latest victim Susan he then sat at Preece's desk and pondered the previous day's events.

It caused him to shiver, with a definite tinge of regret, as he remembered leaving poor Susan in the cellar alone.

The office door opened.

"Morning Detective Sergeant, you're early, take your arse off my chair and organise a cup of char, white with plenty of sugar, that's a good boy"

Inspector Davy had arrived!

Morgan didn't say anything; he just left the office and surprisingly to himself, went about the 'cup of char' duty diligently.

When Morgan returned to the office, Detective Inspector Davy was checking the case information on the wall chart.

"What did Preece think about the obvious change of direction by the 'toss pots', not always removing the digit and the head?" queried Davy.

Detective Sergeant Morgan placed the tea onto the desk.

"He thought it was a case of panic, by the perpetrators ".

The Detective Inspector thought for a moment.

He then turned away from looking at the chart and, pointing his finger at Detective Sergeant Morgan, he stressed

"They panicked alright, so much so, they hid in the bloody cellar of that Leila bird's apartment, what do you think of that? And furthermore, they panicked into chopping Susan baby's bloody head off!"

84

"Tell me Detective Sergeant how did they get into the cellar? You had to remove half the bloody floor to get in, No, Detective Sergeant, they did not panic, someone must have followed you, and followed you into the cellar"

"That's impossible, bleeding impossible, we were right next to the stairs. No way did anybody come down the bleeding stairs" Morgan retorted.

"Detective Sergeant, that's…

The phone rang, Davy walked over to the desk.

"Hello, Detective Inspector Davy speaking"

"Morning Commander, how are you enjoying London Sir?"

"What!"

"I thought we had an agreement, Detective Inspector Preece's 'under cover'. What paper? The Daily Journal, It figures, that Bent has always been a wanker, Yes Commander, tomorrow at ten, OK sir, I'll be there, see you then"

Davy replaced the receiver and sat down at the desk.

He looked up at the Sergeant, as he put his hands on the back of his head.

"Detective Sergeant Morgan, we have a problem that Margaret Taylor has been to the media. That bloody woman has been to the Daily Journal, to the biggest 'toss pot' in the newspaper industry, Mr Bloody Jack Bent!"

"Shit, Preece always said that if anyone burst the bubble, it would be her" confirmed Morgan.

Detective Inspector Davy then told Morgan

"We have a meeting with the Commander at ten tomorrow in the Station Superintendant's office, you produce an interim report that we can discuss at the meeting, I need to console Wendy while the Commander is still in London"

CHAPTER NINE

It was just after 0900 hrs when Detective Sergeant Morgan entered the Station canteen, where he obtained a welcome cup of coffee, and then to the office of Detective Inspector Preece, which was now being used by Detective Inspector Davy.

Although, as far as the Sergeant was concerned, the office still belonged to Detective Inspector Preece and he was still the 'hub' of the Leila investigation.

After quickly drinking the cup of coffee, Morgan concentrated on putting the finishing touches to the interim discussion report that Detective Inspector Davy had requested.

As he was looking through some of the files, he came across a request that Detective Inspector Preece had sent to the missing person's investigation team, headed by Inspector Jackson.

Morgan couldn't remember having discussed this request with DI Preece, so he picked up the phone and called Inspector Jackson.

"Oh, Inspector, this is Detective Sergeant Morgan"

"Morning Detective Sergeant".

"Morning Inspector, do you remember the missing person's request that Detective Inspector Preece made, just before he was suspended?"

"I do Detective Sergeant, DI Preece picked up the information himself, why do you ask, don't tell me that our Mr Preece as lost it?"

"Well I can't find it Inspector, could you send me a copy"

"OK Detective Sergeant, I'll sort you a copy, but don't lose it!"

"I won't, many thanks Inspector"

Morgan was just walking back towards the case wall chart, when Detective Inspector Davy entered the office.

"Morning Detective Sergeant, have you finished the discussion document?"

"I have Detective Inspector, here it is"

Morgan handed the report to the Inspector.

"Cheers Sergeant Morgan, now go and get me a cuppa while I give the report my undivided attention"

Detective Inspector Davy took the report and Morgan left the office to attend to his tea duties.

The phone rang.

"Hello, Detective Inspector Davy"

"Well, well, if it isn't the 'tosser' of the world, the 'wishful Boss of Fleet Street', or you would be, if you were intelligent enough to work there"

Jack Bent was on the other end of the line and his answer to the Detective Inspector was to be expected.

"Morning again Davy, you haven't changed, are you still shagging that old Commander's wife? Or has she gone to a more normal person someone with brains"

"OK 'tosser', what do you want?" moaned Davy.

"I've phoned to strike a deal with you, brainless" taunted Bent.

"Why would I want to strike a deal with you 'tosser'?"

"Because if you don't, I will have to have a few words with the Commander, words that won't do your career any good" threatened Bent.

"I suppose your good lady knows about that little Nancy tart" countered Davy.

"No she doesn't, but then, we're not married any more I'm now married to that Nancy tart"

With that remark, Jack Bent started laughing.

This irritated Detective Inspector Davy, mainly because he didn't have anything else he could use to threaten Bent.

"OK 'tosser', what's the deal?" queried a defensive Detective Inspector.

"As you may know, that unfortunate Stuart's sister, Margaret, has told me about the recent murders. The murders that the general public have not been fully informed about and I for one …

Detective Inspector Davy interrupted Bent.

"OK, spare me the sob story you will not go to print if I do what?"

"Simple, brainless, you give me exclusive rights to all the case information and I pay this Margaret Taylor bird to keep her trap shut"

Detective Sergeant Morgan had entered the room and had placed a cup of tea on Davy's desk.

"OK 'tosser', I'll get Detective Sergeant Morgan to ring you and fill you in, he'll phone you this afternoon, don't choke on anything"

With that hopeful statement, the Detective Inspector put down the phone and turned to the Sergeant.

"Who was the 'tosser' on the phone?" queried Morgan.

"Mr Bloody Bent" answered Davy.

"Jack Bent, I have to phone that pig?"

"Yes Detective Sergeant, you have to phone that pig"

"He has agreed not to print the under cover details if we give him, and only him, the pertinent details of the Leila case."

Detective Inspector Davy continued.

"I know it's an arse, but we need to keep the lid tightly closed on the case or we'll be hung out to dry by everyone"

Davy gulped down the tea and grabbed Morgan by the shoulder.

"Now, come on, let's go to the meeting with our useless Commander".

"I think I will be in his good books when he learns of the deal with 'tosser' Bent"

"You never know, he may return to London and I can regain my hold on Wendy's lovely 'lumps'"

After that churlish remark from Detective Inspector Davy, he handed the interim report back to Sergeant Morgan, and they both left the office, and on to the office of the Station Superintendant.

When they entered the Superintendant's suite, his secretary nodded her acknowledgement to them both and pointed to the meeting room.

As they entered the room, they could see that the Superintendant and the Commander were already having a discussion, and were seated at the circular meeting table.

"Come in gentlemen" welcomed the Superintendant and pointed to two empty chairs.

"Morning Detective Inspector Davy, morning Detective Sergeant Morgan" welcomed the Commander.

Davy and Morgan sat down as directed and Commander Steele spoke first.

"Well chaps, what do you make of Jack Bent, getting involved?"

"He won't be, Commander" stated a smiling Detective Inspector Davy.

"I've made a deal with the Daily Journal that has secured the secrecy of the 'under cover' details of the Leila case" he crowed.
"So Mr Bent will not be exposing the sordid details of the case?" queried Commander Steele.
"No sir, he has agreed to co-operate with me and the investigation" confirmed a smug-looking Davy.
"Fantastic" exclaimed the Commander.
Superintendant Kelly and the Commander stood up from their seated positions, walked over to the Inspector and in turn, shook him vigorously by the hand.
"Are you sure Mr Bent will keep his side of the deal?" asked the Superintendant.
"He maybe a plonker, but when he becomes the sole owner of a story, he is a man of his word" confirmed Davy.
This comment almost caused Sergeant Morgan to swallow the ballpoint pen he had been sucking!
"Right, gentlemen, this meeting is over"
"Well done Inspector Davy, I knew you were the one to take this case forward" concluded the Commander.
"Are we going to discuss the interim report regarding the progress of the case, that I have prepared?" asked Sergeant Morgan.
"No Detective Sergeant, we are perfectly happy" answered the Superintendant as he followed the Commander from the room.
Detective Inspector Davy looked at the Sergeant, with an obvious look of total triumph etched on his face.
"OK, Sergeant Morgan, I think you can continue with the investigation, I have to console someone"

The Detective Inspector then left the room, leaving Sergeant Morgan in total disbelief; consequently he just looked around the empty room, as he whispered

"What the Fuck was that all about!"

Detective Sergeant Morgan decided to call on Ted Draper in Forensics, to find out if they had opened the chest, cum tomb, found at the Leila Maisonette.

He left the Superintendants office and took the short journey along the corridor to the Forensics department, knocked on the door and entered the room.

The Manager, Ted Draper, was on the phone, he signalled to Morgan to enter his office, this the Sergeant did, and waited the conclusion of the phone call.

"Detective Sergeant Morgan, what can I do for you?" asked Ted.

"I wondered if you had opened the chest from 37 The Mews."

"37 The Mews, Sergeant?" asked Ted, as he pondered over the address.

"Oh yes, the Leila case"

"I'm sorry to say, Detective Sergeant, but we need to widen the entrance to the cellar, and that will require us to remove half the bloody building in order to get the bloody chest out"

"We've asked one of the local builders to help out and we're meeting them at the apartment this afternoon."

"What have you asked them to do?" asked Morgan.

"They will gain access into the cellar, remove the chest, repair the entry and then deliver the chest to the Station" answered Ted.

"OK Ted, did you leave the apartment secure?" queried Morgan.

"Yes, it's all locked up Detective Sergeant"

"Well I hope so, we have to be very careful with respect to that place, it's the scene of a particularly horrendous murder."

"The chest is crucial evidence, and it would have been better if you had arranged for it to be removed immediately" stressed Morgan.

"Sergeant, we all have priorities and I certainly have mine" Ted Draper then stated his position very clearly.

"I have more important things to attend to Sergeant, and the removal of your bloody chest was not one of my priorities"

"OK Ted, what time are the builders due?" asked Morgan politely, not wanting to start an argument.

"Two" answered Ted impatiently.

"Have you a spare set of keys?" asked Morgan, who was feeling a little let down by the Forensics team.

"Yes Detective Sergeant, I have"

"Good, if you let me have them, Ted, I'll go and sort out the place and when the builders arrive, I'll supervise the chests removal and its subsequent journey to the Station."

Ted Draper opened one of the drawers of his desk, removed a set of keys and placed them on his desk.

"I want them back when the job is done" he demanded.

"Of course" replied Morgan, as he picked up the keys.

The Sergeant left Ted's office, feeling rather disgruntled that Ted did not seem to understand the importance that the chest could be to the investigation.

He then returned to Inspector Preece's office and threw the prepared Leila case notes on to the Inspector's desk.

"All that bloody preparation time, and nobody was the slightest bit bloody interested" he muttered.

He sat down at the Inspector's desk, and started thinking about his imminent return to the Maisonette.

In his mind he rekindled the visit that he had made with Susan, and a sense of great regret, and to some degree, apprehension appeared!

"Sod it!"

"Am I a man or a bloody mouse?" he muttered.

He obviously decided that he was a man, as he strode manfully from the office.

Detective Sergeant Morgan pulled up in the parking area adjacent to the river.

He removed his torch from the glove compartment as he left his car, and walked purposely towards the Maisonette.

His feelings became a little on edge when he entered the front garden of the property, as he could see that the door of the premises was wide open!

However, Detective Sergeant Morgan was in a determined mood and nothing was going to stop him, so as he purposely walked through the open door, he drew his telescopic truncheon, he was expecting everything, and hoping for nothing.

He walked over to the cellar opening and shone his torch down into the darkness.

Standing at the top of the cellar stairs, he directed the torch beam into the cellar covering each and every corner, he then repeated this sweep, he was now certain. The chest, it had gone!

CHAPTER TEN

Morgan was close to panic, but to his credit, he decided that he was not about to break the '100 metres world record' again, for he had already decided, that he would, enter the cellar.

Just as he was about to tread into the unknown, he noticed a length of cable leading into the cellar and down the stairs.

Morgan's eyes followed the cable to a plug in the kitchen he walked over to the plug and pushed the switch to the 'on' position.

Much to Sergeant Morgan's delight, the cellar 'lit up' and all his fears just disappeared.

'"Thank god for Ted Draper and his gang" he muttered.

Sergeant Morgan entered the cellar and from the centre of the room, he surveyed the area.

It looked like the room had just been excavated and he walked along its perimeter touching the wall as he walked.

"How the bleeding hell did they get the chest out?"

"Ted was saying that he would have to remove half the bloody wall!"

There was a sound from upstairs.

"Christ" He exclaimed, fearing the worst.

He ran up the cellar stairs, just in time to see the back of a young man disappearing out of the Maisonette door.

Morgan followed the youth to the open door, but too late, the youth had disappeared.

Sergeant Morgan turned and walked into the apartment lounge, empty cans and empty pizza boxes littered the floor.

It looked like the locals had decided to use the Maisonette as their own meeting and eating place.

Morgan returned to the cellar and started to walk round the perimeter again, as he shouted.

"How the fuck did they get the bleeding chest out of this place?"

After a while he just shrugged his shoulders, turned, walked out of the cellar, closed the rear door of the premises, and returned to his car.

He phoned the Station and informed the Desk Sergeant on the state of things at the Maisonette, and asked him to send someone to secure it.

Morgan also asked the Sergeant to send a message to Ted Draper regarding the missing chest, and that he should cancel the builders, as they wouldn't be needed.

Morgan returned to the Station and went straight to DI Preece's office.

He noticed an envelope on the Inspector's desk, and as he picked it up he noticed that it was addressed to him.

"Ah, this must be the reply from Inspector Jackson regarding the missing persons file I requested" he muttered.

Morgan opened the envelope and sifted through its contents.

"Bleeding hell" he exclaimed.

He lifted one of the photographs from the envelope and it immediately 'rang a bell' in his mind, he walked over to the Leila case wall chart and compared it with the photograph of Leila.

"Jesus Christ, it's her"

"It's her" He shouted.

Morgan then started to sift through the rest of the contents of the envelope in order to obtain more details of the person in the photograph.

It became clear, that the person that he knew as 'Leila', was in fact, called Sandra Barak, a 23 year old graduate who lived with her parents and who had been missing for 3 months.

"Just when the 'Leila bird' first surfaced" he mused.

Morgan picked up the phone.

"Hello is Inspector Jackson there?"

"OK"

"Hello, Inspector Jackson?"

"Its Detective Sergeant Morgan, it's about the file you sent me"

"Yes, we have a match"

"Sandra Barak, she is our Leila"

"Have you had any luck tracing this Sandra, Inspector?"

"No, well it looks like we find Leila we find Sandra"

"Thanks for your assistance Inspector, keep in touch and I will do likewise"

"Thanks again Inspector"

Morgan returned the phone to the desk.

He pondered what to do next, he then muttered.

"I'll phone Ted Draper"

He picked up the phone and dialled Ted at Forensics.

"Ted, we need to talk. OK I'll come straight round".

Sergeant Morgan replaced the receiver and left the office on his way to the Forensics Department.

Once in the Forensics Office, he walked over to Ted Draper who was looking at some photographs that he had laid out on his desk.

As Morgan approached, Ted pointed at one of the photographs.

"This chest was two and a half metres long, two metres wide and two metres in depth; we estimate that it weighed 200 Kilos"

"You say that it is missing from the cellar?"

"Certainly is" stated Sergeant Morgan.

"Well Detective Sergeant, as far as I am concerned there are only two ways to remove it; to dismantle the bloody thing or, as I have already mentioned, to widen the cellar entrance".

"So what are you saying Ted?" Morgan queried.

"What I am saying is… "

Ted paused, and then admitted.

 I don't know what I am saying"

He continued, still in disbelief.

"It's bloody impossible!"

"It must have been dismantled"

"OK, so it must have been dismantled, but what do you think it was made of?" questioned Morgan.

"Now that's something else Detective Sergeant, we didn't have much time to inspect the chest, and again, I have to admit I've no idea"

"It was not metal, it felt like wood, but it wasn't, I've no bloody idea"

Ted Draper concluded, with the following admission.

"To be perfectly honest Detective Sergeant Morgan, I feel completely useless, I really can't help you, I'm very sorry"

"OK Ted, thanks anyway, lets hope we can find it and you get the chance to make a more definite examination" answered Morgan sympathetically.

With that, Morgan left the office and made his way back to DI Preece's office.

Just before he reached the office he heard a voice behind him.

"Well fancy meeting you here Detective Sergeant Morgan".

Morgan turned round walking behind him was Jack Bent.

"Oh, hello Mr Bent, I was just going to ring you" lied Morgan.

"Yes, course you were" was Bent's sarcastic remark.

No one in the Station liked Bent, he was thought of belonging to the 'old school' regarding newspaper journalism.

He would report the facts, but he was also a very untrustworthy person, and the facts could be 'adjusted' to suit sales.

"Come, I'll show you the Leila case information" Morgan reluctantly replied.

They both entered the Inspector's office and Morgan led Bent to the case wall chart, where they both pondered over the compiled information.

Sergeant Morgan pointed to the CCTV photographs of Leila.

"We now feel that this girl is a missing graduate called Sandra Barak"

Morgan's mobile phone rang.

It was Inspector Davy.

"Hello Detective Inspector, I'm just going through the Leila case details with Mr Bent"

"Tell that 'tosser' to bollocks" was the Inspectors reply.

"Sergeant, be in my office first thing tomorrow, we have to talk, and don't give the 'tosser' too much information, keep the bloody pillock in the dark"

With that, the Detective Inspector ended the phone call rather abruptly.

Detective Sergeant Morgan continued to discuss the pertinent details with Jack Bent, trying to look like he was interested, but he was only passing time until he could get rid.

Eventually, Bent seems satisfied with the information he had received and he left the office with this parting statement.

"Don't forget to tell that brainless Detective Inspector Davy, that I will only keep the lid on this case as long as I am kept in the loop, stress that to the useless bugger, 'as long as I am kept in the loop', catch you later Sergeant."

Meanwhile, some twenty miles to the east of the Police Station, Heather Langley and her daughter Julie were walking by the river side.

It was a nice sunny day and she had taken the opportunity to walk her dog and to spend some time with her young daughter. They had been walking near to the river for nearly two hours, and Heather decided that it was time to return home.

"Julie, go get Henry, it's time to go home, and don't let him go in the river"

"OK Mummy" said Julie.

Julie ran off towards the river to look for Henry.

She ran between two small bushes at the side of the river that led to a small sandy area.

Henry was barking as he looked towards the bushes.

"Henry, stop barking, we have to go home" said Julie.

But Henry kept on barking, and suddenly, he started to growl.

Julie just walked towards the dog, and grabbed his collar, "Now Henry, come, we have to go home".

Henry was now looking behind Julie and he quickly pulled away from Julie's grasp, and ran away in apparent terror.

The movement in the bushes became more pronounced, and as Julie started to turn around, and for no apparent reason, her head was quickly and efficiently removed, and just as quickly, her headless body was thrown into the river, just like a piece of rubbish!

Heather was already walking towards her car, when Henry ran up to her. She looked at the dog, he was very dirty, and it was plainly obvious, that the dog had been frightened in some way.
"Henry, what's wrong and where have you been?" she asked.
Heather then realised that Julie was not following the dog as she expected.
This signalled a feeling of panic!
She ran along the river bank, back in the direction of where the dog had just appeared.
Heather was calling her daughter as she ran, but to no avail. She became concerned that Julie may have fallen into the river, so she ran closer to the river bank, nothing.
Heather by now was in total panic, as she started to shout her daughters name again and again.
"Julie, Julie, where are you? Where are you girl?"
"It's time to go home" she pleaded.
Heather then noticed something floating in the river, her worse fears seemed to have been realised and she started to cry uncontrollably as she ran closer having recognised that the something floating in the river was, in fact, her daughter's body.
Heather started to scream, but there was nothing that she could do, as the body of her daughter disappeared over the weir and out of sight.

CHAPTER ELEVEN

Next morning when Detective Sergeant Morgan arrived at the Station, he saw Inspector Jackson in the Reception Area.

"Morning Inspector" called Morgan.

"Oh Sergeant, just a minute, can I have a word"

The Inspector guided Morgan into his office, just down the corridor.

They entered the Inspector's office and sat down at his desk.

"Sergeant Morgan, I have some terrible news, we pulled the body of a young girl from the river last night".

"A little earlier, a woman called Heather Langley reported that her daughter had fallen into the river, so we assume that the girl found was her daughter, 8-year-old Julie Langley".

"Oh, that's awful, Inspector" sympathised Morgan.

"It's more than that Detective Sergeant, the poor sod's head was missing!"

Sergeant Morgan's heart seemed to stop.

A sense of great sadness came upon him, his complexion changed to a ghostly colour, and he almost fainted.

Inspector Jackson recognised the effect his statement had on the Sergeant, so he offered him a glass of water.

Morgan accepted the glass, and after drinking all of its contents, he cleared his throat and with his 'Police head on', answered the Inspector, with a question.

"Bloody Hell Inspector, so this is obviously linked to the Leila case?"

"Most definitely, the head was removed in the same clinical way, it's definitely linked." Jackson stated.

Sergeant Morgan then made a rather sad request.

"We must initiate 'under cover' Inspector."

"I have already done so Detective Sergeant, but we can't keep saying to the family members, that their loved ones are still bloody missing"

Inspector Jackson continued, stressing very loudly

"And in this case, the mother knows that her daughter is missing presumed drowned, but she won't wait for ever, before she will expect us to find her daughter and to produce her bloody body"

"I know Inspector, I'll discuss the situation with Detective Inspector Davy, I agree, we have to move on"

"Move on and bloody quickly Sergeant, I look forward to hearing from Davy."

"OK Inspector, I'll deal with it as soon as Detective Inspector Davy arrives at the Station, thank you for your understanding in this matter"

They shook hands and Morgan left the office and walked to DI Preece's office.

When he entered the office, Detective Inspector Davy was sat at his desk with his hands covering his face.

"Morning Inspector"

"Is, it? Who said so?" Davy retorted.

"Sorry Inspector, but I've just heard some distressing news, and we need to discuss it urgently"

"You have some bloody distressing news Sergeant? Well so do I, that Bloody Wendy is pregnant!"

"What? You are joking, is it yours?" asked Morgan, rather foolishly.

"Course its bloody mine, that bloody husband of hers has forgotten how"

Detective Sergeant Morgan understood the predicament that the Detective Inspector found himself in, but the matter of an eight year-old girl's body was more important to Morgan.

Morgan did not want to look unsympathetic, but he had to stress that there was a more pressing matter that they had to address. He decided to 'take the bull by the horns' so to speak.

"Detective Inspector, we have a headless child, 'under cover'!"

Detective Inspector Davy moved his hands from his face and placed them on the desk.

"What!" he shouted.

"Yes Inspector, uniform pulled a young girl from the river last night, headless, they haven't told the family about their daughter's condition, but we can't keep it a secret for long"

"Bleeding hell, have the bastards struck again?"

"Well Inspector, it seems very much like it, I have discussed it with Inspector Jackson, and we both agree that we have to sort this 'under cover' situation, before it explodes in our faces"

"Well Sergeant, that's for the 'toss pot' Commander to sort, not me!"

Detective Inspector Davy then stood up from his desk.

"Sort out a meeting with the old 'Toss Pot' Commander, and give me a ring when you have a time, I'll be in the bloody pub!"

"But Detective Inspector" pleaded Sergeant Morgan.

"But Detective Inspector bollocks!" answered Davy.

And with that outburst Davy left the office.

Sergeant Morgan sat on the Inspector's desk and pondered his next move.

He decided to phone the Commander, set up the meeting for tomorrow and carry on with the Leila investigation.

Morgan then rang Commander Steele and arranged a meeting for 0900 hours the following day.

He then centred his mind on his next step in the investigation. Morgan suddenly remembered Detective Inspector Preece stating that they should check two addresses Leila's Maisonette and Stuart's flat.

He phoned Forensics, Ted Draper answered.

"Ted, it's Detective Sergeant Morgan, do you have the keys to 17 Norton Lane?"

"You do, is the flat still secure?"

"Are you sure? I'm only kidding Ted, my little joke".

"I need the keys, I need to check the premises at Norton Lane I'll be round to your office directly"

Sergeant Morgan left the office to pick up the keys to Stuart's flat and then to follow up on Preece's advice, and check out the place.

Detective Inspector Davy had sat in his car with his eyes shut for over two hours, before he heard the sound of the pub doors opening.

Davy then locked his car and slowly walked across the car park and into the pub.

Once sat at the bar, he entered into some sort of trance.

All he did was order whiskey after whiskey and just stare into space!

"What's wrong Mr Davy, you been sacked?" asked Dennis the barman.

"I often wish I had Dennis, I often wish I had" Davy responded. And then back into his trance like state.

After some forty minutes and too many whiskeys, an unmistakable voice could be heard.

"Well, what a place to find a brainless copper"

Jack Bent had just entered the bar.

Davy turned his head to face Bent.

"Hello 'tosser' what's wrong, run out of lives to ruin"

"I thought I might come over and ruin yours" was Jack Bent's response.

"Mines already ruined, sit down, I'll buy you a beer"

"YOU buy ME a beer? Now there is definitely something up the shit for you to buy me a beer!"

"Shut up and sit down, Dennis, give the 'tosser' a drink."

It was like a marriage made in Hell.

It was totally against their working relationship, but the more alcohol they both consumed the more they seemed to enjoy one another's company.

Davy, much the worse for the drink, confided with Bent.

"Jack, I'm in a total fucking mess"

"That bloody Wendy has got herself pregnant!"

"She hasn't got *herself* pregnant" was Bent's obvious response.

"You, Detective Inspector Paul 'fucking' Davy, have got her pregnant, you, dick head, and you alone!"

Inspector Davy agreed.

"Yes, I mean I have, but what the fuck can I do Jack?"

"Tell her to get it aborted, tell her to have an abortion" stated Bent

"She'll never do that. Anyway, what are you doing in here?" Davy enquired.

"Well Detective Inspector, one of my colleagues was giving me a lift to the Station, when I noticed your parked car, so here I am."

"It's that Taylor bird, she's asking for more money"

"Yeah, I'm not surprised, birds like that don't keep quiet for long" Davy conceded.

He then continued.

"Anyway, we have to pull the plug on this 'under cover' thing we have another body, a young girl"

"You are fucking joking, a young girl?" exclaimed Bent.

"Yes, its true Jack, we are in the fucking mire, Detective Sergeant Morgan is to arrange a meeting with the Commander tomorrow maybe he will have the answer"

"For all our sakes I hope so, I bloody hope so." said Bent.

They ordered more drinks and continued to talk nonsense, and for the first time since they met, they seemed to get on!

Eventually Davy seemed to regain some sort of sense he picked up his keys from the bar and asked.

"Right Jack, I have to go, can I give you a lift?"

Bent answered, with a twinkle in his eye.

106

"I have a better idea, firstly, you have drunk too much to drive, and secondly, we should pay a visit to that Lap Dancing Club, over on Lloyd Street."

"Don't be daft Jack, that place will cost a fortune, and that's just to get through the bloody door!" retorted Davy.

"Trust me Paul, I can get us through the door for nothing, come, let's go, it's a chance to forget your problems with the Commander's wife" stressed Bent.

Davy thought for a moment while he assessed the situation, when taking the alcohol he had consumed into account, driving was not an option.

He shouted to the barman Dennis.

"Dennis, call us a Taxi, we're going to peer at some young arse!"

"That's it Detective, you know it makes sense" said Bent, as he ordered another round of drinks.

The Taxi duly arrived, Davy and Bent drank up, and said goodbye to the barman, and off they went to the Lap Dancing Club.

The doormen at the Lap Dancing Club duly recognised Jack Bent, and they waved him and Davy inside the Club without payment.

They both walked through the Reception of the Club and headed straight for the bar, Davy with his mouth so wide open his bottom lip was almost touching the ground!

He had never been to such a Club, and the state of 'undress' surprised him.

Davy was also surprised regarding the atmosphere of the place, he had expected a dull, dark and seedy sort of environment, but what he was experiencing was the exact opposite, a place that seemed full of life, with many sounds of laughter and obvious enjoyment.

"What's your poison Paul" asked Bent.

"I'll have a Gin and Tonic, with plenty of Ice" replied Davy.

It only took a few more moments, before a nubile young 'lady' walked up to Davy, and spoke in a whispered sexy voice.

"Hello stranger, my name is Belinda, would you like some company?"

This almost caused Davy's knees to collapse from under him, his hand started to shake, causing the ice in his glass to perform some kind of dance with a tinkling tune.

He quickly composed himself and looked at the young 'lady', she was dressed in a really skimpy bra, which really didn't cover much, and panties that just did!

She had long black hair, and the sexiest of smiles.

Davy pulled himself more upright, trying to look taller, but failing.

"I certainly do, you gorgeous girl, I certainly do." he answered, as he allowed Belinda to link arms and guide him to a table close to the Pole Dancing Floor Area.

Jack Bent, who had been deserted at the bar, just stared in disbelief.

However, Bent wasn't alone for long, for a few moments later, he also was approached by an equally scantily clad young 'lady' called Juliet, and, as with Davy, he allowed her to guide him to the same table that Davy and Belinda occupied.

Davy was the life and soul of the party, so much so, that it didn't take too long, before he'd removed his shoes, shirt and trousers, crossed the floor to the Pole Dancing Area and attached himself to the Pole!

Unfortunately, he was about to prove that Paul Davy was no Pole Dancing expert.

The rest of the crowd encouraged him to perform, but as soon as he tried to climb he only got about a metre up the pole before his grip failed, and he ended up in a crumpled heap on the floor.

But Davy was no quitter, and he tried a further three times to climb the pole before a couple of the security personnel encouraged him to take up some other occupation.

This they did, by removing him from the Pole Dancing Area and back into his seat at the table he had so enthusiastically vacated, with the insistence, that he replace the discarded clothing and behave himself.

Although his newly-found friend had brought much laughter and amusement to most of the Club, Jack Bent realised that they were on the verge of being thrown out, so he helped Davy back into his clothes and told him to calm down.

Davy reluctantly accepted this advice from Bent and settled back into the party mood, by redirecting his attentions to Belinda, and to a lesser degree, Juliet.

Time passed and although Davy was very much under the influence, he still had enough of his wits about him, to realise that he had spent his way to an empty wallet!

Jack Bent noticed his predicament and whispered.

"Do you want to borrow some money Paul?"

At first Davy was going to say yes, but rather surprisingly, he sensibly declined.

"Sorry Belinda my darling, but I have to go, its work tomorrow" was his lame excuse to the young maiden that he had been trying to entertain.

As for Belinda, she had satisfied her terms of employment, so she just said goodbye, and left for pastures new.

Jack Bent also decided to leave, so he detached himself from his attentive and rather expensive young girl Juliet, and asked the barman to call a Taxi.

The Taxi duly arrived and both Bent and Davy left the bar area of the Lap Dancing Club and walked very unsteadily to the Reception Area, saying goodbye to the doormen as they walked towards the waiting Cab.

They were so much under the influence of the alcohol they had consumed, that at first, the Taxi driver refused to let them into his Cab.

It wasn't until Jack Bent forced a number of ten pound notes into his hand, that he relented and allowed them to enter.

As the Taxi set off for the respective homes of Bent and Davy, the rain was bouncing about six inches off the ground.

They had only been on the journey for a couple of minutes, when, as the Taxi was waiting to turn right at some traffic lights. "WATCH IT!" shouted Bent

A large truck skidded on the wet surface, and it hit the Taxi like a runaway train!

The Taxi and its occupants were pushed across the road by the truck which ended on its side, with the Taxi turned over on to its roof.

You could hear the screams for help emanating from within, but suddenly, the Taxi Cab burst into flames, and as it burnt, all sounds and life, were quickly extinguished.

CHAPTER TWELVE

As Sergeant Morgan walked along the riverside approaching 17 Norton Lane, he couldn't help thinking how much the area was similar to where Leila's Maisonette was situated.

He entered through the door at the rear of the premises which led straight into a kitchenette and this led to a large lounge, with a single bed located in one corner.

"Not much of a place to live" he muttered to himself.

As he looked around the flat, he realised it was very dusty and it didn't look like anyone had lived there for at least two to three months.

He gasped!

Someone had grabbed hold of his shoulder… he jumped forward and turned to face the culprit.

"Bleeding hell, I thought my time had come" he shouted.

It was Detective Inspector Preece.

DI Preece gave him a little time to compose himself and then asked.

Well, Sergeant, are you going to say hello, or something?"

"Yes Detective Inspector, how are you, how are you enjoying your suspension?"

"I'm well, Sergeant, more to the point, how's the 'Leila case' progressing?"

"Not very well Inspector, we had a most upsetting episode the other day"

Sergeant Morgan continued to bring the Detective Inspector up to date on the investigation and how the latest murder could mean that his 'under cover' decision may have to be abandoned.

DI Preece disagreed, but he didn't argue the point, he just changed the subject.

"Sergeant, I have been watching this place for a couple of days and there are some strange happenings, so strange, I almost broke into the apartment"

Preece continued.

"I would just stand amongst the bushes, you know, the ones just off the path adjacent to the river, and strange lights would appear from inside the flat. Yet, I never saw anyone enter or leave the place and when I looked through the window, nothing, there wasn't ever anyone to be seen"

"I wish you hadn't said that. This place is starting to give me the creeps" confessed Morgan.

"You say you found a cellar at Leila's place?"

"Well let's see if there's something similar here"

And with that, DI Preece started to walk about the flat, looking for any sort of disturbance to the building that could back up his last comment.

Morgan followed the Inspector as he searched, but all he wanted to do was get out of the place and quick.

He did not want to go through another experience like he'd had at Leila's Maisonette!

They started to knock on the walls, to knock on the floors they moved the bed and the only wardrobe, nothing.

Preece beckoned to Morgan.

"Give me a hand to move this table Sergeant and we'll clear the kitchen, I want to remove the lino from the floor."

Morgan reluctantly agreed and they both cleared the kitchen and rolled up the lino, which they discarded through the open rear door of the flat.

Morgan's heart nearly jumped from his chest!

A section of the kitchen floor boards had definitely been disturbed.

"Not another bleeding cellar" he mused.

Sergeant Morgan's fears were realised when Inspector Preece levered open, a trap door to a cellar.

"Let's get the fuck out of here Inspector!"

"Let's go, come on, let's go" shouted Morgan.

"Calm down Sergeant" stressed Preece.

DI Preece reached into his coat pocket and pulled out a revolver.

"Inspector, Let's go, we need to get the armed response team over here, come on, let's go!"

Morgan was pleading, almost begging the Inspector to leave.

"Sergeant Morgan, get a grip, we are trained Police Officers, we will deal with the situation."

Morgan turned to leave, but the Inspector grabbed his jacket.

"Sergeant, I am not leaving, so you go, and have it on your conscience for acting like a coward."

The Inspector relaxed his grip on Morgan's jacket and Morgan stood staring into the blackness of the cellar.

He did not want to enter, but Detective Inspector Preece was right, and he knew that he had to comply.

They both looked at each other for a moment, and then just nodded.

Preece took a small torch from his jacket pocket and led Morgan down the stairs and into the gloom.

They stood at the bottom of the stairs and, much to Sergeant Morgan's fears, in the far corner was a very large Chest.

That was the signal for Morgan to try and break the one hundred metre world record again, and nothing was going to stop him!

He had just turned, with the intention of sailing up the cellar stairs when the whole cellar area was suddenly lit with a kaleidoscope of light.

The main beam then centred on both Preece and Morgan.

Sergeant Morgan realised that his world record dream was to be shattered.

The beam had frozen both himself and the Detective Inspector to their respective positions.

A rather demanding, but strangely comforting voice descended from the beam, with a strange, but well intended message;

Detective Inspector Preece and Detective Sergeant Morgan, I require your attention.

My name is Taurus I am from the planet Jude, one of many planets that are part of a parallel universe to your own.

We are in the year 4000 on Jude, so we have surpassed your world's development both intellectually and scientifically.

We are sorry for the deaths that we caused in your world, but it was totally necessary for our world to survive.

We needed the Bone, blood and DNA of the chosen victims; these we used to rectify an inbred virus that had made our men folk impotent.

We had to leave 'the follower' entombed on your planet, until the tests on the body samples could be verified as sufficient, we realise now, that it was a mistake".

"We have now concluded our tests successfully and can leave your planet.

It is with regret, that the follower was disturbed at his hibernation place.

It is also with regret that the follower continued to collect samples, especially the last sample of the unfortunate girl.

To this end, we will replace the missing body parts to all the unfortunates and we will assist you with the necessary cover up activities.

We are now leaving your world, May I express our eternal gratitude to your world in our hour of need.

You will not remember any of what I have said to you, but I needed to express both our thanks for what your world provided, and our sympathy to the ones your world has lost.

The beam disappeared, and the cellar darkness returned, with the only light from the beam of the Detective Inspector's torch. Detective Inspector Preece turned to Detective Sergeant Morgan.

"See Sergeant, I told you not to worry, the bloody cellar is empty!"

"Sorry Detective Inspector, but I have had some very painful memories of my last visit to a cellar" confided Morgan.

"Let's go Sergeant; it is plainly obvious that there is nothing here to investigate" concluded the Detective Inspector, as he walked towards the stairs of the cellar.

They both then left the cellar, much to the delight of Detective Sergeant Morgan, who ensured that the apartment was left secure.

Detective Sergeant Morgan and Detective Inspector Preece headed along the riverside to where their cars were parked.

"What will you do now Detective Inspector?" asked Morgan.

"I don't know Sergeant, maybe I'll leave the investigation to you and Detective Inspector Davy"

DI Preece then warned Morgan

"If you don't find the suspects Sandra Barak and Stuart Taylor soon, both you and Detective Inspector Davy could find yourselves looking for a New Job"

They shook hands and exchanged pleasantries before they departed to their respective destinations, Detective Sergeant Morgan to the Station and Detective Inspector Preece to his garden.

A feeling of 'To Hell with the Investigation' had inexplicably overcome them both.

CHAPTER THIRTEEN

Not only did Detective Inspector Preece and Detective Sergeant Morgan have their memories 'erased' with regards to the Leila investigation, but so did all the relevant personnel at the Police Station.

In other words, everyone who had some sort of involvement with the Leila murders and the subsequent investigation had their memories regarding the headless state of the bodies erased. Instead of the Police Morgue containing headless bodies, it now contained the same bodies, but with only the little finger of the left hand missing.

Detective Sergeant Morgan arrived back at the Station just before 1600 hours, and as he walked inside he sensed an environment of complete calm.

A Calmness, that was far away from the usual manic situation that usually existed.

Morgan just accepted this he walked straight to what he now accepted, was Detective Inspector Davy's office, and sat down at the Detective Inspector's desk.

He sat back in the chair, placed his hands on to the back of his head and closed his eyes.

In his mind, it was unclear what to think about the events he had just witnessed at 17 Norton Lane.

His brain seemed to be a little scrambled, and he found it difficult to concentrate on the recent events at the flat. So much so, that he sprang to his feet shouted "bollocks" and left the office for his own flat.

Next morning just before 0630 hours Detective Sergeant Morgan entered the Police Station in a much more positive mood, once in Detective Inspector Davy's office, he immediately started to apply himself to the work at hand. Normally, he would wait for instructions from Davy, but he decided to make the decision himself.

To this end, he phoned HNT Associates and Mr Quarmby, regarding the occupational conditions surrounding their properties rented by Leila and Stuart Taylor.

He informed them, that their properties' could now be re-let, and that the respective keys could be obtained from the Police Station at their convenience.

Sergeant Morgan kept looking at his watch, he had now been at work for over two hours, and there was still no sign of Detective Inspector Davy.

Morgan picked up his mobile phone and phoned Inspector Davy's number, no answer.

Sergeant Morgan was now feeling a little worried, remembering the problem that the Inspector had regarding the condition of the Commander's wife Wendy.

He was also worried about the Inspector's state of mind.

Morgan then realised that the arranged meeting with the Commander at 0900 hours was imminent, so he decided to attend the meeting and continue trying to contact Davy once the meeting had ended.

As he entered Superintendant Kelly's office, no one else had arrived, so he just sat at the round meeting table and waited.

After a couple of minutes, Commander Colin Steele and Superintendant John Kelly entered the office, closely followed by Inspector Peter Jackson and Sergeant Colin Whitehead.

Sergeant Whitehead was of a similar age to Detective Sergeant Morgan, but perhaps he was more reliable and less likely to jump to conclusions.

As they all took their places around the table, Morgan could see from the expressions on their faces, that something was very much amiss.

There weren't any pleasantries, the Commander just welcomed everyone to the meeting and added.

"Sergeant Whitehead has some very disturbing news."

He then waved to the Sergeant, the signal for him to speak.

Detective Sergeant Whitehead stood up from the table, and with his voice at breaking point, tried his best to speak coherently.

"This morning, I have had some terrible news from the General Hospital three bodies were pulled from a burning Taxi Cab last night.

They informed us that they have just found the remains of a Police Security Card on one of the bodies, it would appear that it was the card belonging to Detective Inspector Paul Davy"

This news had the effect of a kick in the guts to Detective Sergeant Morgan.

Sergeant Whitehead continued.

"I've sent uniform to contact the Taxi firm and to clarify who ordered and actually used the said Taxi Cab."

"I have also sent Detective Inspector Davy's DNA records to the Hospital, but unfortunately, at the moment, it looks like the Inspector has gone."

The Sergeant re-took his seat at the table the Commander then thanked him and spoke.

"It goes without saying that we all hope that there has been some kind of mistake with the security card, but unfortunately, we have to be realists and accept that's unlikely, and we have in fact lost the Detective Inspector."

"Sergeant Whitehead and his staff will confirm the situation as soon as possible, and in the meantime, we all must carry on with our respective duties."

The Commander then changed the subject.

"Now gentlemen, I must confess that I've checked my diary, and I can't remember why I called this meeting."

"Can you Superintendant Kelly? Or you Detective Sergeant Morgan?" he asked.

They all looked rather silly, looking at one another in complete wonderment, but no one could think of the reason for the meeting.

The Commander took control of the meeting once more, and made some surprising announcements, especially regarding Detective Sergeant Morgan.

"In view of the present circumstances, I am promoting Detective Sergeant Morgan, to Acting Detective Inspector, with immediate effect."

"Also, I am assigning Sergeant Whitehead, to assist the Acting Detective Inspector, with special regards to the Leila case, and I'm sure, its speedy conclusion."

The Commander then tried to lighten the environment.

"Now, during what looks like a terrible situation, I have, to me anyway, a joyous announcement"

"My wife Wendy is pregnant with our first child"

This was the signal for many surprised handshakes of congratulations, apart from the now Acting Inspector Morgan, he'd been told by the real father, Davy!

The Commander continued.

"As you all know, I'm not the youngest copper around, and with the impending birth, my wife and I think it is time for me to take early retirement."

"This will take effect in one month's time and Superintendant Kelly will be my candidate to fill my boots, and I will also propose that Inspector Jackson takes over as Station Superintendant."

More shaking of hands and congratulations ensued, and the meeting concluded in a really jolly mood, with Acting Detective Inspector Morgan returning to HIS office to ponder on the developments.

As he took his seat behind his desk, he had two overriding emotions; one of surprising grief, on the possibility of Detective Inspector Davy's death, and one of total delight, on his much desired promotion.

Then suddenly Morgan's mindset changed completely, for some unknown reason, Acting Detective Inspector Morgan began sorting through the Leila investigation case files, and various papers and photographs were shredded.

His mind seemed to be confused, so he just accepted that the probable death of Detective Inspector Davy could be the reason. However, it didn't take long before he realised, that the Leila case was far from solved, and he still didn't have any idea regarding the whereabouts of Sandra Barak and Stuart Taylor. The searches of their last known addresses had produced nothing, and there had been no sightings.

Morgan was starting to feel rather insecure, he may have been promoted, but he was far from comfortable with regard to his own performance during the investigation.

He continued to evaluate the files for another couple of hours, and at least all the pertinent files, photographs etc. were in a much more tidied state and sorted in chronological order.

There was a knock on the office door, and Sergeant Whitehead entered the room.

He didn't sit down and he spoke in a whisper.

Furthermore, the information he was to provide was NOT REALLY what Acting Detective Inspector Morgan wanted to hear.

"I'm sorry Detective Inspector, but it has been confirmed that Detective Inspector Davy, did in fact meet his death in the Taxi Cab incident last night".

"One of the other victim's was a reporter from the Daily Journal, a Mr Jack Bent".

"Jack Bent!"

"Davy was sharing a Taxi with Jack Bent" exclaimed Morgan.

"Excuse the pun Sergeant, but Detective Inspector Davy wouldn't 'piss on' that pillock if he was on fire!"

He had only been promoted for a couple of hours, but Morgan seemed to be already acting more like his old boss, DI Jim Preece.

Morgan sat down at his desk and put his head into his hands, after a few moments, he realised that he had been too abrupt and disrespectful to Davy and to the Sergeant.

"I'm sorry Sergeant Whitehead, please take a seat and carry on, I shouldn't interrupt and talk crap"

The Detective Sergeant sat adjacent to the Inspector's desk and continued.

"The Detective Inspector's car was found in the car park of the Royal Oak Public House, and according to the barman, this is where he met Mr Jack Bent".

"Obviously, the Detective Inspector left his car in the car park, and both he and Mr Bent, journeyed to the 'Valley of Dolls' Lap Dancing Club, unfortunately, during the Taxi journey home, they were in collision with an Articulated Lorry".

Morgan stood up from his desk and started walking around the room, rubbing his chin with one of his hands as he mumbled to himself in amazement.

"Detective Inspector Davy drinking with Jack Bent, and visiting a Lap Dancing Club!"

He returned to his desk and sat down, he then spoke surprisingly tenderly.

"Colin, I am going to be really candid with you, I never really got to know Detective Inspector Davy"

"Furthermore, I thought he was a womanising plonker!"

"That said, he could be a bloody good copper, and in a strange way, I'll miss him, thank you for the speedy and efficient way that you conducted the gathering of the facts, it holds well for our future work together."

Morgan then reached inside one of his desk drawers and handed Sergeant Whitehead some selected papers and photographs.

He was now speaking as an Acting Detective Inspector.

"Detective Sergeant Whitehead, that's some light reading material, first thing tomorrow we start to work as a team and to conclude the Leila case"

Acting Detective Inspector Morgan arrived at the Station at
0700 hours and walked straight to the canteen.

He got himself a cup of coffee and made his way to his office.
As he walked inside the office, he was greeted by Sergeant
Whitehead, who was placing some of the 'light reading material'
onto the Leila case board.

"Morning sir, I hope you slept well?"

"Yes Sergeant, I did, and less of the sir"

"Just call me Inspector".

Morgan sat at his desk, with both hands folded on the back of
his head.

"Right Sergeant Whitehead, what have you learned?"

"Well Inspector, from what I can see, the investigation seems to
have been conducted in a very sensible and orderly fashion".

"However, I have one question; Apart from Mr Billy Watson,
better known as 'Bantam', all the other bodies are still under
Police custody, why?"

Morgan removed his hands from his head, with his left hand, he
started to rub his chin and with a slight frown he answered.

"I agree it looks a little strange, in the early days of the
investigation Detective Inspector Preece was in charge, there
was a lot of stupid speculation by the press, and the Detective
Inspector decided that the bodies should remain under Police
control."

Morgan continued and stressed.

"It looks like, just before Detective Inspector Davy's demise, he
was trying to satisfy the press speculation, thus the meeting with
Jack Bent."

"On reflection, controlling the bodies, and NOT communicating properly with the press could have been a mistake, but you have to remember, we still don't have the missing digits"

Morgan concluded by admitting that there may have been what some would call fundamental mistakes, but the investigating staff were under a great deal of pressure both from the press, and to a greater degree, the Police Management.

"Right Sergeant lets put the past to one side and concentrate on the present."

"We need to plan our next move, we need to find Sandra Barak and Stuart Taylor, they are the integral players and without them, the investigation will fail"

"O.K Inspector, I can understand the points you outline, but with regard to the missing digits, what if we never find them?"

"It's our job to make sure we do Sergeant".

"We find Barak and Taylor, and everything will fall into place, everything will just fall into place." stressed Morgan.

There followed a detailed discussion regarding several ideas on how to proceed; with the following initial steps agreed.

Acting Detective Inspector Morgan would call on the suspended Detective Inspector Preece to talk over the case, and to re-explore all the salient facts.

Sergeant Whitehead would take a visit to West's Supermarket's Warehouse, to talk to the personnel who worked with and knew all of the victims, especially Stuart Taylor.

This visit would also give the Sergeant his opportunity to gain a possible insight into the 'atmosphere' that surrounded the team prior to the murders.

Finally, Morgan stressed

"Sergeant, two things; one, go and sort out the meeting with West's, and two, sort out your desk and set it up in this office."

"I will now ring Detective Inspector Preece and arrange to meet with him. We'll meet again tomorrow to discuss any further developments".

Sergeant Whitehead nodded and left the office and Morgan picked up the phone and dialled DI Preece.

"Hello Inspector, this is Serg......

"Oh, I mean Acting Detective Inspector Morgan, are you well?"

"I'm very well, I heard about Davy and I'm very sorry, so you're 'Acting the Goat' now" joked Preece.

"Yes Inspector, I wonder if we could meet, I'd like your advice on some matters".

"Of course we can what about dinner tonight?"

"The wife makes a bloody good 'Spaghetti Bollock Naked' I'll tell her that you'll be here at six".

With that suggestion, Detective Inspector Preece hung up.

Morgan just sat at his desk, wondering what he had just agreed to, or was the Detective Inspector just drunk.

Anyway, he did want to see Preece again, so go to dinner he would.

126

It was dead on 1800 hours when Morgan rang the doorbell. The door was opened by DI Preece's wife Janet.

"Oh, come in Sergeant, Jim's just setting the dinner table, make your way to the lounge, I'll tell Jim you're here."

"I've brought a bottle of wine Mrs Preece, I hope you like it?" answered Morgan, as he gave the bottle to Janet.

"Oh, it's Valencia Medium Dry White, one of my favourites, it goes really well with Spaghetti Bolognaise" thank you very much Sergeant.

Morgan walked into the lounge he was dying to correct her about his title, but decided to remain silent.

A few moments later Detective Inspector Preece entered the room.

"What's your 'poison' Acting Inspector?"

"Would you like Whiskey, or would you prefer Brandy?"

"I'll just have Tonic Water, if that's O.K Inspector" answered Morgan.

"Please, let's just stick to Jim it's more comfortable that way" Preece then poured the drinks, Tonic Water for Morgan and a large glass of Whiskey for himself, and they both sat down in the lounge.

There followed an in-depth discussion about the Leila case, but nothing new was forthcoming.

It seemed to them both, that the only likely progress would be something gained from the public; a sighting, or evidence regarding the whereabouts of Barak, or Taylor, or both.

They both also agreed that the main disappointment was the lack of evidence at Leila's Maisonette and Taylor's apartment.

Janet interrupted their conversation when she shouted from the kitchen, for them to go to the dining area as the meal was ready.

This they did, Preece opened and poured the wine, and Morgan pondered the entrance of 'Spaghetti Bollock Naked'.

Half way through the meal, Janet asked a question.

"Sergeant Morgan, in that 'headless' case, when will you be releasing the bodies to their families?"

This question took Morgan by complete surprise!

"What headless case, Mrs Preece?" he queried.

Jim Preece intervened.

"Janet, there are no 'headless' bodies and there never were. What you are talking about, are the mutilated bodies that were found, not headless."

"But Jim, you said that they were headless" insisted Janet.

"No love, you are mistaken; I never said they were headless"

"They were just mutilated"

Morgan felt he had to back up the Detective Inspector.

"I can assure you Mrs Preece; there never were any bodies that were headless."

Janet looked at them both in turn, with a rather quizzical look on her face, and then she just shrugged her shoulders and carried on eating.

The meal was finished in relative silence, broken only by general chit chat, but Morgan had been stunned by Janet's comments.

He kept thinking, why would she say such a thing, and be so insistent that it was true?

After the meal, Preece and Morgan retired to the lounge, leaving Janet to the washing up.

Morgan did offer to help, but Preece said that she enjoys it. They were more relaxed when Janet wasn't there, and the atmosphere was very jovial.

Out of the blue, Preece made a very serious statement.

"Morgan, I've really enjoyed my life in the force, and I've always considered myself a bloody good Copper."

"However, Janet and I have decided it's time for me to take early retirement, it's time to enjoy ourselves while we still can."

Morgan wasn't surprised about Jim's statement, and he answered truthfully.

"Well Detective Inspector, You WILL be missed, and I for one will be sorry to see you go."

Morgan shook Preece's hand and wished him and Janet all the best for the many years ahead. Preece thanked him, and then shouted to Janet.

"Janet my love, leave the bloody pots, come here, we're going to have a toast."

Janet appeared from the kitchen Jim Preece opened the drinks cabinet and produced a bottle of champagne.

He then produced three glasses, popped the cork on the champagne bottle, poured the contents into the glasses, and proposed a toast.

"Here's to a long and happy retirement, doing exactly nothing, apart from loving my wonderful, wonderful wife."

"Cheers" they all shouted, as the contents of the glasses were emptied by one and all.

Janet then fell into her husband's arms, and as they began kissing, it became obvious that it was time for Morgan to disappear.

He made his excuses, thanked them for a lovely meal, and made his exit.

Preece and his wife just waved goodbye, without breaking from their embrace.

Morgan began laughing to himself as he made his way to his car, but as he entered the car, he remembered the comment that Janet had made, 'headless bodies'!

CHAPTER FOURTEEN

Morgan arrived at the Station just after 0700 hours. He signed in and went straight to the section where the Morgue was situated. As he entered, he could see Alan Longhurst, one of the attendants.

"Good morning Alan, how are you today?" he greeted.

"Not too bad Pete, or should I say, Acting Detective Inspector Morgan" answered Longhurst.

"Pete will do, Alan, I need to take a look at some of your customers."

"I just need to satisfy myself, that they all have their, would you believe, their head's attached."

"Acting Inspector, have you been drinking? Why would you think their heads would be missing? We don't' deal in 'body parts'" commented Longhurst, sarcastically.

"Alan, just humour me, I just need to take a look."

"OK Pete, which of the lucky buggers would you like to meet?"

"Any of the victims of the Leila investigation, you choose, any will do"

Longhurst walked over to the cabinets, made a selection, and pulled the door open, exposing the bagged body within.

"This is one of yours. Sergeant Mick Cooney."

Longhurst opened the sheet covering the corpse, and stood to one side to allow Morgan viewing access.

Morgan stared at his one time colleague.

He was overcome with a sense of regret seeing him in such a situation, and regret that he had been so stupid as to listen to Janet Preece and her insistence of 'headless bodies'.

Morgan turned to Alan Longhurst, and with an ever-increasing sense of remorse, he thanked him.

"Thank you Alan, you have been very understanding, I won't bother you again"

"Call anytime Acting Inspector, we aim to please."

This last comment did not register with Morgan he was already halfway down the corridor on his way to his office, churning over and over in his mind.

"Why did I listen to that silly bugger Janet?"

When he entered his office, he threw his jacket on to the coat stand, still feeling a little like a mug.

The phone rang and Morgan reluctantly picked it up, still feeling a little daft.

"Hello, Acting Detective Inspector Morgan",

"Morning Superintendant, the time of Detective Inspector Davy's funeral OK, thanks for phoning."

Morgan had just been informed by the Station Superintendant of the details regarding Davy's funeral in three days time.

Morgan would be attending, but only as a mark of respect to Detective Inspector Davy, and not as part of the organised 'send off' by the Police Federation.

He walked over to Sergeant Whitehead's desk, and he noticed that the Sergeant had already brought his papers etc. into the office, but hadn't placed them inside the desk.

He couldn't stop himself from flicking through the papers, and one set of documents caught his eye, he picked them out of the pile and started to read.

They concerned a case that the Sergeant had obviously been involved in, a long standing investigation within the local drug scene, specifically concerning two very well known drug 'Barons', Messer's Tony Bailey and Neil Cooke.

The names of the Barons were known to Morgan, he had tried to arrest them on a number of occasions when he was in uniform, but as the documents outlined, evidence was always at a premium, and not sufficient for a conviction.

He returned the documents to the Sergeants desk and turned to check the information on the Leila case board.

But Morgan couldn't get the statement from Janet out of his mind, so he decided to re-check all the data again.

He was still sorting through the papers and photographs, when Sergeant Whitehead entered the office.

"Good day Inspector" greeted the Sergeant.

"Hi Sergeant, how did your meeting at West's go?" replied Morgan, still checking the case board.

"It went as expected Inspector, Ron Judge the Despatch Manager, confirmed most of what we already knew, except for one thing. He had heard that 'Bantam' character, mention headless bodies."

Morgan looked up from the case files he was checking, at first he spoke in a very measured tone.

"Sergeant, this morning I have had a most humiliating experience in the Morgue. I stupidly checked the condition of one of the so called headless bodies.

I have just, for the umpteenth time, checked through the case notes, believe me Sergeant there are NO FUCKING BODIES THAT ARE HEADLESS!"

Morgan walked over to his desk and sat down, and, pointing at the Sergeant, he again stressed.

"Sergeant Whitehead, the mention of bodies with anything apart from a finger missing, IS NOT to be a subject for discussion in this office. Do you agree?"

All the Sergeant could do was nod, this he did, and rather quietly sat down at his desk.

This started a very quiet period, with them both just attending to tidying their desks, especially Acting Detective Inspector Morgan, he was just sitting quietly, letting his blood return from boiling point.

After a few minutes, Morgan decided he had to apologise, so he looked up from his desk.

"Sergeant, please take my previous comments as unusual, I didn't want to sound like an arse ole, I lost it, and I apologise."

Whitehead just answered

"Apology accepted", although, he felt that the Inspector had reacted, very much over the top.

Morgan decided to change the subject.

"Sergeant, what do you know about the two 'tossers, Bailey and Cooke?"

Sergeant Whitehead was surprised that the Inspector knew about the two drug 'barons', after all, they were not openly talked about within the Station.

With this in mind, he answered with a certain amount of caution.

"Obviously I've heard of them, but I'm not up to date on their recent activities."

Morgan realised that the Sergeant was not being entirely truthful, so he asked again.

"Sergeant, surely you remember, you were involved in a very extensive investigation regarding these two villains? And before you start talking 'crap' I've seen the case notes on your desk".

"And furthermore, before you start accusing me of shifting through your files, you left them lying on your bloody desk, even the bloody cleaner could have read them."

Sergeant Whitehead wanted to punch the Inspector, but he realised that he had brought the Inspector's comments upon himself, and he should have been more careful with important documents. He had to concede, that he had been foolish, so he admitted it.

"OK Inspector, you're right. I did assist in many investigations regarding those two, and yes, I should not leave important files lying around."

Morgan sensed that both he and the Sergeant were acting like enemies, so he decided that he should keep to a subject that they both agreed on.

"Sergeant, the Leila case has calmed, so let's concentrate on the two druggies. Maybe we could make a contribution?"

"Get out your information and let's see what we can do."

"That's as maybe Inspector, but Inspector Jackson, and to some extent, the Commander, were in charge of the original investigation and should we not ask them before we act?" Morgan answered with another question.

"I accept your answer, but Jackson will need all his energy when he becomes Station Superintendant".

"So we could make a real contribution, and, at the same time help to clear Jackson's case file, being the Station Superintendant is a full time job, is it not?"

"OK Inspector, you win" answered Whitehead, in a bit of a whimper.

Sergeant Whitehead retrieved the documents from his desk, and both he and the Inspector interrogated the material together.

After sifting through all the pertinent documents, Morgan had a question for the Sergeant.

"Sergeant, what's your opinion on the relationship between Bailey and Cooke?"

The Sergeant answered, emphatically.

"There's no doubt about it! They are both Bloody Gay, they've had a gay relationship for years."

Another question emanated from Morgan.

"So if they've had a good relationship for so long, they will have kept their 'criminal files' in the one place. In the place, where they both lived, or worked, do you agree Sergeant?"

"I agree Inspector, but we have never been able to take them by surprise so to speak", conceded the Sergeant.

"Exactly" answered Morgan, excitedly, as he continued.

"And that's exactly what we need to do. Visit them when they least expect it."

"That's easier said then done" said Whitehead.

"Don't worry Sergeant, we will make a plan, we'll sleep on it."

Morgan concluded the discussion, by saying.

"We'll talk some more tomorrow; it's time I wasn't here."

Morgan took his coat from the coat stand, and with a wave left the office.

Sergeant Whitehead just sat at his desk, he kept wondering what the Inspector had meant?

'Visit them when they least expect it.'

He churned this statement over in his mind, and concluded; regardless of when we visited them, they always expected it. He then shouted out loud.

"Anyway, we're not on that bloody investigation!"

Sergeant Whitehead stood up from his desk, placed all the confidential paperwork into the desk drawer and locked it; he didn't want Acting Detective Inspector Morgan moaning about cleaners again.

Then he also walked over to the coat stand, picked up his coat, and decided to follow in the footsteps of the Detective Inspector, and have an early night.

He left the office still pondering the discussions regarding the 'Barons', and started to wonder,

"Maybe the Inspector is right, maybe we should re-start the investigation."

It was just before 0530 hours Tony Bailey and Neil Cooke were checking the Bar and Restaurant receipts from the previous night at one of their night clubs, the Bailey Projectile.

"Neil, make sure the bloody door's locked will you love? I need to open the safe."

"OK luv" was Neil's answer.

Tony had just reached down to open the safe when he heard a thud, he turned around just in time to see his partner fall to the floor, blood spurting from the back of his head.

Tony cried out "What the Fu…"

A second thud and Tony Bailey also fell to the ground, shot through the temple.

A lone figure removed the safe key from the hand of the dying Tony and casually walked across the room to the safe.

The safe had a combination lock, but the figure, for some unknown reason, already knew the combination, the numbers were entered and the key used and the safe opened, once opened various documents and papers were removed.

These were checked, some were replaced in the safe, and the safe locked, the other documents were placed in one of the drawers of the adjacent desk along with the safe keys.

An already prepared suicide note that was signed by both Tony and Neil was then placed on the desk.

The figure's attention was then directed towards the bodies of the two victims and these were very carefully arranged on the floor, so that they were facing each other, each having one of the two guns used, placed in one of their hands.

Finally, the office door was checked and left locked.

The figure then walked back to where the two bodies lay, readjusted their positions slightly, and vanished as silently and as quickly, as it had appeared.

CHAPTER FIFTEEN

Morgan walked into the Station canteen just after 0730 hours. He saw Sergeant Whitehead talking to Inspector Jackson, so he decided to first get a cuppa, and then to join them.

"Morning guys" was Morgan's greeting.

Both Sergeant Whitehead and Inspector Jackson looked up, and recognised Morgan with a wave.

"Good morning Acting Detective Inspector" they both answered.

Inspector Jackson and Morgan had never been the best of friends, so Morgan was pleasantly surprised to get a friendly wave from Jackson.

Morgan got his coffee and sat down next to Sergeant Whitehead. Inspector Jackson, trying his best to be accommodating, told Morgan that they had just been talking about the Barons.

"Detective Inspector, we have just agreed that the Barons case should be re-assigned, and that you are the one to take it forward."

Morgan was surprised by this comment, but he answered amicably.

"I'm very honoured that you both think that I could contribute to the case, and both Sergeant Whitehead and I, will do our utmost, to crack it."

Inspector Jackson continued.

"The Sergeant has told me that you both have already looked through most of the case files, and if I can be of any assistance, you only have to ask."

"That's very much appreciated Inspector Jackson, we will certainly get you involved if needs dictate" answered Morgan.

There followed a general discussion, mostly regarding the forthcoming funeral of Inspector Davy.

Of which, Inspector Jackson joked.

"It looks like he will have to carry his own bloody coffin it's been very difficult to find any volunteers."

"I'm not surprised, he's always been his own man, maybe we should ask Commander Steele." suggested Morgan sarcastically.

"Ah, Ah, very funny." said Whitehead.

Morgan stood up and placed his empty cup onto the canteen serving hatch.

"Right, Sergeant, shall we go and start the day's proceedings?"

"Sounds a good idea Detective Inspector" answered Sergeant Whitehead.

Inspector Jackson also stood up.

"I'll have a look into the 'Barons' files that I have, there may be something there that Sergeant Whitehead doesn't have".

"If I find anything, I'll pass it on."

He continued

"It would be a real bonus to this Station, if we can sort out those two bleeders, once and for all."

Morgan was very surprised, but he found himself agreeing with Inspector Jackson.

"Very unusual" he mused.

Both Sergeant Whitehead and Detective Inspector Morgan left the canteen and made their way to Morgan's office.

Once in the office, Morgan was yawning as he went straight to his chair and sat down without removing his coat.

"Too many late nights Inspector?" asked Whitehead.

"You said it Sergeant" answered Morgan, still yawning.

Sergeant Whitehead started to collate the files of the Barons investigation and began sorting them on his desk.

Morgan's phone rang, so Morgan picked up the phone.

"Hello, Acting Detective Inspector Morgan."

"Inspector Jackson, have you found some more information?"

"What!"

"Where did you say?"

"Right, we're on our way."

Morgan replaced the receiver, and almost danced towards the door.

"Come on Sergeant, we may have had a break"

"Where are we going?" asked Whitehead.

"We are going to the Bailey Projectile."

"We are going to the Bailey Projectile!" was Morgan's repeated triumphant call.

Sergeant Whitehead tried to clarify the situation by asking.

"What the Bloody hell is the Bailey Projectile?"

But Morgan had already exited through the office door.

All the Sergeant could do was to follow, and get an explanation once he caught up with the Inspector.

Morgan duly explained the situation during the journey.

The Barons had been found dead in the office of one of their clubs, the Bailey Projectile.

Two Uniform Constables were in attendance when Acting Detective Inspector Morgan and Sergeant Whitehead arrived at the Club.

The Constables ushered them both to the crime scene, the upstairs office.

Morgan observed the crime scene as he walked between the two bodies and with his hands in his pockets he observed and read the suicide note that was lying on the desk.
It read:

> To our entire worldly, lovely, and beautiful long lasting friends.
> The time has come to say our goodbyes to one and all.
> We both have enjoyed the journey, but it is time to go.
> We both hope to meet with you all again, on the other side.
>
> Signed Neil and Tony

Morgan asked one of the Constables
"Who discovered the bodies?"
"The cleaner, Mavis Booth, Detective Inspector, when she opened the office this morning, round about 0700 hours."
"Where is she now?"
"She's downstairs Detective Inspector."
Morgan turned to the Sergeant.
"Go and have a talk to her Sergeant, confirm that she hasn't touched anything, and find out if she knows what time the rest of the staff would have left for home."
Sergeant Whitehead left the office and Morgan re-checked the desk.
He put on his gloves and started to check through the drawers of the desk.
As he read some papers from one of the desk drawers Morgan's face lit up with an expression of great delight.

So much so, that he sat on the chair adjacent to the desk to flick through and read them again, and as it turned out, with even greater satisfaction.

"Eureka" he exclaimed.

"This IS my lucky day" he shouted.

Sergeant Whitehead returned to the office.

He informed the Inspector that, as far as the cleaner was concerned, the club closes at 0300 hours, and that most of the staff would have left some thirty minutes later.

Morgan stood up from his interesting reading material, and surveyed the scene again.

"Well Sergeant, it doesn't look like anyone else was involved anyway."

"The position of both of the bodies, the firearms that they both hold, and last but not least, the bloody suicide note."

"It's cut and dried, they had a suicide pact."

He walked back to the desk and bagged the papers he had been reading.

"Furthermore, these little beauties, will give us enough evidence to put away the rest of the gang."

"Right Sergeant, you'll need to get a warrant so that we can open the safe".

"Bag the suicide note, get the Tech Guys down here, and find out who else has keys to this office. I'm going back to the Station to see Luke Morley and the Drug Squad."

"It's not the Tech Guys it's Forensics Inspector." answered Whitehead as he thought 'what did your last bloody slave die of.'

"Yeah, OK, Forensics." answered Morgan.

Morgan continued.

"Oh, and before I forget, find out if our cleaner lady has any form."

"And we will need to find out if our 'love birds' have any long-standing medical problems."

Morgan was running in overdrive, so much so that he almost flew out of the office, leaving Sergeant Whitehead to secure the crime scene and to complete the tasks he had just been given.

The Sergeant kept looking at the position of the two bodies; yes it certainly looks like a suicide pact, but surely they could have found an easier method to die, he mused.

Once back at the Station, Acting Detective Inspector Morgan went directly to the office of the Drug Squad, and in particular, to see Detective Sergeant Luke Morley.

As he walked into the office, he was immediately recognised by Morley.

"Bloody Hell, look what the 'cat's' dragged in, Acting Detective Inspector Morgan." commented the Sergeant.

Morgan and Luke Morley had spent a lot of time together when they were in uniform, and since then they had maintained a loose and friendly relationship, but were not close friends.

Luke Morley was one year older than Morgan, but the way that they both acted, professionally and personally, and the very similar styling of their blond hair, anyone who didn't know them, would swear they were brothers.

"The 'cat' has dragged in some documents that are going to make your life a bloody lot easier. Mine's coffee, black no sugar" Morgan continued triumphantly.

Detective Sergeant Morley produced the required drink and sat down with Morgan to read through the documents.

As Luke Morley read through the papers, he kept stopping to talk to himself, with expressions like; "I bloody knew it", "So that's how they move them", "that little tosser" and "wait till I get my hands on him" and so on.

As soon as Morley had finished reading, Morgan asked for his response.

"There's absolutely everything here. Names, pick up dates, distribution personnel, it's bloody great, if you weren't so bloody ugly I'd kiss you." was Detective Sergeant Morley's very happy response.

Sergeant Morley then hesitated.

"Just a minute, this is some sort of bloody joke? Where did you get these documents from? Acting Detective Inspector"

Morgan answered reassuringly.

"Don't worry Detective, I obtained the documents from the offices of the Bailey Projectile club this morning, surely you have heard on the grape vine that the two owners of the club have passed away? Fortunately for us, and may I say, especially for you. They left these documents in their desk."

This statement was just what Detective Sergeant Morley wanted to hear.

"No I didn't hear about the two unfortunates. Some kind of suicide pact eh, well I never."

"Tough!"

Morley continued.

"Well Acting Detective Inspector Morgan, you are a bloody Saint. For this information I will buy you a pint, No, I'll buy you bloody gallons!"

Morley stood up and aggressively shook Morgan by the hand. "My team and I have work to do, I'll give you a ring later Detective Inspector, we should have some celebrating to do." Morgan just laughed as he walked to the door he turned and added the comment

"I hope you realise, that I'm very expensive Detective Sergeant Morley" as he left the office.

As Morgan entered his own office, the phone was ringing he walked over to his desk and picked up the receiver.

"Hello, Acting Detective Inspector Morgan".

It was Journalist Steven Dukes, calling from the Daily Journal. Steven Dukes was a younger version of the deceased Jack Bent, but with one exception, he was true to his word, and was liked by all that knew him.

"Yes I remember Jack Bent, I was very sorry to hear about his accident, what can I do for you Mr Dukes?" asked Morgan.

"You've been contacted by a Margaret Taylor?"

"Yes, I know of her."

"She said WHAT!"

Dukes had just informed Morgan that Margaret Taylor wanted the same understanding with the Daily Journal, which she had with Jack Bent, or she would blow the whistle on the 'headless corpses'.

Acting Detective Inspector Morgan's head nearly blew off! Consequently, he replied in a rage.

"Tell that Fucking Margaret Taylor…"

He paused, put his hand to his mouth, took a few deep breaths, and answered again, but calmly this time.

"Yes, Mr Dukes, I've heard that rumour before, why don't you come to see me at the Station, and I'll show you the so-called headless bodies."

He continued, stressing very clearly,

"Let's see if we can put an end to the money-grabbing antics of Margaret Taylor, and prove once and for all, WE DO NOT HAVE ANY HEADLESS BODIES IN THE STATION MORGUE!"

Steven Dukes agreed to Morgan's request, and they arranged to meet at the Station at 1600 hours that afternoon.

Morgan was just starting to calm down, when Sergeant Whitehead entered the office.

He immediately noticed that the Inspector's face looked a little red,

"What's wrong Inspector?" he asked.

"Are you having a 'hot flush'?" he joked.

"Hot flush, I'll give you bloody hot flush, it's that bloody Margaret Taylor, she's still talking about headless bloody bodies!" he retorted.

Detective Inspector Morgan could feel himself getting hot under the collar again, so he changed the subject, asking the Sergeant "How did you get on with our investigation at the 'lover boys' club?"

"Very well, Inspector, I think I've covered all the queries you had."

The Sergeant then reeled off answers to the questions posed by the Inspector at the Bailey Projectile club.

"Yes Inspector, we have secured the scene and the club will be closed for the next few days."

"The warrant will be issued tomorrow, so we can have a look in the safe".

"As for the 'lover boys', I have requested uniform to find out about any medical problems, and it seems only the 'lovers' and the cleaner, Mavis Booth, have keys to the office. And last but not the least… the cleaner has no form."

"Great work Sergeant, great work." said Morgan gleefully.

Morgan then updated the Sergeant,

"I took the desk documents to Sergeant Morley of the Drug Squad, and he was ecstatic. It looks like we have had a good result, a bit by chance, but a good result."

"Oh, by the way, when Morley locks up the rest of the 'tossers', he's going to buy the drinks."

"What, Morley buys the drinks? That I have to see" exclaimed Whitehead.

"Let's go celebrate, I'll buy the coffees" said Morgan.

With that comment from the Detective Inspector, they both left the office for the canteen.

As they sat down in the canteen, Sergeant Whitehead had a question.

"Inspector, There still is one problem."

"And what is that?" asked Morgan.

"Forensics checked the suicide note for finger prints"

"So?" queried Morgan.

"There weren't any." stated Whitehead.

"Well, that is strange, but as long as the two signatures are genuine ones, so what!" answered Morgan.

There was a shout from the doorway.

"Acting Detective Inspector Morgan, there's a chap from the Daily Journal to see you."

"Oh shit!"

"I have to show this bloody Journalist our so called headless troupe"

"Sergeant, you carry on sorting out the 'lover boys' investigation, and I'll catch up with you later."

The Detective Inspector left the canteen and made his way to the Station Reception.

He met Steven Dukes and took him to the Morgue, where the attendant allowed Dukes to visually check as many of the Leila case victims as was necessary.

Once Dukes was satisfied, Morgan guided him through to the canteen, where they sat and had a drink.

"What do you want me to say to Margaret Taylor?" asked Dukes.

"Just ignore her, she'll eventually, just go away" said Morgan.

CHAPTER SIXTEEN

It was the day of Detective Inspector Davy's funeral. Acting Detective Inspector Morgan and Detective Sergeant Whitehead sat in Morgan's office, discussing the 'lover boy' case.

"Inspector, from what has transpired, what's your thinking on our next move?" asked Whitehead.

"Well Sergeant, Morley and his Drugs Squad, are very happy with their part of the investigation, and very soon we should be treated to a free night out. As for us, well, the opening of the safe produced nothing"

"There's no evidence of third party involvement. There hasn't been any tampering with the office door lock, and finally, the lack of fingerprints on the suicide note. But in this case, the absence of such finger prints could only mean that when they signed the note, they wore gloves. So as I see it Sergeant, it's over!"

"The verdict is suicide"

"Inspector, not many people would sign such a note wearing gloves" Sergeant Whitehead suggested.

"I've just covered that point Sergeant" stressed Morgan. Morgan took time out to think again about the absence of fingerprints, and the possibility of signing the suicide note wearing gloves, before he gave his final answer.

"Well, that does appear a little odd and could be a problem Sergeant, but as I have already said, when they signed the note, they must have worn gloves. Anyway, I'm not going to spend time trying to prove, or disprove it."

Morgan then outlined what he saw as their situation away from the 'lover boy's' case, and what their immediate investigatory direction was.

"Sergeant, we need to concentrate on other matters, especially the Leila case, we need to up the anti."

Morgan continued.

"We need to concentrate on the whereabouts of the two suspects, Barak and Taylor; to this end I will ring our new friend, Mr Steven Dukes at the Daily Journal. I'll invite him to a drink tonight, and ask him to run the story, it's time we updated the general public."

"Sergeant, you go and get the most recent photographs of our suspects, and I'll phone our friend".

The Sergeant half-heartedly agreed and left the office, Morgan then phoned Steven Dukes at the Daily Journal.

"Hello Steven, this is Detective Inspector Morgan, we need to talk, how do you fancy meeting for a drink tonight?"

"If you're paying Inspector, it sounds good to me" was Dukes expected answer.

"OK, I have Detective Inspector Davy's funeral at two, I'll give the reception a miss, let's say the Black Bull at half past four?"

"That's fine by me Inspector, I'll see you then."

Morgan put down the receiver, and sat back in his chair, his hands resting on the back of his head.

He knew that he was expected to attend the post funeral 'get together', but he felt that moving the Leila case forward, was more important.

Sergeant Whitehead returned to the office and placed the two requested photographs on Morgan's desk.

"Did you make arrangements with Steven Dukes Inspector?" he asked.

"Yes Sergeant, it's all done. I'm meeting him after the funeral let's hope we achieve the desired result. However, it does mean that I'll miss the jollies after the funeral service, thank God."

As Acting Detective Inspector Morgan and Detective Sergeant Whitehead entered the church, they noticed DI Preece and his wife Janet, seated close to the door and decided to sit next to them.

"Good afternoon, Sergeant Whitehead and Acting Detective Inspector" acknowledged Preece.

Both Morgan and Whitehead acknowledged the Detective Inspector, and said hello to Janet.

After a few more minutes, Detective Inspector Davy's coffin entered the church and the congregation stood up with their heads bowed.

Morgan nudged Whitehead and whispered.

"I'm surprised to see that they managed to convince six uniforms to carry the coffin after all."

"Don't be so disrespectful" commented Sergeant Whitehead.

After just less than two hours, the service was complete, and Morgan found him self stood next to Janet, at the grave side.

"How's the Detective Inspector finding retirement?" queried Morgan.

"He seems to be coping alright Sergeant, but to be honest, I never seem to see much of him, and when I do, he's always so tired." said Janet.

She continued. "I think I saw more of him when he was still working."

"You need to take a holiday, so you both can relax and decide what to do in the future, retirement can be difficult" stressed Morgan.

"I agree Sergeant, but I'll need to get him drunk first before I even try to mention it" Janet joked.

Detective Inspector Preece tapped Morgan on the shoulder, and whispered.

"How are you getting on with the Leila case Inspector?"

"We seem to have stalled" Morgan admitted.

He continued

"We are going to try and stimulate the public's interest through the Daily Journal."

He then whispered to Preece.

"That Margaret Taylor raised the headless issue again, I may have to pay her a visit" he joked.

"Well all the best, Acting Detective Inspector, when you visit that pillock Taylor, give her a slap from me" said Preece, not joking!

After the burial and general chit chat was concluded Detective Inspector Morgan made his excuses and left the cemetery for the Station.

He'd forgotten the photographs of Barak and Taylor.

Once the photographs were collected, he would make his way to the Pub, and his meeting with his journalist friend, Steven Dukes.

As Morgan entered the Black Bull, he could see Steven Dukes sat at the bar, so he joined him, and asked

"What can I buy you Steve?"

"I'll have a pint of lager Detective Inspector, by the way, how did the funeral go?"

Morgan ordered a pint and a Tonic Water for himself, and then answered Dukes.

"The funeral went really well, I was surprised to see so many there, especially as Detective Inspector Davy wasn't the most respected or even liked Officer at the Station."

Morgan placed the two photographs on the bar, and pushed them over to Dukes.

"So Detective Inspector, these are the principle suspects?" queried Dukes.

"Yes, but unfortunately, they are the ONLY suspects!" stressed Morgan.

He then presented his proposal to Dukes.

"Steve, what we need to do, is to place these two into the public domain. Your article could be the deciding factor in bringing an end to this investigation."

"It's good that you feel so positive when dealing with the press, it's a pity most of the other Coppers don't feel the same way" commented Dukes.

"I don't know much about the feelings of other Police Officers, but I certainly want to be positive" answered Morgan.

Morgan did not want to talk about the relationship between the Press and Police, so he was pleasantly surprised, when Dukes changed the subject.

"What about you, Peter, are you married?" asked Dukes.

"Never ever tried it, but you never know, if I meet a rich, gorgeous girl, I may have to try it" joked Morgan.

There followed a detailed discussion on how to present the article, with them both agreeing that the 'Front Page', was a must!

After a couple more drinks, and surprisingly to Morgan, in total agreement, they parted, with the following final comments.

"I'll speak to the Editor first thing tomorrow morning, and if he gives the go ahead, I'll prepare the article for the late edition" said Dukes.

"That's great"

"I will owe you one Steve" confirmed Morgan.

"All you will owe me is total licence regarding the Leila case, and I mean total", stated Dukes.

"Don't worry Steve you will be the only journalist in the frame, you have my word" assured Morgan.

It was the early hours of the morning Margaret Brown (nee Taylor) and her husband Ian were fast asleep within their bungalow, on the outskirts of Manchester.

Unknown to them, there was a lone figure silently moving within the kitchen area of the bungalow.

Very carefully and silently, all the gas taps on the oven top were turned on, allowing the gas to flow.

The figure then moved silently towards the bedroom area.

The gas boiler was situated within the bedroom where Margaret and Ian were sleeping.

The figure moved towards the boiler, and just as silently the gas input pipe was quickly loosened, allowing the gas to escape freely.

The figure then paused from its activities, and allowed the escaping gases to filter to all parts of the bungalow.

The speed and silence of the figure ensured that the sleeping couple were not disturbed and were unaware of their pending demise.

After a pre-determined time lapse, when the figure was satisfied that the gas flow had covered all parts of the building, there was a spark, followed by a massive flash of flame, and an all-encompassing destructive explosion.

The roof of the bungalow was totally removed by the blast and the walls flattened, turning a well-looked-after home into a pile of flaming rubble containing the extinguished lives of Margaret and Ian Brown.

The lone figure had already disappeared, just as quickly and as silently as it appeared.

Next morning at 0805 hours, Detective Inspector Morgan entered his office, placed his coat on the coat hanger, quickly turned, and made his way to the Superintendant's office.
He knocked on the door.
"Come in" was the answer.
Superintendant Kelly was at his desk, as Morgan entered.
He asked Morgan.
"What can I do for you this morning Acting Detective?"
"Morning Superintendant, I just wanted to update you on the Leila case" said Morgan, as he yawned.
"What's wrong Detective Inspector Morgan? Too much to drink after the Davey funeral?" queried Superintendant Kelly.
"No Superintendant, I think I may have a cold" answered Morgan.
"Well then, update me" stressed The Superintendant.
"Right, well yesterday, I had a meeting with Steven Dukes of the Daily Journal. He agreed to speak to his editor and try and get the 'Leila' suspects and their whereabouts, into the public domain."
"He has agreed to put a spread on the front page of the Daily Journal."
"That sounds good Detective Inspector, we could do with a break in the case, let me know what transpires"
Superintendant Kelly was really busy, and unless there was a pending arrest in the Leila case, he wasn't really interested in updates.
"Is that all Detective Inspector?" he asked abruptly.
"Yes Superintendant, that's it, I'll keep you up to date."
Morgan said goodbye and left the office.

As he made his way to his own office, he encountered Sergeant Whitehead as he came out of the canteen.

"Morning Sergeant, how did the funeral reception go?

"Very well Inspector, Detective Inspector Davy had a good send off, it's a pity you weren't there" was the sarcastic answer from the Sergeant.

"You know why I wasn't there Sergeant. I had other very important discussions to conduct. Now less of the stupid questions, and let's get on."

They made their way to Morgan's office, with Sergeant Whitehead feeling rather miffed with Morgan's attitude.

The Sergeant felt that Morgan had let the department down, by not bothering to attend the funeral function.

After a while, it became obvious that there was an atmosphere within the office, Morgan recognised this, and decided to act.

"OK Sergeant, come on, tell me why I should have been at the send off to Detective Inspector Davy?"

"Because he wa......

The phone rang.

Morgan answered.

"Hello, Acting Detective Inspector Morgan"

"You are kidding!"

"It's for real?"

"Thanks for letting me know, I really appreciate it."

Morgan returned the receiver, and turned to Sergeant Whitehead.

"Sergeant, forget about our feelings regarding Detective Inspector Davy, we have something to celebrate. That was Manchester Division, Margaret Taylor and her husband died last night. Apparently, the family home was destroyed by a gas explosion, OH DEAR!"

Morgan sat back in his chair.

The death of Margaret Taylor seemed to remove the monkey from his back.

"Sergeant, we need to celebrate."

"I think I'll ring Luke Morley. If I'm not mistaken, he owes us a few drinks" said Morgan gleefully.

He picked up his mobile phone.

"Hello Detective Sergeant Morley, this is the guy that you owe a night out. You were just going to ring me? You have? Well that's great news"

"When and where are you taking us? Tonight, great, we'll see you there, six thirty it is."

Morgan put his mobile phone back into his pocket and turned to the Sergeant, his phone call to Sergeant Morley had certainly changed his mood.

"Sergeant that was our friend Luke Morley, after the help that we gave him, he has arrested and charged six druggies, and he's buying the drinks at the Black Bull tonight."

Sergeant Whitehead's mood was also lifted by this news, so much so, that he even started to smile.

"Well Inspector, I can't wait."

"I think I will even order champagne" Whitehead joked.

Morgan agreed, but he then spoke a jovial word of caution.

"I don't think you will get away with that Sergeant, But you may as well try."

The atmosphere in the office became rather silly, more like a carnival atmosphere with both the Inspector and the Sergeant, working at their desks whistling joyfully, if really badly.

This continued for the next thirty minutes or so, before Morgan remembered that he had to ring Steven Dukes at the Journal. This he did.

"Hi Steve, this is Peter Morgan, how did your meeting with the Editor go?"

"You are kidding, Bloody Hell. This day gets better and better!" Morgan had stood up and had thrown his arms into the air.

"Right matey, get yourself down to the Black Bull tonight, we're celebrating. Great stuff, see you down there, six thirty."

Sergeant Whitehead just sat at his desk and smiled, this was indeed turning into a significant day.

Morgan started to wander around the office, he couldn't stand still!

"Sergeant, we have to buy some bloody lottery tickets. The way this day is going, we're bound to win."

Morgan calmed down a little, walked over to his desk and sat down.

"Oh, I forgot, Steve Dukes said that the Editor at the Daily Journal is going to extend the evening edition. They are 'plastering the front page with information on our missing suspects."

It was now Sergeant Whitehead's turn to lose it. He stood up from his chair, walked to the centre of the office, and performed a sort of jig come moon dance that even Michael Jackson would have been proud of!

Morgan and Whitehead entered the Black Bull just after six thirty.

They could see Detective Sergeant Morley and three of his colleagues sat at the bar, and it was obvious from the noise they were making that they were out to enjoy themselves.

As they joined them at the bar, Morgan made Sergeant Whitehead's request for him:

"Get out the Champers Morley, we're here to party"

This request conjured up the expected answer from Morley.

"You know what you can do with your 'Champers' Inspector."

"You and the Sergeant will have to make do with a normal drink."

"Talking of drinks, what can I buy my new found 'friends'?"

Morgan ordered a pint of bitter and Whitehead a pint of lager, which Luke Morley duly paid for.

Morgan and Whitehead were then introduced to the rest of Morley's crew and the laughing and drinking began.

After a further ten minutes, Steven Dukes joined the party.

Detective Sergeant Morley had always had a rather 'uneasy' relationship with the Daily Journal, but on this occasion, he just wanted to have a drink, and to Hell with the past.

To complement this, he welcomed Steven Dukes with a genuine hand shake, much to Dukes' surprise, but welcome.

Luke Morley then asked.

"What can I get you Steven?"

"Cheers Luke, I'll have a pint of lager"

Dukes had brought with him a copy of the Journal's late edition, and the entire party took it in turns to inspect the front page.

Morgan responded very positively.

"Well Steve, this is exactly what we wanted, cheers mate"

Sergeant Whitehead added to the Inspector's delighted comment.

"I had my doubts, but you've come through with flying colours, well done Steven"

The party continued throughout the evening, until just before eleven, when, worse for the drink, Morgan, Whitehead and Dukes unsteadily fell into a shared Taxi, leaving the Drug Squad still at the bar and still drinking!

Morgan was the first to be dropped off at his flat and as he staggered way from the Cab, he stuttered a goodbye.

"Well chaps, I've had Hic! A bloody great Hic! Night, Hic! Let's have another one when we catch the Hic! Leila buggers Hic!"

It was early the same evening, just after six, when Charlotte Johnson of HNT Associates, opened the door to the flat at 17 Norton Lane.

She was showing a potential tenant, Andrew Atkinson, around the premises.

"This way Mr Atkinson, I'm sure you will find this is just what you are looking for."

She continued with the obvious sales spiel:

"As you can see, it's a very good, self-contained apartment it's well decorated, and coupled with its prime position adjacent to the riverside, a really much sought-after rental."

"If you would like to follow me, Mr Atkinson, I'll show you the bedroom."

They walked towards the bedroom, and Charlotte opened the door and ushered Mr Atkinson inside.

As she followed him, she wondered why he had come to an abrupt halt.

She was going to ask what the problem was when she noticed the bed.

"Oh My God"

"Oh My God!" echoed Charlotte.

Lying side by side on the bed, were the bodies of Sandra Barak and Stuart Taylor.

CHAPTER SEVENTEEN

Sergeant Whitehead arrived at the station at 0800 hours, feeling a little light headed, he walked straight into the canteen and a welcome cup of coffee.

He had a brief conversation with a couple of uniformed officers about the Davy funeral, and then headed for Acting Detective Inspector Morgan's office.

Once in the office, he sat at his desk, closed his eyes and just sat there, wishing the day would quickly pass and he could return to his bed.

The phone rang.

"Hello, Acting Detective Inspector Morgan's office. Oh, morning Inspector. You're where? You want me to join you? Why?"

"OK I'll be there directly."

The Sergeant had learned that Morgan wanted to meet him at 17 Norton Lane, but he had not told him why.

As the Sergeant approached the premises, he noticed the Morgue van parked outside the flat he knew then that something significant had occurred.

When he entered the apartment, he saw Acting Detective Inspector Morgan talking to Forensic Officers, so he waited until they had finished their conversation before greeting Morgan.

"Good morning Inspector."

"Ah, good morning Detective Sergeant"

"Come, I have a pleasant surprise for you."

Morgan signalled for Whitehead to follow him into the bedroom, where he pointed to the two bodies on the bed.
"There you are Sergeant, not only did we enjoy our party last night, but Christmas has come early."
Sergeant Whitehead stared at the bed.
He couldn't get his mind to register what he was seeing, he was totally speechless.
Morgan sensed this, so he grabbed the Sergeant and pulled him across to the bedside table.
"OK Sergeant, I can see you've lost your voice. So just read that, it's a suicide note." He pointed to a note on the table.
Whitehead focused his eyes and read the note.

> Both Sandra and I have been through a terrible few months. The voices would not go away, and we had to do their bidding. We are sorry for the things that we did, so we thought the best thing to do was to leave this place, please forgive us.

At last Sergeant Whitehead regained his voice.
"Fucking Hell, it's them Inspector, and the paper only went out last night!"
Detective Inspector Morgan put his arm around the Sergeant.
"Sergeant, the Front Page doesn't work THAT fast."
He continued.
"The Forensics team say the bodies have been here at least twenty four hours, and it looks like they died of a heroin overdose. Now, take a look at these."
He pointed to the glass at the side of the suicide note, and its contents.

"Yes Sergeant, they are the missing digits!"

"We can now release the bodies" he joyfully shouted.

Sergeant Whitehead's mind, almost reluctantly started to register what Morgan was saying, and he belatedly joined in Morgan's celebration.

Answering the Detective Inspector with an expression of total relief etched on his face.

"Bleeding Hell Inspector, that's it, the end, the end of the Leila case, the bleeding end of the investigation."

"Yes Sergeant, its over, the Station can now return to normality, come, let's leave Ted Draper and his team to finish here, we have to organise the release of the victims to their respective families."

Sergeant Whitehead was now fully up to speed, and gladly followed Morgan from the flat to return to the Station.

Back at the Station the news of the discovery had filtered through to all departments, consequently, here too, there was a feeling of relief that at last they could put the Leila case to bed. Everyone was in celebration mode, even Superintendant Kelly, who was smiling like a 'Cheshire Cat'.

The Superintendant almost walked through the door as he entered Acting Detective Inspector Morgan's office.

He shook Sergeant Whitehead and Detective Inspector Morgan vigorously by the hand, as he spoke.

"It's a bloody good day for the Station, we've had this bloody investigation hanging over our heads for long enough, we did our best, but nothing seemed to fit".

The Superintendent then continued

"I must go I have to phone the Commander and Detective Inspector Preece."

Then he quickly turned on his heels and was gone.

"Well Inspector, I wonder why the Superintendant is in such a good mood" Whitehead joked.

"Never mind the Superintendant, Sergeant, you go and organise a release warrant, we need to give the victims back to their families, I'm going to see Sergeant Cooney's mother, Christine."

"OK Inspector, give her my regards" answered the Sergeant, as they both left the office.

As Acting Detective Inspector Morgan pulled up outside Mick Cooney's mother's house, he noticed that Detective Inspector Jim Preece's car was parked outside.

He walked up the path and rang the doorbell, the door was opened by Jim Preece, who welcomed him and ushered him inside.

"Nice to see you again Sergeant Morgan" was the welcome from Janet Preece.

"Nice to see you Mrs Preece" answered a slightly miffed Morgan.

Christine Cooney was seated next to Janet.

She motioned with her hand her recognition to Morgan, but she was sobbing into her handkerchief, so didn't speak.

"I'll make some tea, come and help me Detective Inspector" motioned Preece.

Morgan excused him self from the ladies and followed DI Preece into the kitchen.

"You arrived pretty quickly Detective Inspector" queried Morgan.

"We were already here when Superintendant Kelly phoned" answered Preece.

They then talked over the Leila case and the unexpected ending, both acknowledging that it was about time. If it had gone on much longer, it would have caused the community to question the ability of the Station, and the Police in general.

Preece then asked Morgan a question.

"When will you be releasing the bodies Detective Inspector?"

"Sergeant Whitehead is sorting the warrant, as we speak, so it will only be a couple of days" answered Morgan.

They completed making the tea and returned to the lounge to join Christine and Janet.

As they entered, Christine had stopped crying and was talking to Janet she seemed to be coming to terms with getting her son back.

She spoke to both Preece and Morgan.

"I know you've always done your best, but it's been so long, Michael being in that place."

"I missed him so much."

She started to cry again, overcome with the emotion of getting her son back and being able to say a proper goodbye and above all, to place him to rest.

Morgan stayed at Christine Cooney's house for just over an hour, during which it was decided that Preece would assist Christine with the funeral arrangements.

Before Morgan left he restated his condolences to Christine, and asked Jim Preece to let him know when the burial date was known.

Morgan didn't go back to the Station, the events of last night and the emotion of finally closing the Leila case, had left him feeling mentally and physically drained.

So it was hardly surprising that he decided to go straight home, and to bed.

Next morning, Morgan arrived at the Station feeling refreshed, as he entered, Commander Steele was talking to one of the uniformed officers in the Reception Area.

"Ah, Acting Detective Inspector Morgan, I think congratulations are in order?" Steele remarked.

"Well thank you Commander"

The Commander then invited Morgan to see him in his office, as he had an important, and maybe surprising statement to make.

They entered the office and, when seated, the Commander sprang his surprise statement on Morgan.

"I think we can remove the 'Acting' don't you?"

He continued.

"Come and see me at ten thirty, and bring Sergeant Whitehead."

"Well thank you Commander, we'll be there" said a delighted Morgan.

Morgan left the Commander's office and made his way to his own office.

As he entered he encountered a rather quiet and worried-looking Sergeant Whitehead sat at his desk.

"Morning Sergeant, you look like you've lost a pound and found a tanner" said a still delighted Morgan.

He then asked "What's wrong?"

The Sergeant looked up.

"Morning Inspector, Forensics checked the Barak and Taylor suicide note, it's the second such note that didn't have any finger prints. Do you find that rather strange Inspector?"

Morgan sat at his desk, stared at the ceiling for a couple of moments.

He then went into a sort of Rap.

"The bodies were there",

"The bloody missing fingers were there",

"The suicide note was there",

"And finally Sergeant, I don't bloody care about finger prints."

Morgan stood up, took a deep breath, and exhaled the air slowly. He then walked over to Sergeant Whitehead and sat on his desk. He looked directly at Sergeant Whitehead and spoke to him in a rational and sympathetic manner.

"Sergeant, we have been investigating the Leila case for months, and to put it bluntly, we never looked like solving it."

"Then, all of a sudden we get a break; Barak and Taylor are found on the premises where Taylor used to live. There is a suicide note that explains their reasons for committing the murders, and there's no evidence of any involvement by person's unknown."

The expression on Morgan's face then changed to bewilderment, and he shouted

"So why the Fucking Hell, have you got a long face?"

"Get a fucking grip Sergeant"

"The bloody case is over, fucking over, live with it!"

Morgan slowly returned to his desk, leaned back in his chair and, placing both hands on the back of his head, calmly stated.

"By the way Sergeant, the Commander has invited us to his office at ten thirty."

Sergeant Whitehead sat up in his chair. He took a few moments to think about his response, clearing his throat before answering. "Inspector, I am only trying to perform my job to the best of my ability and the points that I raise are pertinent to an accurate conclusion of any investigation. However, I do respect your greater experience and judgement, and because of the nature of the Leila case, I am prepared to listen, and live with it."

Just like the Inspector would, and trying to 'cool' the atmosphere, the Sergeant changed the subject.

"Why doe's the Commander want to see us at ten thirty?"

"It looks like he wants to give us both a massive pay rise" Morgan joked, he then added

"The Commander is retiring in a couple of weeks, and he probably wants to invite us to a party."

He didn't mention his immediate promotion.

Morgan then asked the Sergeant about the release warrants and the likely timescale.

"The coroner's department say that all the bodies will be available for release in two to three days, depending on the circumstances of the relevant families" answered Whitehead.

"That's great, the sooner the better for all concerned" answered a relieved Morgan.

"Now then Sergeant, come, let's go to see our Commander, we can call to see the Morgue staff on the way, and make sure everything is progressing as per your statement".

They both then left the office, with Morgan in celebratory mood, and Whitehead with more of a 'suck it and see' mood.

After a successful visit to the Morgue where Whitehead's statement regarding the readiness of the victim's bodies was confirmed, they walked the short distance to Commander Steele's office.

As they entered the office, the Commander was sitting at the meeting table talking to Superintendant Kelly.

"Come in Detective Inspector, come in Sergeant, take a seat" was the Commander's greeting.

Commander Steele opened the meeting by firstly talking about the conclusion of the Leila investigation.

"It goes without saying, that we, the Police, and of course, the public at large, are glad to see the end of the investigation."

"I, for one, would like to congratulate all the personnel involved with the case, and I will be putting out a statement on the Station Website".

"I will also be issuing a press release outlining the importance that the Daily Journal played in the investigation, with particular reference to one of their journalists, Mr Steven Dukes."

"Now, as far as the actual investigating team is concerned, as from today, Acting Detective Inspector Morgan is promoted to Detective Inspector."

Sergeant Whitehead looked at Morgan, the size of whose smile was trying to split his face into two parts.

The Commander continued.

"As mentioned previously, it is now confirmed that Superintendant Kelly will be taking over as Commander upon my retirement."

The Commander then turned to Morgan.

"Now Detective Inspector, would you update the meeting regarding the release of the bodies residing in the Morgue?"

"Well Commander, Detective Sergeant Whitehead has been dealing with the specifics, so it's only fair that he should speak on this matter." Morgan answered, as he beckoned to the Sergeant to speak.

Whitehead was feeling down hearted, everyone involved with the case, seemed to be recognised, except him. But he decided to remain positive.

"Thank you Detective Inspector, and may I take this opportunity to congratulate you on your promotion."

"With regard to the victims of the Leila case, we have been assured that all the arrangements are in place, and all the respective families will be satisfied by the end of the week."

"Thank you Detective Sergeant, may I also congratulate you, for your participation in the investigation, I'm sure it won't be long before it's your turn for promotion" said the Commander, as he tried to reassure an obviously disappointed Sergeant Whitehead.

The Commander then concluded the meeting and Morgan and Whitehead left the office with differing opinions and moods, one very happy, the other very much undecided, their relationship again very much strained.

As they both headed back to their office, they came across Detective Inspector Preece talking to the Desk Sergeant. Morgan stopped for a talk, but Whitehead just nodded and carried on to the office.

"Fancy meeting you here DI Preece. Don't you have better things to do?" joked Morgan.

"Hello Detective Inspector Morgan, I often call in for a natter, but today I'm here to sort out the release of Mick Cooney" answered Preece.

"Well don't forget to tell me the funeral arrangements when they are completed" requested Morgan.

"I will it should be in four to five days."

Preece and Morgan shook hands and Morgan carried on to his office pondering whether he and Sergeant Whitehead would still be talking.

He decided that he would make the first move, so when he entered the office he surprised the Sergeant with a suggestion.

"Sergeant Whitehead, I've been thinking, I think that I should recognise your contribution to the Leila investigation."

"So I am proposing to take you for a curry, tonight."

"You are joking Inspector when did you ever put your hand into your pocket?" was Whiteheads sarcastic comment.

"Well, I'm putting it in now Sergeant, so what do you say, shall we go, just the two of us?" replied Morgan, trying his best to cheer up the Sergeant.

Sergeant Whitehead paused, and thought for a moment, 'why am I being so confrontational?'

He decided that he also had to make an effort and to lighten up his attitude, and accept the invitation in the spirit it had been intended.

"OK Detective Inspector, you have a deal" he answered.

"Great Sergeant, I'll book a table for two at the Heavens Gate, Indian Restaurant, for eight tonight, you won't regret it" confirmed a delighted Morgan.

CHAPTER EIGHTEEN

Next morning, it was just before eight as Morgan entered the office Detective Sergeant Whitehead was on the phone.

As soon as Whitehead saw the Detective Inspector he handed him the phone, saying;

"It's your new friend from the Daily Journal, Steven Dukes.

Morgan took the phone from the Sergeant and greeted Dukes.

"Good Morning Steve. Who? When? Where from? O.K, give me the details"

Morgan paused while he speedily noted what Steven Dukes was telling him.

"Yes we will be very discrete, you can depend on me and Sergeant Whitehead, I'll speak to you later Steve when we have checked it out. Yes, it will remain confidential, don't worry. Speak to you later, bye."

Morgan put the phone down and looked at Sergeant Whitehead, it was obvious to the Sergeant that the call had the Detective Inspector worried.

He sat on his desk and started to relate the call's content to the Sergeant, but had to hurriedly stop.

"Bloody Hell, sorry Sergeant, but I have to go to the toilet."

Detective Inspector Morgan dashed from the office, leaving Sergeant Whitehead in hysterics.

When Morgan returned some ten minutes later, his face was as white as the white paint on the walls!

"Well I don't regret the visit to the Indian restaurant, but maybe you do?" laughed Whitehead.

"Never again Sergeant, never again" commented Morgan.

Morgan again sat at his desk and finished telling the Sergeant about the phone call from Steven Dukes.

"Steve has a local business friend, a Mr Brian Murphy, who owns the local shopping centre, The Mansion Centre, along with various other Retail ventures."

"One of his daughters, Kathryn, who is eleven years old, and who attends St Mary's Catholic School, has been kidnapped. Brian Murphy has received a ransom note, demanding two million pounds. Like most kidnappings, he has been told not to involve the Police or his daughter's life will be at risk."

"Kathryn was taken as she walked home from school at approximately 1630 hours yesterday, unfortunately, there were no witnesses."

Morgan stressed to the Sergeant the importance of confidentiality.

"As I see it Sergeant, we have to handle the investigation alone, and I mean ALONE."

Morgan then continued.

"And with some Speedy Police Work, and a little luck, we will return Kathryn to her family, and sort out the bloody kidnappers before the ransom is due."

Sergeant Whitehead agreed with everything Detective Inspector Morgan had said, and he confirmed this by stressing.

"I'm with you one hundred percent Inspector, one hundred percent. As you know, paying a ransom to kidnappers doesn't always end happily."

There followed an urgent discussion on their next move, with particular attention paid to their immediate actions.

They decided that Sergeant Whitehead would interrogate the Police computer to outline all known criminals that had been in the past, or would be expected to be, involved in kidnapping. And he would pay particular attention to any criminals that were local to the immediate area.

Detective Inspector Morgan would arrange a meeting with Brian Murphy, through Steven Dukes, to obtain a recent photograph of Kathryn and to determine the likely route she would take from school.

One action they did not want to take was to follow Brian Murphy as he carried out the instructions for delivering the ransom money.

This would be a last resort, and as they had already discussed, not an action that usually worked.

As time was crucial, Morgan would meet Whitehead in his office, as soon as they had completed their tasks, regardless of the time.

It was just before 2100 hours when Detective Inspector Morgan returned to his office, noticing that Sergeant Whitehead had already returned.

The Sergeant had completed his task, and he had listed, with last known addresses, all the possible perpetrators.

Morgan related the expected route from Kathryn's school to her home, and produced the required photograph.

He had also ascertained that Brian Murphy had three days to raise the demanded funds.

He informed Sergeant Whitehead that Steven Dukes was to talk, also discreetly, to some of his contacts, just in case someone may have heard something from any 'street talk'.

They both diligently checked the list of possible criminals that could be involved that Whitehead had produced, and two names stood out.

Conrad Sykes and Trevor Tindale, both local criminals with a string of convictions, Sykes in particular, had 'form' regarding restricting the movements of another individual.

They both agreed that they needed to keep moving quickly, so Morgan would take on Sykes, and Whitehead would take Tindale.

They would start first thing tomorrow, and this meant very discreetly, following their targets from their homes and staying with them all day.

Obviously hoping that at least one of them was involved, and consequently, would lead them to where Kathryn was being held.

Both Morgan and Whitehead were a little apprehensive that the plan would work, but as they saw the situation, they had two days to try, knowing that failure was not an option to be considered.

Detective Inspector Morgan arrived at the Station at 0700 hours. As he entered his office, he was thinking, what a waste of bloody time yesterday was.

All Sykes did was hang around the local pub all day, eventually going home pissed.

He sat at his desk hoping that Sergeant Whitehead's day had been more productive, although, when the Sergeant had rung at midday, it didn't look so good.

He started to flick through the other names of likely perpetrators that Sergeant Whitehead had printed out from the computer.

Unfortunately, no other likely names stood out.

Sergeant Whitehead walked through the door.

"Please tell me you have our kidnapper" pleaded Morgan.

"It doesn't look likely Inspector, although, I think we could get Tindale for dealing in dodgy cars" moaned the Sergeant.

The atmosphere in the office dropped to 'Morgue level', both of them were physically and mentally drained.

Early the same morning, Kathryn Murphy was lying on a makeshift bed, made out of a number of flattened boxes when she opened her eyes.

She had been locked in some sort of old building and she could see by looking out of a very small window, that it was starting to get light outside.

She had been given a sandwich and a bottle of water by her kidnapper, but she wasn't really interested and she had just left them on the floor.

She had cried during the course of the kidnap, but she was of a strong mind and character, and had partially accepted her situation and remained positive.

She knew her father would eventually rescue her.

There was only one person involved with the kidnap, a 31-year-old local thug called Damian Foster, he had acted, not directly on impulse, but basically in total desperation.

Foster had found himself drifting more and more into dangerous drug taking, and misguidedly, thought that taking someone like Kathryn and demanding a ransom, would be his way out.

At this point, he had no idea how he would organise the money pick-up while keeping his identity secret. He had just bundled Kathryn into his car and driven off.

The only sort of plan in the exercise was the hideout, an old deserted barn on the outskirts of town. Damian Foster was walking around outside the barn, churning over his next move in his mind, when a figure appeared out of the early morning sunrise. "What the…"

Before Foster could react, he was knocked unconscious with one lighting blow.

The figure then tied and gagged him and placed him in the boot of his own car, the figure then moved quickly towards the barn. As Kathryn heard the door opening, she tried to hide in one of the dark corners of the barn.

"Don't worry Kathryn, I've come to take you home, come, we have to go".

The stranger held out his hand, at first Kathryn was reluctant to leave her hiding place, but for some strange reason, she felt safe with this stranger.

She walked from her hiding place and approached the stranger and he took her by the hand and led her outside.

"You sit in the passenger seat of the car Kathryn, while I make a phone call" he said reassuringly.

He guided her to the car and as she settled herself into the seat, the stranger made the call.

Back at the Police Station, Morgan's phone rang.

"Hello Detective Inspector Morgan. Where? Who is this?"

"In the bloody boot"

If you are some sort of crackpot I'll …"

"Hello Kathryn, are you OK? I'll be there directly"

Morgan threw down the phone. "Come on Sergeant, we have to go, Kathryn's at the old Miller Barn. Come on!"

Kathryn saw the Detective Inspector's car approaching, so lent out of the car window and shouted to inform the stranger.

The stranger had already seen the car, so he acknowledged Kathryn's shout, and spoke quietly and reassuringly to her.

"It is time for me to go Kathryn, don't worry, you will soon be back with your family."

He then walked a short distance from the car and disappeared!

After a few seconds Detective Inspector Morgan and Detective Sergeant Whitehead arrived at the scene and walked up to the car, with Sergeant Whitehead opening the car door and ushering Kathryn out.

"Hello, my name is Colin I believe you're Kathryn Murphy, are you OK?"

"Yes, I'm well thank you, it was that nice man that let me go" Kathryn answered, as she looked around wondering where the stranger had gone.

"What nice man?" Morgan asked.

"A nice, friendly man, he just disappeared." She answered.

The Detective Inspector and the Sergeant, didn't press her any further, they just assumed that she was suffering from her ordeal.

As Sergeant Whitehead ushered Kathryn into Morgan's car, Morgan opened the boot of the car Kathryn had been seated in. Sure enough, as he had been told on the phone, there was the kidnapper, all tied up.

Morgan then phoned Brian Murphy and told him of the happy conclusion to Kathryn's ordeal.

Morgan also told him that he would take his daughter straight to the Police Station and that they should all meet there.

Morgan concluded the call and turned to Sergeant Whitehead.

"Right Sergeant, you drive the 'toss pot's' car back to the Station and see that he is processed".

"Oh by the way, leave him in the bloody boot for the journey."

Detective Inspector Morgan parked his car in the Station car park, took Kathryn by the hand and led her towards the Station Reception Area, only to be besieged by her mother and father and the rest of the Murphy family.

Morgan just stood to one side, while the hugs and kisses flowed. When they finally broke apart, the Murphy family members duly ushered Kathryn into the Station Reception Area.

Everyone was jubilant, with handshakes all round, especially towards Detective Inspector Morgan, who, as far as the Murphy family were concerned was some kind of Saviour, a Saint! Suddenly, Kathryn shrieked

"That's him, that's him" as she pointed to a framed picture of Commander Steele that hung in the Reception Area.

"That's my nice friend he is the nice man that let me go!" Detective Inspector Morgan just smiled, and looking at the Desk Sergeant, he joked

"She's been through one hell of an ordeal the unknown stranger that helped her must resemble the Commander"

She obviously doesn't KNOW our Commander"

The Desk Sergeant agreed with Morgan, and added.

"I agree Detective Inspector it takes the Commander until dinner time to get out of bloody bed"

"There's more chance of Elvis Presley being the stranger than the bloody Commander!"

Commander Steele was fast asleep in his London Hotel bedroom.

A figure that had just left his body had materialised in the adjoining bathroom.

The globe in the figure's pocket lit up;

Elder;

Julius, you are overdue, please return to Jude.
You have assisted the Earth being for too long, you must return to Jude.

Julius;
There is so much to achieve on this Earth I request that I am able to remain here and fight evil.

Elder;
That is not our way, the Earth beings' bodies may not stand your occupation for long periods and our transition methods to and from locations may also be detrimental.
They must be allowed to develop their own body transit and subsequent materialisation technology.
You Must Return!
Julius;
I understand I will depart immediately.

However, Julius's answer was rather ingenious.

CHAPTER NINETEEN

It had been some two months since the conclusion of the Leila case, and Detective Inspector Morgan had formed a compatible and friendly partnership with his Sergeant, Colin Whitehead. Commander Steele had retired to the Seychelles, with Superintendant Kelly being promoted to Commander. Inspector Jackson was promoted to the Station Superintendant, and rather surprisingly to Morgan, seemed to be doing a reasonable job.

Even more surprising was Morgan's relationship with Steven Dukes of the Daily Journal. They had become very friendly and often spent the weekends drinking together in the local bars.

Detective Inspector Morgan awoke from another most disturbing sleep that contained another episode of the same strange dream.

He had experienced this dream, since the end of the Kathryn Murphy case, which made it all the more strange, because the dream was not about Kathryn Murphy.

His mind seemed to have been working overtime throughout the dream, so much so, that instead of feeling rested and refreshed, he felt totally drained.

The dream had seemed to centre on some sort of intensive instruction course regarding the unknown technique of Body Transit and subsequent Materialisation.

Not for the first time, Morgan had ended up sitting on the side of his bed, relating to himself the message and the instructional content of the dream.

This made reliving the dream easy; because of its unrelenting frequency the dream was impregnated into Morgan's memory, as thus;

I am Julius;

I have experienced your world and the problems that your crime officers encounter.

I have to return to my own world, but before I do, I have decided to implant into your brain, the expertise and ability of Body Transit and subsequent Materialisation.

This will assist you greatly in your fight against evil and crime. To initiate the technique, will need to enter a key word into your memory. This will act as a trigger that will instruct your brain to start the transit process. Initially, you may experience a little difficulty, but don't worry, you need to persevere.

Remember, before transit, you need to visualise the destination. However, be warned this ability must be used carefully and you must not discuss the transfer method with anyone.

You are the chosen one; Remember, only use your given ability in pursuit of the common good.

The dream seemed to centre on an alien being, which had visited this Earth and was now preparing to return home.

Leaving instructions to Detective Inspector Morgan, on how to transport his body from place to place, by only using his thought processes.

All he had to do was to think of a place he wanted to go to, and the power of his mind would take him there.

"Bloody impossible, you would need a better mind than I possess" Morgan muttered.

He dragged himself from his bed and walked into the bathroom, where he immersed his face in cold water.

He started talking to himself as he started to get dry.

"Fancy, just thinking of a place, and ZAP, You're there"

"Bloody silly, so if I thought of going back into the bed……

"Shit!"

Morgan found him self sat on his bed.

He still had the towel in his hands, so he knew he had been in the bathroom, but he didn't remember walking back into the bedroom.

"O.K, so I'm going senile" he countered.

"I obviously did walk back, but I'm still a little sleepy and I just don't remember walking back."

"So I'll think of going back to the bath……

Morgan found him self in the bathroom!

This unsettled Morgan, he was now starting to think that he WAS going senile.

He started to slap his face with both hands, hoping that this would wake him.

As far as he was concerned, he could be still asleep and still dreaming.

"No, I'm NOT still a bloody asleep!" he shouted.

He was still in the bathroom, and he was NOT asleep.

His mind was in overdrive.

He was afraid to 'think of a place', just in case he found himself there.

The sound of the Sunday paper falling through the letter box made him jump, and his mind thought about the paper shop.

"Christ" he exclaimed.

Morgan stood in the paper shop dressed only in a pair of shorts! Fortunately, he had materialised at the back of the shop, behind the shelving, and no other customer saw his appearance.

"Think man" he whispered to himself "Think bedroom"

This had the desired effect, he materialised in the bedroom, but it was not his!

He could hear the noise of someone showering in the adjacent room and looking at the clothes that were spread on the bed he instantly knew that he was in the bedroom of a woman.

"Bleeding Hell, where the hell am I?"

"Think bathroom".

He appeared in his own bathroom.

The cry of relief shook the flat.

"What the Fuck can I do?" he shouted.

"I can't 'THINK' anymore … "I can't live like this"

He ran through the instructions from the dream in his mind, and started to mutter to himself.

"That's it my brain needs a 'key' word."

"I need a word that comes naturally to me, something that I would not forget"

He walked back into the bedroom, and stretched out on the bed, he closed his eyes, trying to enter into 'thinking mode'.

"Now what can I use" he mused.

"That's it"

"The word will be PETER!" he shouted triumphantly.

"I would be senile, if I forgot my own bloody name" he mused.

He then started to whisper.

"Now let's see, how do I tell my brain that the word is Peter?"

"I'll just think PETER!"

With his eyes still closed, he lay there thinking, Peter, Peter, Peter.

After a few moments, he stood up and, first thinking Peter, and then visualising the location, he thought 'bathroom'

"Yes!" he shouted.

"I'm in the bloody bathroom"

He then thought PETER, visualise bedroom.

"Bloody easy" he shouted as he sat on his bed with his arms raised.

The realisation of what he had just done, and what he could achieve, both professionally and, perhaps, personally, started to sink in.

The technique of body transit and subsequent materialisation, was years beyond the present world. Why him? Why was he the 'chosen one'?

The phrase 'pursuit of the common good' came into his mind. Morgan didn't know why he had been chosen, but he decided, sitting there on his bed, that he would uphold the ethos for which he had been chosen.

He thought PETER, Visualise; Lounge.

Standing there in the lounge of his flat, he smiled, but still feeling a little uneasy regarding his newly found abilities.

He picked up the Sunday Paper, and as soon as he started reading the scandalous headlines he knew he was back in the 'real' world!

Sitting in his favourite chair, Morgan turned to the back pages of the paper to read about the week's sporting events.

After some forty five minutes, everything of slight interest had been read and Morgan placed the paper in the magazine rack.

He looked at the wall clock; it was ten to eleven.

Morgan stood up, stretched his limbs and walked into the bathroom.

He was meeting Steven Dukes in the Victoria Hotel pub at twelve thirty, so it was time for a shower.

Morgan showered and dressed, and soon he was ready for a Sunday afternoon drink.

Should he think 'Peter' and 'Victoria' he mused.

The decision was to walk he didn't want to use his new ability in a flippant manner.

Anyway, the sun was shinning and he needed to get his legs and arms moving normally in the warm sunshine.

As he walked the mile or so to the pub, Morgan started to think about the circumstances where body transportation would be of benefit.

The overriding conclusion was;

All his Police Work would benefit from such a technique, in other words, to lock up the 'toss pots' that were creating havoc on his patch.

Morgan entered the Victoria Hotel and took a seat at the bar.

One of the barmaids, Julie, walked up and greeted him.

"Morning Peter, what can I get you?"

"I'll have a pint of bitter and a date" he answered, rather hopefully.

"I've told you before Peter, I'm a married woman and I'm not putting my marriage to one side, for a date with you."

"Just remember Julie, when you've had enough of that husband of yours, Ill be waiting".

Julie just shrugged her shoulders, smiled and started to pull the pint.

Morgan had only taken one sip from his drink, when Steven Dukes appeared at the bar.

"Mines a pint of lager Pete" he requested.

"Do you wait outside while I order before you come in?" Morgan queried.

"Course I do, you know I'm a tight sod" joked Dukes.

Morgan waved at one of the other barmaids, Brenda, and requested a pint of lager.

"Brenda, if you are quick, you can take me out" he joked.

"If I was quick, I would have disappeared into the other bar, before you ordered" was Brenda's glib reply.

"What is it with you Pete?"

"You try it on with Brenda and Julie every week, and you always get the same answer; Piss off, said nicely" stated Dukes.

"Aw it's only a bit of a joke, but one day it'll work" replied Morgan.

He continued.

"Enough talk about the girls, what's happening in the world of the Daily Journal?"

"Not a lot, we're going through one of those quiet periods" replied Dukes.

"Same here, it seems like once Commander Steele retired, all the criminals retired with him" joked Morgan.

"Maybe we should...

Morgan's mobile phone rang, it was Sergeant Whitehead.

"Hello Sergeant, are you coming down for a drink?"

"You're where? I'm on a day off."

"What's wrong with the rest of the Dicks?"

"She has what? And she may have been raped?"

"OK Sergeant, I'll be there in ten minutes, bye".

192

"It looks like the criminal's have just returned from their retirement!" Morgan joked.

"I'm sorry Steve, but I have to go" he moaned.

"You mentioned rape" asked Dukes.

"I'm afraid so, a young lady has been murdered and possibly raped." Morgan answered.

Her body is in the red light area on Wilson Street."

"Oh shit!"

"I've left my bloody car at home" exclaimed Morgan.

"I can give you a lift home, I need to go down to the crime scene anyway" offered Dukes.

"OK, let's go, but remember, you didn't hear about the incident from me"

"Don't worry, if anyone asks, I'll say the paper received a call from a member of the public" assured Dukes.

They both said their goodbyes to Brenda and Julie and left the Victoria Hotel, leaving their half finished drinks on the bar.

CHAPTER TWENTY

Morgan pulled up in Wilson Street, parked his car and walked over to where Sergeant Whitehead was talking to a member of the Forensics team.

"Afternoon all, what do we know Sergeant?" he queried.

"Hi Inspector, we have a young woman, maybe in her twenties and possibly foreign" answered Whitehead.

"The Forensics has conducted a primary check on the body, it is obvious that her neck was broken and she was possibly raped."

"They reckon she could have been dead for some twelve hours." The Sergeant then pointed to a grassy area.

"She was found under those bushes by a Mr Greaves, just before one, he was taking a short cut from the canal road, on his way to visit his mother."

Morgan walked over to the van where the body had been placed and lifted the sheet that covered the body.

"Bloody Hell, the pillock has twisted her head nearly 360 degrees" he exclaimed.

"Sergeant, have we any idea who the poor sod is?"

"Not at this stage Inspector, we've checked through her clothing and nothing" confirmed the Sergeant.

Detective Inspector Morgan walked around the crime scene, being careful not to disturb anything. It was just a grassy area adjacent to the general footpath and the main road.

Sergeant Whitehead noticed Steven Dukes parking his car.

"Bloody Hell, look who's turned up." he said.

"Never mind the press, you should be used to them by now, have you found a handbag, or any bag?" asked Morgan.

"At this stage Inspector, it looks like she didn't have any sort of bag, if you ask me, I would say that she was dumped here" replied Sergeant Whitehead.

"I agree Sergeant she must have been dumped, we need to check for any CCTV cameras in the street".

"I've already sent a uniform to carry out that check Inspector."

"Great work Sergeant, you are so good, I think I'll go back to the pub" joked Morgan.

"Seriously Sergeant, we need to identify the victim, I'm going to the Station, you finish here, but remember, only tell Steven Dukes the basics, and I'll see you back at base."

"OK Inspector, I shouldn't be more than an hour, see you back at the Station around three."

The Sergeant continued to work the crime scene and Detective Inspector Morgan left for the Station.

Detective Inspector Morgan was sitting in the Station canteen when Sergeant Whitehead approached his table and sat down.

"Well Sergeant, what's the latest?" Morgan queried.

Sergeant Whitehead started to relate the latest information on the murder;

"Uniform has determined that the 'Midtown Bank', at the opposite side of the road to the crime scene, has CCTV cameras."

"They have obtained the address of the key holder and are in the process of obtaining the relevant tapes"

"Forensics are processing the victim, with regard to the time of death and all the injuries, which will include the determination of rape or no rape."

"As for the identification of the victim, at this point, we have no idea."

"Good work Sergeant"

"Let me buy you a coffee, and then we'll go to our office and start the case file."

"What is it Sergeant? Black without sugar?" asked Morgan.

"That's it Inspector".

Morgan collected the coffees and they walked to the office. Once inside, Morgan removed his jacket and placed it on the coat stand and then sat at his desk.

"Right Sergeant, first things first, what did you tell Steven Dukes?"

"Not a lot, he asked if the victim had been raped."

"I wonder where that idea came from?" asked Whitehead, looking accusingly at the Detective Inspector.

Morgan could see that the Sergeant knew about his occasional drink with Steven Dukes, so he came clean on the matter.

"O.K, you've got me."

"Steve was in the pub having a drink with me when you rang and he obviously heard some of our conversation."

Morgan continued

"What about the victim?"

"I didn't have a detailed look at her, were all of her clothes intact?"

"Yes Inspector, although Forensics said that her trousers and under clothing were disturbed, hence the possibility of rape".

There was a knock on the office door.

"Come in" shouted Detective Inspector Morgan.

It was PC John Dunn, the Officer responsible for collecting the CCTV tapes.

"We have the tapes from the Midtown Bank Detective Inspector, and Ted Draper is ready to show them in the Forensics department."

"Great stuff Constable Dunn, come on Sergeant, let's go and see if we can obtain any benefit from the tapes."

"We can also get an update from the Forensic guys" said Morgan, as they all left the office.

"Afternoon Ted" was Morgan's greeting, as he, PC Dunn and Sergeant Whitehead entered the Forensics department.

"Afternoon Detective Inspector, before we show you the tape, let me update you on the victim"

"We haven't been able to identify the victim, but she was NOT raped, she wasn't wearing a bra and her underclothes were torn, hence the initial prognosis, but she had definitely been messed with."

"Ted, are you saying, that the poor sod's neck was broken, and then she was dressed by the assailant?" asked Morgan.

"Exactly, and it gets better Detective Inspector, we have already looked at the tapes, and…"

"Well, let's look."

They all moved over to the DVD and Ted Draper started the tape, fast forwarding to the pertinent section.

He started to give a running commentary, but was stopped by Morgan.

"Ted, just let the bloody tape run, we can all form our own judgments".

Everyone settled down and watched with great interest as the drama contained on the tapes began to unfold.

The scene was very clear, a car pulled up, the tape showed the time as ten minutes before midnight, and a man got out, pulled the victim from the boot, dumped her under the bushes on the grassy area, returned to the car and drove off.

"What kind of idiot would do such a thing?" exclaimed Whitehead.

"A desperate one Sergeant, a desperate one" replied Morgan.

"Yes Detective Inspector and a very stupid one" agreed Ted.

"You will also have observed the registration number of the car, as he zoomed in on the number plate, it's not very clear, but after a little tweaking we think it's YX56 HGF, a Black Ford Fiesta ST."

"We've had it checked out, and the owner of the car is a Mr Jeff Thorne, of 16 Pointer Street" Ted Draper concluded.

"Great work Ted. You work on the victim's identity we need to pay this Mr Thorne a visit."

"Come on Sergeant, let's go, time is of the essence, let's nail the bastard."

Detective Inspector Morgan and Sergeant Whitehead were already walking towards the door, when PC Dunn spoke.

"Can I say something, Detective Inspector?"

"Course Constable, what is it?" asked Morgan, as he turned around.

"Could you re-run the tape, to where the 'man' bends over the boot to lift out the victim?"

"OK Ted, re-run the tape for PC Dunn, would you?" requested Morgan, as he walked back from the office door.

Ted Draper ran the tape until the part in question was reached.

"There, slow it down, Yes!"

"I've never seen a backside like that, on a man!" exclaimed the Constable

This statement took the others by complete surprise.

Ted Draper ran the scene again, and again, and finally again, this time in close up.

"Bloody Hell, You could be right Constable, you could well be right" said Morgan.

"What do you think Sergeant?"

"Looking at the tape in close up, the arse definitely looks female"

Sergeant Whitehead continued

"Also, in close up, the person's hair doesn't look right, my bet is that it is a wig, so I think that John is right, we are looking at a woman."

"Do you agree Ted" Morgan asked.

"The person could well be a woman, but why was the car number plate not disguised in some way?" he queried.

"I agree Ted, but let's not bother too much at this stage."

"As I asked, you concentrate on the identity of the victim, and Sergeant Whitehead and I will call on this Thorne character, and let's see what transpires."

Ted Draper agreed, and Morgan and Whitehead left the Forensics Office.

As Detective Inspector Morgan's car pulled up outside 16 Pointer Street, a petite blonde-haired woman was just leaving the premises via the front door.

Sergeant Whitehead quickly jumped out of the car, followed closely by Morgan.

The Sergeant moved ahead and quickly moved to the front gate, and to wait, as the blonde-haired woman approached.

"Excuse me, I'm Sergeant Colin Whitehead and this is Detective Inspector Peter Morgan, can we have a word madam?"

"Why yes, but why?" asked the woman.

"Am I to assume that you are the owner of the property you have just left?" asked Morgan.

"Yes, I'm Lucy Thorne, what's this about Detective Inspector?"

"Can we go inside Mrs Thorne, it will be easier to talk" Morgan asked.

"Is this about my husband Detective Inspector?"

"Can we go inside Mrs Thorne?" Morgan repeated firmly.

This time, Morgan guided her through the garden gate and up the path towards the front door.

Once inside the house, Lucy Thorne walked with them into the lounge, where she sat down on one of the sofas, beckoning to both Morgan and Whitehead to also sit.

"It's about my husband isn't it?" she asked.

"Where is your husband? Can we speak to him? Morgan asked.

"Oh, I thought that was why you were here, to tell me where he was"

"So you are telling us that your Husband is missing?" queried Sergeant Whitehead.

"Yes, he walked out some six months ago" confirmed Mrs Thorne.

"Six months ago? Did you report this to the Police?" asked Morgan.

"No Inspector" stuttered Lucy.

"Mrs Thorne, your husband has been missing for six moths, and you never informed the Police?" stressed Morgan.

Lucy Thorne hesitated before answering.

"Well I just expected him to come back, every day I just expected him to come back."

Her manner troubled Morgan, so, temporality, he changed the subject.

"Did he take the family car with him, a Black Ford Fiesta ST with the registration number YX56 HGF?"

"No, I still have the car, I've lent it to a friend for a couple of days." was Mrs Thorne's rather stuttered reply.

"Who was that?" asked Sergeant Whitehead.

"Oh she's just a friend" answered Mrs Thorne, somewhat cagily.

"So Mrs Thorne, could we have the name of this friend" asked Morgan.

"Why do you need to know Detective Inspector? She is just a friend" pleaded Mrs Thorne.

"We need to know Mrs Thorne, because, we need to know, and furthermore, we also need to know, because she's in possession of the car that belongs to your husband."

Again Morgan stressed his point, raising his voice significantly.

"And this is a bloody husband, Mrs Thorne that you don't seem to miss!"

Detective Inspector Morgan continued, again stressing very clearly.

"We also need to know, because the very car in mention is pertinent to our present investigation. Now, who is the friend who has borrowed your car?"

Mrs Thorne looked visibly shocked and it was obvious she had something to hide, but what?

"OK Inspector, her name is Elaine Southern she's my Personal Trainer and Health Guru".

"So, she's your Health Guru, so where do we find this Health Guru?" asked Detective Inspector Morgan sarcastically.

"She works at the Bodyline Gym and Health Spa in Ascot Street it's just round the corner from here. In fact Detective Inspector, I was just on my way there, when you and the Sergeant turned up."

"Will this Elaine Southern be at the Gym now?" asked Sergeant Whitehead.

"Yes Sergeant, I have my lesson at five, after which, I will be getting my car back" confirmed Mrs Thorne.

"OK then Mrs Thorne, the Sergeant and I will accompany you to the Gym, and you can introduce us to your friend" suggested Morgan.

Lucy Thorne agreed and they all left for the Bodyline Gym and Health Spa.

As Morgan's car pulled into the car park, Sergeant Whitehead pointed out the car in question, to the Inspector; it was parked close to the Gym entrance.

"We will need to check out your car Mrs Thorne, so we'll need the keys from your friend" said Morgan as they all walked through the main entrance to the Health Centre.

"OK Inspector, I'll just go and tell her" answered Mrs Thorne.

She then walked away from them both, heading towards the ladies changing area, before Sergeant Whitehead caught hold of her arm.

"Sorry Mrs Thorne, but you need to stay with the Inspector and I you can make a call through Reception."

"Just ask them to call Elaine Southern, and that she should meet you in Reception" stressed Detective Inspector Morgan.

With this in mind, they all approached the Reception Desk and Mrs Thorne made the call.

As they waited, Sergeant Whitehead started to wander around the Reception Area.

As he was looking at the advisements board, one picture caught his eye; it showed all the Training Instructors employed at the Gym and Health Spa.

One of the Instructors, a tall slim woman with short red hair was of particular interest to the Sergeant.

His mind returned to the CCTV tape and the person removing the victim from the car. He instinctively knew that the woman in the picture was that person.

"Inspector, have you se…

The Sergeant was distracted.

The Ford Fiesta ST was leaving the car park!

Sergeant Whitehead turned and as he ran towards the Reception entrance, he was shouting to the Detective Inspector.

"Inspector, the bloody car, it's leaving the bloody car park!"

Morgan looked out of the window just in time to see the Ford Fiesta turn into the main road and speed away.

He followed Sergeant Whitehead into the car park and they both just stood there, with Morgan thinking.

"Why had they been so bloody lax and stupid?"

They returned to the Reception Area, where there was another surprise waiting for them, Mrs Lucy Thorne had gone.

"Where is the bloody bitch" shouted a disappointed Sergeant Whitehead.

"Oh Christ" said Morgan.

There wasn't anyone at the Reception Desk, so Sergeant Whitehead ran into the ladies changing area.

A couple of women were in the process of getting dressed, and when he entered they were surprisingly calm, they just looked in disbelief that a man could have entered the room.

"It's OK, I'm a Police Officer" said Sergeant Whitehead, trying to reassure them.

"Did you see a woman with blonde hair come in, or pass through here?"

They both just shook their heads, obviously still a little stunned.

Sergeant Whitehead ran back into the Reception Area where Morgan was returning from a side door adjacent to one of the gyms with one of the Health Centre employees.

"She's bloody disappeared" said the Sergeant, feeling totally useless.

Detective Inspector Morgan just paused for a moment, taking time out to think.

"OK Sergeant, you survey the immediate area, she can't be far, and I'll get the address of that Elaine bird, and drive over there, I'll ring you when I get there, if there are any problems, you'll have to ring the Station for a lift back."

Sergeant Whitehead agreed and he set off through the main entrance to begin his search.

Detective Inspector Morgan then asked the Health Centre employee to contact the Duty Manager, so that he could obtain the required address of Elaine Southern.

The Manager duly arrived and after proving his identity, the Inspector was given the required address.

It was some fifteen minutes later when Detective Inspector Morgan pulled up in his car outside Flat.45 the Meadows.

He first tried the front door to the flat, but it was locked, so he walked round to the rear of the premises.

At the rear there was a short garden with a water feature in the centre, but no sign of the Fiesta car in question.

Morgan then tried the rear door, and as it was unlocked, he gingerly walked inside the flat, shouting out the name of Elaine Southern as he entered.

All was quiet, and it quickly became obvious to Morgan that the flat was empty.

He checked the lounge and the kitchen area, and then he walked through to the bedroom.

Once inside, he was presented with a state of total disarray, he could plainly see a number of the dresser drawers had been pulled out on to the floor and the wardrobe door was wide open.

There were many items of clothing left strewn across the floor, of which, some were a mixture of fancy dresses and a variety of wigs.

It was obvious to Detective Inspector Morgan, that someone had grabbed a few items and hurriedly left the scene.

CHAPTER TWENTY ONE

It had been a couple of weeks since the disappearance of both Mrs Lucy Thorne and Elaine Southern, the only relatively positive outcome, was the discovery of the Black Fiesta ST, that had been found abandoned at Heathrow Airport.

Both of the suspect's premises had been searched, with nothing forthcoming.

Photographs of them both were obtained and circulated throughout all Police Areas of the country.

As for the victim, she was identified as Miss Martina Vitti, who originated from a small town called Celano, in the Province of L'Aquila in central Italy.

She had worked in the UK for 18 months and had been a member of the Bodyline Gym and Health Spa for a couple of these months.

Detective Inspector Morgan was talking on the phone to Steven Dukes of the Daily Journal.

"Unfortunately Steve, the whereabouts of our two suspects still isn't known, so far all of our endeavours have produced absolutely bloody nothing."

"What was that?"

"What source is that?"

"Are you sure?"

"Just a minute, I'll get a pen, right, give me that address again."

Detective Inspector Morgan wrote down the address that Steven Dukes had suggested to him.

Dukes had told Morgan that one of his sources knew about an apartment that Elaine Southern used in St Pauls Bay, Malta.

"Right Steve, leave it with me, I'll be in touch if something develops."

Morgan put down the phone, leaned back in his chair, and wondered.

"What if I used my 'New Ability' to check out the place?"

Sergeant Whitehead entered the office.

"Right Sergeant, I have to return home, I seem to have misplaced my wallet."

"Well I can lend you so…

Too Late, Detective Inspector Morgan had left the office.

Once in his flat, Morgan researched the internet, he needed to find the exact location of the property.

The internet indicated the following address;

Villa 'Les' Konverzjoni, Just off Gillieru Harbour St Pauls Bay, Malta.

Morgan also checked the weather and indications were that it should be around 30 degrees Centigrade.

"Well I will just have to change into shorts and sandals" he laughed excitedly.

He sat on his bed and took a moment to steady himself and to prepare mentally, for the upcoming journey.

"Think PETER, Visualise; Gillieru Harbour, Malta."

As he materialised, Morgan lost his footing on the rocks and he fell head first into the warm choppy waters of the Mediterranean Sea.

After the shock of the unprepared entry to the water, and the initial shock of his predicament, he surfaced with a gulp and struggled back on to the rocks, and to relative safety.

"What a pillock" he shouted

This caused a lone fisherman to turn around, and, looking at a soddened Morgan, just shook his head.

Morgan smiled in the fisherman's direction and dragged himself from the rocks and onto the Harbour walkway.

He walked towards the fisherman, and sitting on the rocks behind him he asked.

"What sort of fish are you hoping to catch?"

The man answered, in broken English.

"I fish for Octopus, very good stew."

He then asked Morgan a question

"You swim? Very silly and very dangerous."

It took Morgan a while to understand how the fisherman could catch anything, all he had were a few white ribbons tied on to the end of the line and no hook!

The fisherman just let the tied feathers float beneath the surface of the water, pulling and tugging and guiding them in and out of the rocks.

After a couple of minutes, he pulled the line tight, and very carefully reeled it in.

Much to Morgan's surprise, a small Octopus was pulled from the water.

The fisherman removed it from the grip it had on the ribbons, placed it into a small sack, and tied the sack to a mooring post. Needless to say, the sack starting wondering all over the place!

Morgan sat there in the warm sunshine, until his clothes were dry, although, he wasn't looking forward to walking without the sandals he had lost during his swim.

"It is time to find the Villa" he muttered to himself.

He waved goodbye to the fisherman and walked off, or rather hobbled off.

"Walking without sandals was like walking on burning embers", he mused.

Nevertheless, he hobbled on towards the 'Villa Les', and much to his surprise, he found what looked like the Villa's premises in less than ten minutes.

He approached with great care, the last thing he needed, was for one of the occupants to see him, and even worse, if they were the ones he expected, to be recognised.

The Villa had a wall surround of about two metres in height there was a pool in the front garden and a double garage to the rear of the property.

Morgan hobbled slowly around the perimeter of the walled garden, until he was sure that he had not been spotted, then quickly climbed the wall and hobbled towards the patio and the front door entrance.

Not until he was positive that the front part of the villa was unoccupied did he start the transit sequence;

Think PETER, Visualise; Patio Lounger.

Once he materialised in the living quarters he listened for any occupational noises.

The only noises to be heard were noises coming from the bedroom area, so Morgan approached carefully, and then started to smile he had recognised that the noises were of a scxual nature.

"It's a good job no one's watching, I must look like a bloody pervert" he mused.

The bedroom door was ajar, so he positioned himself just to one side of the door, so he could see through the slight gap caused by the positioning of the door hinges, and close enough to aid hearing.

Once he settled into position, he confirmed that the noises were of a sexual nature, and even more obvious, that they would soon be celebrating a climax.

Looking through the hinge gap, he could see that the participants were both female, furthermore, he recognised Lucy Thorne straight away, and the distinctive short red hair of the other woman, indicated he was also looking at Elaine Southern.

The climax of the activity, came, and again, and again, and eventually, the noises subsided and everything was quiet, for what seemed like a minute or two.

Then the tall red headed woman left the bed and headed for the adjoining bathroom, where she started the shower.

Fortunately, this caused Lucy to talk a little louder, when communicating, and what she said, was more than Morgan could ever have dreamt of.

"Elaine darling, how long do you think we need to stay here?" she asked.

"I don't know we will have to return to the UK at some stage, I'm not sure"

"I'm worried Elaine, what if they find Jeff?"

"Don't worry lover, the Stork has him well and truly covered" joked Elaine.

"I'm still worried may …"

Elaine interrupted.

"Stop worrying, come and join me in here, I need my back massaging" she sexily instructed.

Morgan observed Lucy leave the bed and walk into the bathroom.

He decided that he had better take this opportunity to leave the Villa and make his way back to the UK.

He needed to arrange to have them both picked up by the Maltese Police, before they moved location.

Walking was not to be advised, so he went straight into transit mode;

Think PETER, Visualise; Morgan's bedroom UK.

As he sat on his bed, he turned over in his mind, parts of the conversation that Lucy and Elaine had in Malta.

"The Stork has him well and truly covered."

He thought about this statement.

"The Stork has him well and truly covered."

"Fucking Hell" he shouted.

Morgan picked up his phone.

"Sergeant Whitehead, where are you?"

"You're still at the Station?"

"Right, meet me at Elaine Southern's abode, organise a couple of uniforms and a shovel, and ask Ted Draper and his team to come along."

"What, the Superintendant?"

"Or I'll see him when we return to the Station."

Morgan continued.

"I need to talk to Superintendant Jackson anyway".

"OK Sergeant, time is of the essence get the guys moving."

Morgan jumped from his bed, dressed in his work suit and left the flat on his way to Flat 45 the Meadows.

Detective Inspector Morgan arrived at the property before Sergeant Whitehead and parked his car at the rear of the premises overlooking the small garden.

"That's it"

He remarked joyfully, as he looked over to the garden feature, an ornament of a stork!

Sergeant Whitehead and the others duly arrived and they also parked at the rear of the property.

As Detective Inspector Morgan hobbled towards them, Sergeant Whitehead commented.

"What the bloody hell's wrong with your feet Inspector?"

"Oh nothing Sergeant, I may have a touch of gout, nothing to worry about."

"If you have gout, you've a LOT to worry about" replied the Sergeant, laughing.

He then continued

"If I was you, I'd make for the Doctors, and pronto."

"Yes Sergeant, when we've sorted this little problem" confirmed Morgan.

"Now get the uniforms into gear and tell them to dig beneath that bloody stork" he ordered.

During the dig, Sergeant Whitehead asked.

"Where have you been all morning Inspector? The Superintendant has been going mad."

"Where's your phone? Did you have it turned off?"

The Sergeant continued.

"And what gave you the idea of digging under the bloody stork?"

"Sergeant, Sergeant, for Christ's sake. All wi…."

"Afternoon Detective Inspector" greeted Ted Draper, as he and two of his team entered the garden.

"Why all the rush to come down here?" he asked.

"We've found something Detective Inspector" was the cry from the diggers.

The uniforms were pointing to the appearance of a body of a man, within the hole they had just dug.

"That's the reason why you're here Ted. That's the bloody reason", was Detective Inspector Morgan's triumphant cry.

They all walked over to the area of the dig.

Ted Draper pulled on his gloves and he and his team started to inspect the body.

After a couple of minutes, Draper turned to Morgan.

"It looks very much like his neck is broken Detective Inspector."

"He may have been here for four or five months."

This comment caused Sergeant Whitehead to turn to Morgan.

"I don't know about you Inspector, but it looks like we have found the missing Jeff Thorne."

"I know Sergeant, I know" was Morgan's smug reply.

CHAPTER TWENTY TWO

When they all arrived back at the Station, Detective Inspector Morgan and Sergeant Whitehead decided that they needed to go straight to the Superintendant's office.

Superintendant Jackson was not very happy with Detective Inspector Morgan's, morning disappearing act.

"Where the Hell, were you Detective Inspector?"

"Do you not remember that when you clock in you are always on duty?" he snapped.

"Yes Superintendant, I do appreciate what you say, but I had lost my wallet, and then my mobile phone and I spent most of the morning locating the bloody things" answered a slightly blushing Morgan.

Morgan then explained the call from Steven Dukes about the Malta information as obtained from one of his informers.

This brought a smile to the face of the Superintendant, and he immediately phoned the Commissioners office.

As he wasn't available, the Superintendant asked his secretary for him to return his call as soon as possible.

The decision that the Superintendant next made, did not sit too well with the Detective Inspector.

"Well done Detective Inspector Morgan, I'll arrange with the Commissioner to ask the Maltese Police to check out the address you have outlined, and hopefully to apprehend Messer's Thorne and Southern".

"If all goes to plan, we will need to send our own officers to Malta, to bring the perpetrators back to the UK, and for this task, you, Sergeant Whitehead, along with WPC Alice Waterman will be sent."

The Superintendant continued.

"Sergeant Whitehead, in the meantime, please Leave us, and take the opportunity to inform WPC Waterman regarding the envisaged trip, and to make sure your travel documents are up to date."

"Yes Sir!" replied a delighted Sergeant Whitehead as he left the office.

Inspector Morgan just sat there totally flabbergasted.

"What about Me?"

He pleaded.

"I have a more important task for you Detective Inspector, much more important."

Superintendant Jackson then started to explain his decision.

"Yesterday I was contacted by a Miss Judy Armitage, Services and Child Care Co-ordinator, based at the East Street Youth and Community Centre"

"What she had to say to me was very upsetting; to me as a father, and May I stress, to me as a serving Police Officer, and the fact that we as Police Officers we don't seem to be able to protect our children."

"Miss Armitage has some rather sketchy evidence that she gained from one of her previous charges at the Centre."

"This evidence is not proven, but very believable, with regards to child prostitution and in some minor cases organised pick pocketing"

"So much so, that I have promised her that we, and in this case I mean you, will work with her and that you will leave no stone unturned until this matter is brought a suitable conclusion."

The Superintendant continued firmly stressing.

"These activities have to stop".

"The Bloody arseholes involved need to be eradicated from our society, and you Detective Inspector Morgan are the man to do it!"

Morgan just sat there looking at the Superintendant, his mouth wide open.

He had never heard the Superintendant speak in such a passionate manner.

After a few moments of thought, Morgan responded, but his remarks were insignificant, in comparison.

"I will do my utmost Superintendant, my total utmost" he spluttered.

"There is one good point Detective Inspector Miss Armitage will not come to the Station as most of her charges do not trust the police, so I have arranged for you to meet her in the Hope Inn on Market Street, at noon tomorrow."

"Just imagine you are on a blind date, put a newspaper in the left side pocket of your jacket, and she will approach you."

"See, Detective Inspector Morgan, you will 'go to the ball' and with my blessing" he joked.

The Superintendant then gave a word of warning.

"You know the procedure, have a few drinks, and strike up a working relationship with Miss Armitage, but remember, you are working"

Detective Inspector Morgan and the Superintendant exchanged a few pleasantries, and Morgan left the office.

When Morgan left the Superintendants office he had mixed emotions.

Yes, he was happy to be trusted with the child prostitution case, but he was far from happy, having to miss out on the pending arrest of Lucy Thorne and Elaine Southern.

Consequently, in order to relieve his annoyance, on his way to his own office Morgan decided to ring Steven Dukes and invite him for a pint at the Victoria Hotel later that night.

It was just before eight when they met, they ordered their drinks and sat in one of the corner booths of the bar area.

They were talking about Sergeant Whitehead's expected Malta trip, when Morgan asked

"Steve, did you find out who phoned the Journal with the address of the Villa in Malta?"

"No Peter, all I know is that it was a woman's voice, and she sounded very sure that both Lucy and Elaine would be there." Morgan pondered Steve's answer.

"Why the Hell, did she wait for more than two bloody weeks, before phoning?" he queried.

"Beats me, maybe we will find out the reason when the two ladies are arrested" suggested Dukes.

He continued.

"Anyway, why has Sergeant Whitehead been selected to go to Malta and not you?"

"The Superintendant thinks I would be more useful on another case that, incidentally, is more important than chasing two lesbians."

"How do you know they are lesbians?" Dukes asked.

Morgan hesitated, had he opened his 'big gob' too soon!

"Well it stands to reason, doesn't it, all the wigs and fancy clothes in Elaine's flat" answered Morgan, hoping that would satisfy Steve.

Steve seemed to be happy with Morgan's answer, because he changed the subject.

"So Peter, what's this other more important case?"

Morgan didn't want to divulge too much, but maybe Steve could be useful.

"Steve, what I am about to tell you is very much confidential, and it goes without saying, that you do not converse with anyone else about it".

"Look Peter, we've worked together as a team for some months now, and I, for one, think that we have a good relationship, a relationship that works for the Police and for the Journal."

Dukes continued, hoping to convince Morgan of his integrity.

"If you say I need to keep information under wraps, that's exactly what I will do."

Morgan lowered his voice he didn't want anyone else in the pub to hear any of the conversation that followed.

"The Superintendant has heard some distressing news regarding child prostitution and child pick pockets on our patch."

"He has put me in contact with a Miss Armitage, a Child Care Co-ordinator, who has the relevant information, and contacts that we feel could take the investigation forward to a successful conclusion."

"I'm meeting Miss Armitage tomorrow, and that's when I'll see how useful her information, and indeed how useful she can be, in tackling the case."

"Needless to say Steve, you will be kept informed, just as you always are".

Morgan then ended in a jovial manner.

"Now get off your fat arse, and get me another pint"

"Yes sir, you pillock" answered Dukes, as he walked towards the bar.

Next morning Sergeant Whitehead entered Detective Inspector Morgan's office, and for some reason, he was still smiling. He placed a cup of coffee on to Morgan's desk, maybe as a peace offering.

"Good morning Inspector, my, you are well presented this morning, what's the occasion?" he asked.

"Morning Sergeant, never mind my appearance, what's the latest on the body we dug up yesterday?"

"What have the Forensic Guys said?" asked a still rather grumpy Morgan.

"Forensics have validated the body as that of Mr Jeff Thorne, as we expected, his neck was broken, and he has been buried for some five to six months"

"Unfortunately, there isn't any DNA or other evidence, that would point towards the perpetrators" stated Whitehead.

"And the Commissioner, has he answered to the request from the Superintendant?" queried Morgan.

"Yes Inspector, photographs have been sent, and the Maltese Police should have apprehended the suspects by now"

"I'm expecting a call from the Superintendant, some time this morning" confirmed Whitehead.

"Good, I hope you and WPC Waterman enjoy your visit to Malta, but remember, you are not on holiday, and keep your grubby hands away from the WPC!" Morgan stated, semi-joking.

Morgan then continued.

"Oh by the way, I had a drink with Steve last night, and he confirmed that his informant was a woman, I think we may have to revisit that bloody so called 'Health Spa'".

"That's interesting Inspector, because I have asked the Superintendant to find out from the Maltese Authorities, who actually owns the 'Villa Les'."

"It will be very interesting if it is owned by someone other than Elaine Southern, someone who also goes to the Spa" said the Sergeant in agreement.

Morgan's mobile rang.

"Hello, Detective Inspector Morgan?"

"Hello, this is Judy Armitage Inspector"

"Hello Judy."

"Did your Superintendant tell you about me Inspector and the arrangement?"

"Yes he did, I'll be there as arranged."

"Bye, see you later."

"Judy?"

"Who's Judy?" asked Sergeant Whitehead.

"Oh nothing for you to worry about Sergeant, I'll tell you more, when you return from Malta" answered Morgan, rather guardedly.

"You have a bird."

"Come on, whose the unlucky lady?" teased the Sergeant.

"I do not have a bird. Now come, let's go and grab a cup of coffee" was Morgan's answer, trying to avoid going into more detail, regarding the phone call.

Unfortunately, Morgan's tactic failed miserably, as soon as they both entered the canteen, Sergeant Whitehead had only one message, to anyone who would listen.

"The Detective Inspector has a bird!"

It was some five minutes, before Sergeant Whitehead settled down and the conversation became more mundane.

Morgan was asking a member of Ted Draper's team about the body of Jeff Thorne, when they were interrupted by Morgan's mobile phone.

It was the Superintendant's secretary; Morgan and Sergeant Whitehead had been summoned to his office.

Once in the office and after the obligatory exchange, the Superintendant made his statement.

"I have just received a call from the Commissioner's office, the anticipated arrest of Messer's Thorne and Southern took place earlier this morning".

"Unfortunately, Mrs Lucy Thorne was the only person in the Villa at the time of the visit, and so was the only one arrested so obviously, Elaine Southern is still at large."

The Superintendant then spoke directly to the Sergeant.

"Sergeant Whitehead, you should finalise your arrangements for your visit to Malta, so that you're able to leave as soon as possible."

"Depending on the situation regarding Elaine Southern, and hopefully, her subsequent detainment, we may decide to extend your trip."

The Superintendant ended the statement by asking for any comments.

"Is that bloody Elaine a bloody clairvoyant or something?"

"She did the same disappearing act at the bloody Health Spa" exclaimed a disappointed Detective Inspector Morgan.

He continued.

"Superintendant, how long do you expect the Sergeant to stay in Malta?"

"At this stage, I don't know, I will be led by Sergeant Whitehead's advice, once he has been able to assess the situation".

He continued, stating hopefully

"The Maltese authorities are monitoring the Airport, so with a little luck, we may apprehend Elaine Southern quickly."

The Superintendant then spoke to Sergeant Whitehead.

"Right Sergeant, off you go, don't forget to call and see me before you leave."

"OK Sir" answered Whitehead.

The Sergeant turned to Morgan.

"I'll also keep you informed Inspector, I'm sure that I'll need to ask your advice over certain matters, especially concerning the ladies."

"Go on, bugger off" was Morgan's reply.

The Sergeant just smiled, and left the office.

"What's that all about?" asked Superintendent Jackson.

"Oh nothing Superintendant, just our little joke" answered Morgan.

The Superintendant then asked.

"Are you ready for your meeting at lunch time?"

"Yes Superintendant, with the meeting in mind, I have made some enquiries regarding the pimps in our area, and one name stands out above all the others; a Kristopher Novak, originating from Czechoslovakia."

"Good, if he is part of the information that Miss Armitage provides, put your foot on his bollocks, and keep it there" stated the Superintendant.

"I'll certainly do that Superintendant" confided Morgan.

"OK Detective Inspector, I'll let you get off, keep me up to date as events unfold."

"You can be sure of that" said Morgan as he left the office.

As Detective Inspector Morgan entered the Hope Inn he had the newspaper in his hand, he ordered a pint of bitter shandy, leant on the bar, and started to read the paper.

After a few minutes, he remembered where he should have the paper, so he quickly folded it and placed it in his jacket pocket.

After a further few minutes, he heard the most accommodating voice.

"Hello, you must be Detective Inspector Peter Morgan?"

Morgan turned around, the woman that he was looking at, did not represent the one he had expected.

Stood before him was a lady, petite in stature, with long blonde hair, full lips and the most engaging smile he had ever seen.

His mouth had suddenly gone dry, so he cleared his throat and somehow mumbled a reply.

"That's correct, and you must be Judy Armitage? What would you like to drink?" as he offered Judy his hand.

The contact of her hand within his sent a shock wave throughout his whole body, Judy seemed to be transmitting something similar to an electric shock, something that Morgan had never experienced before and something that confirmed that as far as he was concerned, Judy was rather special!

"Thank you very much I'll have a Tonic Water with a dash of lemon".

Morgan ordered the drink, and they sat down in one of the lounge area booths.

Initially, it was very difficult for Morgan to concentrate on the matter at hand, as far as he was concerned, he was sitting next to his dream woman.

Eventually, he managed to take his mind and his eyes from Judy Armitage's body, and started the 'work' conversation.

"Judy, you must have some serious concerns about some of the children that you work with, hence the contact with the Station Superintendant"

"Very much so Peter, as you will appreciate, we have a very difficult job, trying to keep some of our charges on the straight and narrow, so to speak."

"The contact, and subsequent conversation with Mr Jackson, was the result of a very disturbing conversation that I had with one of my ex girls, a fifteen-year-old girl called Christine."

"What is Christine doing now?" asked Morgan.

"She has turned her life around, and is now living with foster parents; both of her birth parents were killed in a car crash."

"So in what circumstances did the conversation with Christine take place?"

"Just by chance, Christine rang the centre and we agreed to go for a coffee."

Judy then related the story that Christine had told her.

"Christine said right from the start, that she wouldn't talk to the Police, and that she had only contacted me, hoping that I would know the whereabouts of her friend, Katie".

"She said that she came across Katie a couple of weeks ago, as Katie was on the run from some pimps, she was extremely downbeat and intending to leave the city to seek solace somewhere else."

"Katie had been working in an organised gang of pick pockets, which she didn't seem to worry too much about, but she became aware, that she was being enticed towards child prostitution".

"A direction where Katie would not be forced, so much so, that she attempted to run away, but she was caught, and as a mark of her belonging to them, she had been tattooed with a capital 'K' behind her left ear."

"Does Christine know any of these, excuse me, bloody pillocks?" asked Morgan.

"I asked Christine if she had ever come across the people that had been keeping Katie, but she said that she had not" Judy confirmed.

"Well Judy, we will have to find Katie, what is her full name?"

"She is Katherine Simpson, I don't know her parents' address, but the school that both she and Christine attended was St Joseph's Girls High, in King Street."

"Have you ever heard of a Kristopher Novak?" asked Morgan.

"No why? Do you think he could be involved?" queried Judy.

"It's possible, but first things first, we need to contact Katherine Simpson's parents, I'll get my people to contact the authorities, and it shouldn't take too long to obtain her parents address."

Morgan then started to outline the first phase of the investigation.

"One of the first priorities is to obtain a recent photograph of Katie and to compile a list of her likely haunts."

From a Police point of view, Morgan needed to know of the extent that Judy wanted to be involved within the subsequent investigation, and more pointedly, from a purely selfish perspective, how closely she wanted to be 'involved'.

Hence the next question.

"Judy, are you available to assist me in this investigation, regardless of the circumstances?"

"I am available to help in any way that you see fit, I would hope to be involved in this matter until Katie is found, and the people responsible are brought to justice" She answered.

It was a good job that Judy could not read Morgan's mind.

"That's exactly what I hoped you would say we need to act as a team if the case is to be brought to speedy conclusion" was Morgan's happy reply.

"Now, shall we have another drink to celebrate our new found working relationship?" he asked.

Judy seemed a little hesitant, but she agreed, maybe she was also warming to the proposed union.

"Good, now what would you like, same again?" asked Morgan.

"Yes Peter, it's too early in the day for anything stronger" she said.

Morgan left for the bar thinking

"I need to get Judy out for a social drink, and see how social I can make it."

When Morgan returned to the booth, Judy seemed more relaxed consequently he changed the conversation from Katie, to Judy.

"So, Judy, where do you go to socialise?" he asked.

"Since my boyfriend and I split, I tend not to go out as often as I should" she confessed.

This was music to the ears of one Detective Inspector Peter Morgan.

He tried to sound sympathetic.

"I'm sorry, I didn't mean to open any wounds, how long have you been parted?"

"Oh it's OK, we have been apart for three months now, besides, it's over, and I need to move on" she confided.

"Move on you will" he was thinking.

Then, Judy spoke the words that he hoped he would hear, but never really expected to.

"Have you a girlfriend at the moment Peter?"

"No, I never met the right girl regrettably. Also, my work tends to dominate my life" he answered, hoping for some sympathy. But Judy just smiled.

He then decided to take the 'bull by the horns' and ask her out, without actually asking her out!

"I have a suggestion, let's be positive, we need to work together on this case and we need our relationship to look normal, so when we meet, we meet socially, and enjoy ourselves while we work."

"What do you think of that?" he asked, expecting the worst.

The answer from Judy was a complete surprise, although very much the desired one.

Judy agreed, explaining.

"That sounds like a great idea it will take the pressure from me when I have to explain to people at work, and others, about my meetings with you."

Morgan left his meeting with Judy with a great sense of achievement, hopeful that he and Judy would form HIS kind of a social union and, of course, assist the investigation into the whereabouts of the unfortunate Katie Simpson.

CHAPTER TWENTY THREE

When Detective Inspector Morgan returned to his office, the first thing he did was ring Superintendant Jackson, and to update him on his meeting with Miss Armitage.

He then phoned PC Dunn and asked him to contact the Council, to find out the address of Katherine Simpson's parents and to arrange a meeting with them.

Morgan then listed the information he wanted Constable Dunn to obtain from the meeting;

He was to obtain the most recent photograph of Katie, find out her interests, and, most of all, an indication of the areas of the City that she most liked to visit.

He then phoned Sergeant Whitehead in Malta.

"Hi there you bloody stranger. How's Malta?"

"I hope you're keeping your bloody hands off WPC Waterman."

"Nice to hear that you miss me Inspector" laughed Whitehead.

The Sergeant then gave Detective Inspector Morgan an update on his visit to Malta.

"As you know, that 'Elaine bird' has done another disappearing act, Lucy Thorne says that Elaine had gone shopping when the Police arrived at the Villa."

"So it appears that she must have seen the Police Cars and done a runner."

"Anyway, we've not heard, or seen, anything, she is either hiding somewhere on the Island, or she has already left".

"We are expecting to leave for home in a couple of days, bringing Mrs Lucy Thorne with us, by the way Inspector, she is not saying anything."

"Right Inspector, so I'll see you ….

"Or, I nearly forgot, the 'Villa Les' is owned by a Miss Tracy Bingham, and would you believe it, she also works at the Health Spa."

"You are kidding!" said a surprised Morgan.

"I kid you not Inspector." confirmed Sergeant Whitehead.

"OK Sergeant, enjoy your couple of days, spend it trying to ascertain the likely method of departure by our Elaine, if of course, you don't find her in the meantime"

"I will Inspector, see you soon" answered an obviously happy Whitehead.

Morgan lay back in his chair and started to churn over in his mind, what the Sergeant had just said.

"Tracy Bingham, working at the Spa" he whispered.

"Constable Dunn" he exclaimed.

He picked up his mobile phone.

"Hi PC Dunn, this is Detective Inspector Morgan, where are you?"

"On the way to meet Katherine Simpson's parents"

"Good, when you have seen them, call in at the Bodyline Gym and Health Spa, on Ascot Street. Speak to a Tracy Bingham she is one of the Personal Trainers, you need to ask her to accompany you to the Station."

"If she asks why, just say we need to clarify one or two things regarding Elaine Southern's disappearance."

"What! Well, if she is not there, use your initiative and find her"

"Ring me when you're ready to return to the Station, and I'll meet you there."

"OK, PC, great, speak to you later."

Morgan put his phone down, and started to whisper to himself again.

"Tracy Bingham, I wonder."

After a matter of seconds, his mobile rang.

"Hello Luke, nice to hear from you, what can I do for you today?"

Detective Sergeant Luke Morley of the Drug Squad was on the phone.

"Hi Peter, I may have some very interesting information, that could assist your 'Thorne and Southern' case, fancy a pint tonight?"

"That's the best suggestion I've heard today."

"I'll meet you in the Victoria at about six" suggested Morgan.

"Six it is" confirmed Detective Sergeant Morley.

Detective Inspector Morgan spent the rest of the day doing nothing in particular, just catching up on paperwork, and it didn't seem too long before he was on his way to the Victoria and his meeting with Luke Morley.

Morley was already sat at the bar of the Victoria Hotel, when Morgan entered.

"Mine's a pint" said Morgan.

"It's on the bloody bar" answered Morley jovially.

Morgan sat next to Luke, took a quick sip of his drink and asked.

"Well Luke my boy, what is this very interesting information you have for me?"

"You are at the moment making enquiries regarding the Jeff Thorne murder and getting bloody nowhere, as usual" joked Luke.

"Well Detective Inspector Morgan, I may be able to help".

"Get on with it man!" said Morgan impatiently.

"Calm down, I'm getting there" answered Luke, enjoying a little tease at Morgan's expense.

"Early this morning, we arrested a certain Tina Woodside for the possession and supply of Class A drugs".

"She is well known to us and she has previous, so much so, that if I was a betting man, if the charge is proved, she is certain to get time".

"So bloody what!" Morgan retorted.

"So what, so what if she said, that she had information about Elaine Southern that connected her to the Jeff Thorne murder" Morgan's eyes lit up.

He answered, almost pleading.

"What information?"

"She wouldn't say until we agreed to a deal."

"The deal being, that all charges against her would be dropped." Luke continued.

"She would not expand on the information, but I know this girl, she's a well informed lesbian, an…"

"Did you say lesbian!" interrupted Morgan.

Everyone in the immediate vicinity of their position at the bar turned, and looked in their direction.

"Only a joke" laughed Morgan, as his face started to glow.

He then continued, but now, in a whisper, confirming what Luke had said.

"You said that she was a Lesbian?"

"I did" Luke replied.

"Why is that so important?"

"We think that the main suspects to the Thorne murder, namely, Lucy Thorne and Elaine Southern, are also of that persuasion" explained Morgan.

232

Morgan then stressed what he would like Luke to do.

"You need to arrange for me to interview this Tina, I will speak to the Superintendant, and if he and the Crown Prosecution Service agree, we will give her what she wants, providing, of course, that the information she can provide is sound and will lead to a prosecution."

"I think I can do that" said Luke.

He paused, and allowed a slight smile.

"Providing you tell me about this bird that you're seeing."

"I'm not seeing a b…."

Morgan's mobile phone rang.

"Hello, yes PC Dunn"

"She has what!"

"OK, get back to the Station I'll meet you there in ten minutes, bye."

PC John Dunn had just informed Detective Inspector Morgan, that Tracy Bingham had gone on holiday, and would not be back into work at the Gym for another two weeks.

"I'm sorry Luke, I have to go"

"Don't worry; I'll make it up to you."

Morgan finished his pint and headed for the door.

"Don't forget to arrange that interview with Tina" was his parting comment as he disappeared from the entrance and into the car park.

On his return to the Station, Detective Inspector Morgan went straight to the office of Superintendant Jackson.

He first explained the situation regarding Detective Sergeant Morley's drug suspect.

The Superintendant agreed to the proposed interview and that he would approach the CPS, providing that the forthcoming evidence was first vetted by Morgan and his team.

Morgan then updated the Superintendant on the child prostitution case and the Jeff Thorne murder investigation, and they then talked about Sergeant Whitehead's visit to Malta, and on this matter, they both agreed that Elaine Southern's disappearing act was very disappointing.

Finally, Detective Inspector Morgan assured the Superintendant that he would keep him updated on a daily basis regarding all the ongoing investigations, and left for his own office.

PC John Dunn almost fell over Morgan in the corridor, as Morgan was bent over tying his shoe lace.

"Careful PC Dunn, I'm straight you know" joked Morgan.

"Sorry Detective Inspector, but I've been rushing about like a madman all afternoon!" was PC Dunn's honest reply.

"I know, and it's my fault" admitted Morgan.

"Now, come on, let's go into my office, and you can brief me on the data that you've managed to compile, lets hope you have something tangible."

"And let's hope that you haven't been running about like a madman for nothing."

They entered the Detective Inspector's office and Morgan sat at his desk, folded his arms over the back of his head, and leaned back in his chair.

He beckoned PC Dunn to sit at Sergeant Whitehead's desk.

"Right PC John Dunn, the floor is yours" said Morgan, as he waited with anticipation.

"OK Detective Inspector, firstly, Katherine Simpson's parents were very helpful. They still don't understand why she left home, but they provided this photograph."

The Constable placed a school photograph of Katie on to Morgan's desk.

Morgan picked up the photograph and with sadness in his voice he commented

"It's a bloody shame she looks like such a nice young girl."

He then asked

"Did you find out any of her likely haunts?"

"I'm afraid not Inspector."

PC Dunn changed the subject as he continued.

"Anyway Inspector, as far as the whereabouts of Tracy Bingham is concerned, the Manager at the Health Spa said that she unexpectedly put in a request for a two week holiday, and then just left, not even waiting for her request to be authorised."

"Did you find out where she lives?" asked Morgan.

"Yes, the Manager confirmed that she has a flat next to the river, in the City Centre, Flat 69 Sixth Floor, Cuthbert Heights Valley Avenue."

"Did you pay a visit to the flat?"

"Yes, I couldn't enter the flat, but it was obvious that it wasn't occupied."

"Great stuff Constable, you may end up sitting in that chair permanently." was Morgan's slightly serious, slightly jokey answer.

Morgan thought for a while, then reached into his desk and pulled out a piece of paper containing 'Pimping' information, and a photograph.

He attached the photograph of Katie to the paper, and then passed them over to the PC.

He then stressed.

"Right PC Dunn, this is what you do next, use the photograph of Katie and visit the specific areas of the city marked on that sheet."

"They are the 'Pimping' areas that are used by a certain 'toss pot pimp' called Kristopher Novak he is the one on the attached photograph."

"I think he could be involved in the disappearance of poor Katie, so I want you up his arse, so to speak."

The Detective Inspector reiterated his rather 'basic' statement.

"Wherever that 'toss pot' goes, you go. But remember, be discreet."

"I'll give you a week to prove me right, or to prove me wrong about the toss pot."

Morgan tried to ease PC Dunn's obvious discomfort with the specified task.

"You have always acted very competently, and I have the utmost faith in your ability, but always remember, I'm just at the end of the phone if you ever feel you need some advice."

Morgan continued.

"I'll give you a ring in a couple days to see how you're getting on."

"Thanks Inspector, I'll certainly give it a good go, and I appreciate your belief in me, and of course, your availability for any advice" Dunn answered.

"As for me Constable, I will check out the Tracy Bingham situation, there has to be more to this woman than meets the eye."

They left the office on their way to their separate destinations; PC Dunn, to prepare for his shadowing of Kristopher Novak, and Inspector Morgan, to his Flat.

Once in his Flat, Morgan checked on the internet; he knew that Cuthbert Heights was a recent development, so he expected that there would be advertisements that outlined the Flat interior design.

Once satisfied on the layout, he changed into jeans, a sweatshirt with a hood and a pair of trainers.

He sat on his bed and started the body transit procedure.

"Think PETER, Visualise; the grass verge at the rear of Flat 69 Cuthbert Heights.

As Morgan materialised, he found him self standing on the balcony of one of the ground floor Flats!

He could see through the net curtains, that the occupants were sat round the dining table, enjoying a meal.

"Shit!" he muttered to himself

"It's a good job the balcony doors were closed."

Morgan jumped off the balcony and walked to the side of the building.

"Think PETER, Visualise: the bedroom, Flat 69, sixth floor.

Bingo. Morgan materialised dead centre.

In the toilet, with one foot on the floor and the other foot in the toilet bowl!

Initially, he didn't say anything then he just shook his head and murmured 'Bollocks' quietly.

Morgan started to move carefully around the flat, to ensure that it wasn't occupied.

It was a well presented living accommodation, very well decorated and very tidy.

'I wish I was as bloody tidy' thought Morgan.

He walked over to the computer desk and checked through documents in the desk drawer.

There were a few miscellaneous documents, and photographs; a caravan in Shell Bay, a yacht in Almeria, various pets, family members, but one photograph took his eye, it showed five women, all scantly dressed, not wearing bras, and wearing what looked like male wigs.

He started talking to himself

"I'd like to get amongst that lot."

With his undivided attention concentrated on this photograph, he almost missed a printed confirmation of a Hotel booking.

Morgan started to check the information contained on the booking; one double room for one week at the Hotel Bristol Palace, Genoa.

Morgan then walked over to the phone and switched on the answer facility.

There were various messages, but only one of interest, and what interest.

He was delighted that it was from Elaine Southern, and he could tell from the urgency in her voice, that she was desperate.

"Tracy, the Police have turned up at the Villa. I have eluded them, but I don't have any passport or my mobile phone. I have also left a message on your mobile, but I dare not ring the Health Centre."

"I'll keep ringing you, you have to help me."

The message continued;

"I think I can escape to Genoa via the Ferry at Valletta, perhaps you could meet me there? As I said, I'll keep ringing, Love Elaine."

There were no more messages from Elaine, so Morgan had to suppose that the next time she had rung, Tracy had answered, "So that's why Tracy has taken a hasty holiday, she's gone to bloody Genoa."

He phoned Sergeant Whitehead.

"Sergeant, you were what?"

"I was just going to ring you Inspector, you must be psychic!"

"The Maltese Police have carried out a further search of 'Villa Les' and they found two passports."

"Just listen to this Inspector; the passports were for two men!"

"The Maltese Police are checking the authenticity as we speak"

"I always wondered how the buggers left the U.K" said Morgan.

"However, that fits in with what I was going to say Sergeant, now listen."

Morgan's tone changed, stressing the importance of his information to Whitehead.

"I've had some information relayed to me from a very reliable source."

"It looks like Elaine may have taken the Ferry to Genoa from Valletta and as we now know she won't have a passport, so she could be hanging around in the vicinity of the Ferry."

"I think you and WPC Waterman should get there, pronto."

"OK Inspector, we'll head over there immediately. By the way, who is this source?" queried Whitehead.

"A bloody good one Sergeant and for security reasons it's for only me to know."

"Now get on with my request."

"OK Inspector, we're on our way."

"Oh just one thing Inspector"

"What's that Sergeant?"

"How is your bird? Have you got on yet?"

"Bollocks Sergeant" was Morgan's expected answer.

He continued

"Let me know immediately you have some information, speak to you soon."

Morgan returned his phone to his pocket and decided to move back to his flat.

Think PETER, Visualise; My bedroom.

He materialised on his bed.

He started to speak to himself.

"How is it that I can get my transit right when I come home?"

He then phoned the Desk Sergeant at the Station and asked him to check with passport control at all the Airports; question if a certain Tracy Bingham had left the country, destination Genoa, Italy, we need to be informed.

Morgan then decided to take a bath, he was feeling a little exhausted after all the transit activity he'd just experienced.

So he walked into the bathroom, turned on the hot water tap and disposed of all his clothes in a heap on the floor.

He sat on the side of the bath and watched as the water level rose, tested the temperature and added cold water until satisfied it was just right, he lowered himself into the water, and lying back with his eyes closed, he was in relaxed mode.

After a while, he could hear his phone ringing.

"Fucking bollocks" he exclaimed.

"As soon as I get fucking comfortable, the fucking phone rings." he shouted.

Morgan lifted himself from the water, grabbed a towel, wrapped it around is body, and walked towards the noise that had annoyed him so much.

It was PC John Dunn, who was on the phone.

"I bloody well hope this call is important PC" shouted Morgan.

"I think so Inspector, I've just been informed that a body of a young girl has been found; it would appear it's the body of Katherine Simpson."

CHAPTER TWENTY FOUR

As Detective Inspector Morgan arrived in East Street, he did so with great regret, for he was just about to check on the body of a young girl, too young to be in the situation that she had been found.

As he stepped out of his car, Morgan could see that Ted Draper and his team had erected the appropriate lighting and had tented the crime scene.

Constable Dunn approached the Detective Inspector as he walked towards the tented area.

"I'm sorry Inspector, but she's been strangled, it's such a pity for one so young."

"I agree PC Dunn" was Morgan's rather gruff answer as he continued on his way to inspect the body.

Ted Draper had just finished attending to the victim as Morgan entered the tented area.

"Strangled Ted?" asked a very sad Morgan.

"Afraid so Detective Inspector, I'm afraid so" answered Ted Draper, sympathetically.

Detective Inspector Morgan placed on his gloves and pulled the sheet from the body, he tilted her head to one side, and inspected behind her left ear.

The letter 'K' was tattooed, just where he had expected.

"Bastards" he shouted, as he moved away from the body.

He apologised to Ted for his language, and then moved away from the crime scene.

Tears were appearing in his eyes, Morgan wiped his eyes, and almost shaking, vowed to himself

"I'll get you, you fucking bastards. Regardless of how long it takes, I'll get you!"

Morgan didn't talk again to anyone within the crime scene, not even Constable Dunn, as he just walked to his car and drove home.

Once in his flat, he opened a bottle of red wine and sprawled out on the sofa.

He didn't even bother with a glass he just lay there staring into space drinking directly from the bottle, which was almost empty when his mobile rang.

Morgan just lay there and let it ring.

When the ringing stopped, Morgan drank the unfinished contents of the bottle and left the sofa, throwing the empty wine bottle into the rubbish bin on his way to bed.

Next morning, Morgan had washed and shaved, and was getting dressed when he remembered the phone call.

He picked up his mobile and checked the missed calls.

"Shit, the bloody call was from Judy" he exclaimed.

This reminded him of the awful event that had happened yesterday, and he thought about how he would inform Judy.

He decided that he would ring her once he had checked with Forensics at the Station.

This decided, Morgan finished dressing and left his flat for work.

It was just after 0730 hours when Morgan entered the Station and headed straight to see Ted Draper.

As he entered Forensics, he could see that the office was empty, so he decided to go to his own office and ring Ted later.

As he passed the canteen he could hear the unmistakable voice of Ted, so he entered.

"Ah good morning Inspector Morgan" greeted Ted Draper.

"Morning Ted, can we go to your office and have a talk about the murder last night?" asked Morgan, wanting to keep the talk private.

"Sure" answered Ted, as he picked up his coffee cup.

He continued

"Would you like a cup of coffee first?"

"No thanks Ted" answered Morgan as he walked from the canteen.

They both entered Forensics and sat at Ted's desk.

"There's not much to talk about Inspector, the young girl had been dumped in the alley, she had been strangled, possibly some three to four hours earlier" Ted stated.

"We arrived at the scene just after nine, so she would have met her fate at around five" he confirmed.

"You did see the tattoo?" asked Morgan.

"Yes, it was not a professional job, but I am sure that I have seen something like it before"

"You have? Where?" queried Morgan.

"That's the bloody problem Inspector, I can't bloody remember" confessed Ted, feeling rather silly.

"I'll check all my records, I'm sure that I can locate the case concerned."

"Great stuff Ted, give me a call as soon as you find out, it could be crucial" stressed Morgan.

"No worries Inspector, I'll get straight on it".

As Morgan left Forensics, he reminded Ted of the importance of his search.

As soon as Detective Inspector Morgan entered his office, he rang Luke Morley.

"Morning Luke, I have the agreement of the Superintendant, in principle, regarding my interview with your possible informant, Tina Woodside."

"Can we arrange the interview for some time after ten this morning?"

"The sooner the better as far as I'm concerned Peter, we need to charge her or give her the deal" stressed the Detective Sergeant.

"Right then, ten it is, I'll meet you in the interview room next to the cells, at ten minutes to ten" confirmed Morgan.

"OK Peter, see you then" agreed Luke.

Morgan centred his thoughts onto Judy, and how was he going to tell her about Katie?

He decided that he would invite her out for a meal, and get her slightly tipsy, hoping that the alcohol would soften the blow.

With this in mind, he picked up his mobile, although he was a little apprehensive regarding the call, he knew it had to be made; the conclusion was the sooner the better.

"Hi Judy, how are you today?"

He continued, trying to make an excuse for missing her call.

"I'm sorry I missed your call last night, but if you're willing, I'll explain tonight."

He then tried to lighten the conversation.

"Would you do me the honour of accompanying me to a Restaurant, of your choice tonight, Honey Bug?"

"Nice to hear from you Peter, what's this 'Honey Bug' term?"

"That's my new name for you Judy, you, Honey Bug."

"Well you certainly know how to 'chat' a woman, Peter, you, Peter Bug" answered Judy, trying to enter into the spirit of the conversation.

"Oh you're so complementary, Honey Bug, where would you like to go?"

"Well Peter Bug, seeing that expense is not a problem, I'd like you to take me to the Squires Restaurant in the Queens Hotel" Judy proposed, rather hopefully.

"If that's where my Honey Bug wants to go, then that's where she will go" agreed Morgan.

There followed a lot of really silly talk, that had both of them laughing out loud.

They finally ended their conversation with an agreed plan; Morgan would order a Taxi and pick up Judy from her house at eight sharp.

Morgan's internal phone was ringing, so he said a hasty goodbye, and picked up the receiver.

"Hello, Detective Inspector Morgan."

"Yes Sergeant, she did OK, Sergeant, thanks for the information."

The Desk Sergeant had just informed him that Tracy Bingham had taken a flight to Genoa from Stansted.

Morgan then phoned Sergeant Whitehead in Malta.

"Hi Sergeant, how's your trip to Valetta going?"

"Hi Inspector, not very well, we've had conflicting reports about sightings of Elaine Southern" Whitehead answered.

"The ferry ticket operator thought they had seen someone closely resembling her, but obviously, passport control says she hasn't used the ferry."

"Well, they would say that, wouldn't they" said Morgan sarcastically.

"Anyway Sergeant, we now know that Tracy Bingham is in Genoa, she is staying at the Hotel Bristol Palace. It goes without saying that Elaine will be there too".

"I suggest that you leave Lucy Thorne with the Maltese authorities, and you and your WPC extend your little jaunt, to include Genoa."

"If you both act as tourists, I'm pretty sure that when you come across our Elaine, she won't be suspicious."

"What am I supposed to do for money?" queried the Sergeant.

"Do what you always do, borrow some" joked Morgan.

He then added

"Give Superintendant Jackson a ring and give him an update on the situation, and then ask him to transfer you some funds"

"I have to go Sergeant I have a meeting with Luke Morley. Ring me when you catch the bitch."

Morgan left his office for the meeting with Luke Morley and his druggie informer.

Morley was already in the interview room as Morgan entered. He sat down across the table form the Detective Sergeant and asked,

"This Tina, do you really think we can trust her?"

"Implicitly" Luke stated.

"That's a big word, what does it mean?" Morgan joked.

"It means that I trust every word that she utters, she is desperate to avoid a jail sentence" stressed Morley.

"Well, we have to prove what she says is actually true, before the Superintendant will approach the CPS" confirmed Morgan.

"So, let's hear what she has to say, and then we'll take the appropriate action" Morley concluded.

Morley stood up and left the room, returning a couple of minutes later with the informer, Tina Woodside who he ushered into the room.

They both sat at the table, Morley next to Morgan, and Tina Woodside on the opposing side of the table.

Detective Inspector Morgan opened the session.

"Tina, let me introduce myself. I am Detective Inspector Peter Morgan, and I am the Senior Investigating Officer in the Jeff Thorne murder case."

"We are meeting here today, because you have indicated to my colleague, Detective Sergeant Morley, that you have some information that is pertinent to the case."

Detective Inspector Morgan continued.

"Tina, you have also indicated that you would expect to be excused the Class A drug charges if you provide this information."

Morgan then asked the first question.

"So Tina, what's the information that you think is so important?"

"Oh, first of all, I must mention that our interview is being recorded" he added.

Tina, a drawn-looking woman in her late twenties, nervously fiddling with her hands, looked him straight in the eyes, almost challengingly, and began.

"Firstly Inspector, I want you both to know that I was the person who informed the Daily Journal about the Villa in Malta"

"As for this interview, if I provide the information you seek, will I get off the drug charge completely?"

"We can certainly excuse the drug charge, and as for the phone call, yes, you certainly helped the present enquiry" Morley replied.

Detective Sergeant Morley continued.

"If the information you are to provide is solid and is instrumental in murder charges being proved, yes, we will reassess the drug charge."

Tina hesitated, and took a drink from the glass of water, that had been placed on the table.

"OK then, this is what I know."

She then explained what she knew and the circumstances surrounding the events;

"Elaine Southern and Tracy Bingham both work at the Gym and Health Spa as Personal Trainers, and are lesbians."

"They regularly held lesbian parties over a number of years, and more recently, Lucy, who was Jeff Thorne's wife, me and Martina became regular participants."

"What did these parties consist of?" asked Morgan.

"They were just very silly to start with, we all dressed as men, but as the drugs and alcohol took over, they became more and more sexual"

"When you talk about Martina, who are you referring to?" asked Detective Inspector Morgan.

"Little Martina, Martina Vitti" affirmed Tina.

"You mention dressing up as men, did you ever hear anyone mention passports for men?" queried Morgan.

"Tracy and Elaine always had fake passports available, they used to be heavily involved in drug running, and as you must know, in that world fake passports are a must" Tina pointed out. Detective Sergeant Morley's eyes lit up and he asked.

"Do you know who Elaine worked with?"

"As far as I know, she worked with two Gay men, but they both died."

Detective Inspector Morgan and Detective Sergeant Morley looked at each other; they both knew exactly, the names of the two 'Gay men' that Tina was referring to, even if she didn't.

"OK Tina, carry on with your statement" Morley requested.

"Well, Jeff Thorne somehow found out about Lucy's involvement with the parties that we held, and he confronted Elaine."

"We are talking about Elaine Southern" asked Detective Inspector Morgan.

"Yes Inspector, we're talking about Elaine Southern" confirmed Tina.

She then continued.

"We all knew that Elaine Southern was not a person that you would mess with, she had black belts in both Judo and Karate".

"Anyway, when Jeff went to Elaine's house, they obviously argued and she just attacked him, and as you already know, Jeff ended up with a broken neck"

"How do you know that it was Elaine Southern that broke the neck of Jeff Thorne?" asked Detective Inspector Morgan.

"I was there when Elaine buried him, and I took a photo with my mobile of Elaine putting his body into the ground, that's how."

"Believe me Detective Inspector, as I have already said, Elaine is a very dangerous woman, if she knew that I had such a photo, I would also be dead."

"I assume you can produce this photograph?" queried Detective Sergeant Morley.

"I can Sergeant and it's in a very safe place" Tina stressed. Detective Inspector Morgan thought to himself.

'I believe this woman she must have also taken the photographs that I found at Elaine's flat.'

"Carry on Tina" requested Morley.

"Well, I helped Elaine bury Jeff in the garden, and Elaine then told Lucy what had happened."

"What was Lucy's reaction to the news of her husband's murder?" asked Morley.

"She was glad, she admitted to me that she had always been a lesbian, and that she only married Jeff because of her mother's influence in her life, and her mother liked him."

"So what can you tell us about Martina Vitti?" asked Morgan.

"Martina was a lovely person she wasn't really a lesbian, she just fell in with the wrong crowd, so to speak."

"I felt really sorry for her, but she couldn't stop taking the drugs and that was her downfall"

"What do you mean?" asked Morgan.

"I mean that during one of our parties, Elaine, being under the influence of drugs and alcohol, admitted to the murder of Jeff Thorne, Martina took exception to it, they had a fight and Elaine killed her."

"I don't suppose you have any photographs?" asked a hopeful Morley.

"Sorry Sergeant, No" Tina answered.

Detective Inspector Morgan put his next question to Tina in a very straightforward manner.

"OK Tina, you have been very helpful, all we need now is the photograph."

"Not so quick Inspector" countered Tina.

"Remember our agreement? I need my drug charges to be dropped first. Until I get that agreement from you lot, I won't be producing anything."

Detective Inspector Morgan then made an interesting, and to Sergeant Morley, an incorrect statement.

"Tina, you have my assurance, that when you produce the evidence that you say you have, we will excuse ALL of your pending drug charges."

This caused Morley to give Morgan an accusing look, and he asked Morgan if they could take a short break from the interview.

Detective Sergeant Morley and Morgan left the room and faced each other in the corridor outside.

"What the fuck are you doing? You can't give guarantees like that!" shouted Morley.

"Luke, calm down, what else could I say? We need that bloody photograph" answered Morgan.

After a few more choice words, they agreed that they had to sound more positive, so they re-entered the interview room and continued.

"OK Tina, both Detective Sergeant Morley and I agree that the drug charges will be dropped, providing that you come forward with the said photograph" stated Morgan.

"Sorry Detective Inspector, but I will only give you the photograph when I get confirmation of the dropped charges in writing" answered a very stubborn and determined Tina.

Detective Inspector Morgan could see that the interview had exhausted its usefulness, so he called a halt.

Tina was returned to the cells, Detective Sergeant Morley returned to his office, and Detective Inspector Morgan made his way to the Station Superintendant's office.

As Morgan entered Superintendant Jackson's office, he was greeted by the Superintendant.

"Come in Inspector Morgan, now you're here, you can explain the decision to send Sergeant Whitehead on a holiday to Italy, at the expense of this Station."

"I'm sorry that I couldn't tell you personally Superintendant, but I had to talk to the informer held by Detective Sergeant Morley" was the lame excuse Morgan offered.

He continued.

"The reason for the Sergeant's visit to Genoa is simple we have accurate information that Elaine Southern is meeting Tracy Bingham there."

"And where did this accurate information come from?" was Jackson's sarcastic query.

"I have a very good source that has never let me down, plus the fact that we know for certain, that Tracy Bingham did take a flight to Genoa from Stansted."

"OK then Detective Inspector, I'll accept you acted diligently" conceded Jackson. Stressing

"However, in future you get the OK from me, before you send people abroad."

"Now what's the latest with this Tina Woodside is she going to provide the desired evidence?" he asked.

"It would appear so Superintendant, but not until we can categorically say she will be excused the drug charges."

"However, she did confirm that Elaine Southern had access to fake passports, thus the passports that were found in 'Villa Les' that Sergeant Whitehead told us about" Morgan confirmed.

"Well that's interesting about the passports, but when do you anticipate we will have the required evidence Inspector?"

"We'll have to see what Sergeant Whitehead can turn up in Genoa, and if that's positive, we can move on to a prosecution, and then Tina's evidence would be crucial."

The Superintendant seemed to be satisfied with all that Morgan had told him and thanked him, he then joked.

"The next time you decide to send someone to the sunny Isles of Italy, perhaps you could consider ME."

To which Morgan answered.

"Perhaps I will Superintendant, but only after I've considered ME."

There followed a few more silly comments, after which Morgan left the office to make the journey home, and to prepare for his night out with his new project, Judy.

He had only completed half of his journey when some miscellaneous objects were thrown from the road by the vehicle he was following, and smashed against his windscreen.

"Shit" exclaimed Morgan.

Although he kept on driving, he could plainly see that his windscreen had various significant cracks.

When he arrived home, he inspected the damage to the windscreen, and this confirmed that the windscreen would possibly need replacing.

As he entered his flat, he allowed himself to be consoled by the fact that he was fully covered by the Comprehensive Car Insurance.

With this in mind, he allowed the incident to pass from his mind, the focus being to prepare for his date with Judy.

As Judy entered the Taxi, Morgan knew why he had longed to get to grips with her body!

As far as he was concerned, she was the perfect woman, and with a little bit of luck, she would be HIS woman.

Judy kissed Morgan on the check as she entered, whispering, "Hi, my Peter Bug."

Morgan returned the kiss, whispering,

Hi, my beautiful Honey Bug."

They both chuckled and the Taxi Cab set off for the Queens Hotel.

Once at the Hotel, they were ushered to the bar of the Squires Restaurant, where they ordered their pre-meal drinks.

"What would you like to drink Honey Bug?" asked Morgan.

"I think I'll have a Southern Comfort with Ice, Peter" answered Judy.

Morgan ordered Judy's drink and ordered a Baileys with Ice for himself.

There followed a couple more rounds of similar drinks, before they sat down to eat, and even more drinks, during the meal.

The number of drinks was pre-meditated by Morgan.

He hoped the excessive amounts of alcohol, would help to reduce the pain of what he had to tell Judy.

After the meal, they retired into the Restaurant Bar area, and sat at a table close to one of the windows overlooking the river.

In fact, Morgan was now also feeling the effects of the alcohol, and this could be the reason why he just turned to Judy and stated;

"Judy, I have some very disturbing news."

"What, no Honey Bugs?" joked Judy.

"I'm sorry Judy, but Katie has been found, she's been murdered."

Judy's face turned white!

The radiant smile disappeared from her face instantly.

Her expression changed from one of happiness, to one of despair.

She tried to speak, but she just stuttered, and then she started crying.

Morgan took hold of her and pulled her close, holding her to his chest, trying to give her a gentle squeeze, but only succeeded in 'almost' breaking her ribs!

Judy broke from his embrace, and still crying asked.

"Take me home Peter, please take me home."

Morgan ordered a Taxi and they both left for Judy's home.

During the journey, Judy started to embrace and caress Morgan in a very seductive way, this encouraged Morgan to follow her lead, which led to them kissing passionately.

When the Taxi Cab arrived at Judy's house, Morgan released her from his embrace and asked her

"Will you be OK Judy?"

"Yes Peter, as long as you come inside and look after me?"

It may have been a scene of despair, but this request from Judy, made Morgan ecstatic.

He answered her request, trying his best to sound rather sad.

"Yes of course, and I'll stay as long as you need me."

They left the Taxi Cab arm in arm and entered the house.

Once inside, all hell broke loose.

Judy may have been grieving over the death of Katie, but it did not stop her from quickly removing her clothes, and expertly assisting Morgan to do the same with his clothing.

They did not even have time to enter the bedroom; they were engaged in frantic lovemaking before they hit the sofa!

CHAPTER TWENTY FIVE

Next morning as Morgan opened his eyes, his first thought was that he had been dreaming.

But the proof he hadn't lay next to him, he turned to touch the goddess he had been sleeping with, he then caressed her breasts and kissed them tenderly.

This enticed the response he desired, Judy turned towards him and responded as he had hoped, which resulted in them returning to a repeat of last night's performance.

After a hectic period of lovemaking, Judy left the bed for the bathroom and Morgan laid back in the bed, fully satisfied and feeling really smug.

He looked at his watch.

"Shit" he exclaimed, as he jumped from the bed.

"Look at the bloody time."

"It's twenty past eight."

He shouted in the direction of the bathroom, as he searched frantically for his clothes.

"Honey Bug, I'm late for work, I have to go."

He continued to seek the missing garments and hurriedly get dressed he then wondered over to the bathroom and opened the door intending to tell Judy of his imminent departure to the Station.

"Hello Peter Bug," she pouted, looking up at Morgan from her steaming bath, her nakedness stirring him again, until …

"Oh bollocks to work" he shouted, as he stripped off his just donned clothes in double quick time and joined Judy in the bath, ready for more lovemaking.

When Detective Inspector Morgan eventually arrived at the Station, he was physically drained, but totally full of himself. It was just before midday, and he headed straight for his office. As he sat at his desk, all he could think about was the time he had just spent with the woman of his dreams and how he had eased the news of Katie's death for Judy, and how he was going to enjoy her body again, and the sooner the better!

Morgan picked up his diary, first to enter tomorrow's date with Judy, and then to check through his work arrangements, desperately trying to force his mind back into 'work mode'. His mobile rang.

"Good Morning Sergeant Whitehead" he shouted triumphantly.

"Good Morning?"

"It's the afternoon Inspector" answered a surprised Sergeant.

"Oh yes, so it is" answered Morgan joyfully.

Sergeant Whitehead detected that the Inspector was in a good mood, although he couldn't know the reason why.

But nevertheless, he decided to enter into the spirit of the moment, with his own good news.

"Inspector, I have some good news from Genoa, we have seen our two suspects in the Hotel Bristol Palace."

"That's bloody great news Sergeant" said a still very happy Morgan.

He then managed to return to normality, and warned the Sergeant.

"Listen Sergeant, be very careful, that bitch Elaine is a very dangerous woman, and so might be Tracy Bingham."

"Make sure that you don't let them find out about you or WPC Waterman" he urged.

"Don't worry Inspector, we're keeping our distance, but how do you want us to handle the situation, we can't just monitor their activities?" asked Whitehead.

"Superintendant Jackson is in London for a couple of days, so liaise with the British Consulate and the Italian Police, and arrange to have the two 'lovebirds' arrested."

Detective Inspector Morgan then stressed again.

Be very careful, we don't want any of them to escape our clutches again."

"OK Inspector, we'll tread carefully and will be advised by the local authorities as to the method and timescale regarding the anticipated arrest"

"Good thinking Sergeant, keep me informed, bye."

Morgan replaced the phone with the genuine hope that the Sergeant would keep his promise, and act carefully.

Morgan's mood changed quickly, as his car windscreen entered his mind.

"The damage to my car windscreen, I need to phone for a replacement" he remembered.

So he checked the phone directory for windscreen repairers, and picked out one of the numbers.

"Hello, my name is Peter Morgan, its regarding the windscreen on my Volvo Estate it was extensively damaged yesterday, could you fit me a replacement?"

"Certainly sir, are you covered by Comprehensive Insurance on the car? And if so, who is your Insurance Company?" asked the repairer.

"Yes, I have Fully Comp, the car is covered by Three-to-Two Insurance" answered Morgan.

"Oh, I'm very sorry sir, but we don't deal with that Insurance Company"

"What do you mean? My Broker recommended that Insurance Company" replied a disturbed Morgan.

"Well you will have to talk to your Broker, we cannot enter into any dealings with Three-to-Two Insurance, I'm sorry" and with that the man put down the phone.

Morgan sat back in his chair, in a state of disbelief!

"I spent over £1000 on the bloody Insurance, and the bloody repairer won't deal with them" he shouted.

He phoned two more windscreen repairers, with the same answer; no one would deal with Three-to-Two Insurance.

A very irritated Morgan picked up the phone again.

"Hello, is Clive Brooks there?"

"Ah Clive, this is Peter Morgan, it's about the Insurance on my car".

"I've damage to my windscreen, and no one will deal with Three-to-Two Insurance! Why?"

"Listen Mr Morgan, you opted for Cheap Insurance whatever did you expect?" answered a seemingly disinterested Clive Brooks.

"I bloody well expected windscreen repairers to deal with the Insurance Company that you recommended, and furthermore, I don't call £1000 bloody cheap."

"Well you get what you pay for." and with that comment Brooks put down the phone.

Morgan was livid!

He stood up and walked about his office.

"I don't believe what Clive Brooks just said" he cursed.

But he also realised, that he had made a big mistake in not checking on the Insurance Company suggested when he insured the car.

But as far as he was concerned, he should have received a better service from the Broker, namely, Mr Clive Brooks.

Morgan began to wonder.

He knew that Brooks lived on the Star Estate in the village of Aston, in a detached bungalow overlooking the river, and that he owned a very expensive car.

Aston was a village that Morgan had pleasure visiting many times during his fishing days.

So he decided that he had to make Brooks pay for signing him up with Three-to-Two Insurance.

Think PETER, Visualise; Aston Village, White Horse Hotel car park.

As he materialised, he was relieved, and to some extent pleasantly surprised, that this time he hadn't found himself in a stupid or compromising situation.

Brooke's home was a couple of minutes walk from the White Horse and Morgan headed straight for his intended prey.

As luck would have it, as he approached the property, Mrs Brooks was washing her husband's pride and joy, his nice, expensive Humber Super-Snipe Mk.3 Sports Saloon.

Morgan also noticed that the rear garden of the property had quite a steep gradient towards the fast flowing river.

Morgan moved into a good viewing position of the activities within the garden, ensuring that Mrs Brookes wouldn't be able to observe him.

He then settled down and waited patiently for his opportunity.

After a few minutes Morgan could hear the phone ringing, and when Mrs Brookes went inside the Bungalow to answer, Morgan struck!

As quick as a Cobra strike he was in the car, the handbrake was released, and the car was sent on its journey across the garden and onwards down the slope towards the river.

Morgan returned to his observation position and relaxed as he joyfully watched the car disappear under the surface of the flowing river and out of sight.

Leaning against one of the neighbour's walls he began muttering to himself

"I hope that you have good Car Insurance cover Mr Brooks!"

It was early evening in Genoa, with the hot sun just starting to disappear over the horizon.

Sergeant Whitehead and WPC Alice Waterman had just finished attending a meeting with the Local Polizia.

Consequently, The Genoa Polizia had assigned two female Officers to the investigation, Adelina and Loreto.

They had been directed to assist under the direction of Sergeant Whitehead in the anticipated arrest of Elaine Southern and Tracy Bingham.

A little while later, they were all dressed in civilian clothes, and were sitting in an unmarked police car that was parked outside the Hotel Bristol Palace as Whitehead outlined the plan of action;

The Hotel management had informed the team, that Elaine and Tracy had booked a table for two in the Hotel Restaurant for seven fifteen that evening.

When Elaine and Tracy left their room, they would see Adelina and Loreto having a conversation in Italian some five metres from their room door.

It was expected they would ignore Adelina and Loreto and walk down the corridor towards the lift area.

Once at the lift, they would see Sergeant Whitehead and WPC Waterman apparently waiting for the lift.

Adelina and Loreto would follow Elaine and Tracy to the lift area and then assist the Sergeant and WPC Waterman with the arrest.

"OK everyone, are we fully conversant with what we have to do?" asked the Sergeant.

Everyone nodded in agreement.

"OK then, let's do it."

They prepared to leave the parked car.

"Just a minute" said Sergeant Whitehead.

They all stopped, and looked in the direction that the Sergeant was pointing; towards the entrance of the Hotel.

Tracy Bingham had just appeared on the entrance steps.

She casually walked down the steps and began walking along the Via xx Settembre.

"Bloody hell" said Sergeant Whitehead, as he turned to the rest of the team.

"Alice, you and Loreto stay in the car, Adelina and I will follow Tracy. If Elaine Southern appears, follow her, but don't try to arrest her, and keep your distance".

The Sergeant and Adelina left the car and started to follow Tracy.

They very soon caught up with Tracy as she approached a road Junction, opposite a McDonald's takeaway.

"Good evening Tracy Bingham, my name is Sergeant Whitehead from the British Police and this is WPC Adelina Rossi of the Italian Police Force."

He informed Tracy that she was being arrested in connection with the murder of Jeff Thorne, and furthermore, with assisting a known fugitive Elaine Southern.

"But I am on holiday I haven't been involved in any of those things" pleaded Tracy unconvincingly.

Whitehead and Adelina ignored her pleas and she was handcuffed and walked unceremoniously back to the Police car.

Once she was secured and seated inside the car, Sergeant Whitehead noticed that Alice wasn't there.

"Where is the WPC?" he asked Loreto.

"She followed the other suspect, err, that Elaine woman" answered Loreto.

She continued.

"The woman Elaine, she left the Hotel just after you started to follow the other woman Tracy, she was carrying a small hand luggage type bag and Alice decided that she would follow her and that I should remain in the car."

Sergeant Whitehead tried Alice's mobile.

"Alice, where are you? Where are you Alice?"

The phone just kept ringing, and Sergeant Whitehead started to panic.

Rather uncomfortably, and somewhat late, he remembered the warning that Morgan had given to him.

"That bitch Elaine is a very dangerous woman."

"Fucking Hell" he exclaimed.

"Loreto, which direction did she go?"

"She crossed the Via xx Settembre, and headed towards the Benedict School" she answered, as she pointed in the direction of the School.

The Sergeant jumped from the car, and started running in the direction he had been directed by Loreto.

As he turned the corner, heading in the direction of the Benedict School, he saw a screaming woman running away from the School grounds.

Sergeant Whitehead increased his speed until he entered the grounds, where his heart almost stopped!

A small group of onlookers watched as another member of the public was attending to someone lying on the ground.

The Sergeant ran towards the group, and it was then that his worst fears were horribly realised.

Alice was the person being attended to, she was lying on her back, and the man was trying his best to assess her injuries. Whitehead ran to where Alice lay and fell to his knees, abruptly pushing the man to one side, and urgently checking for signs of life.

There was none!

Whitehead then very carefully lifted Alice's lifeless body, and as he gently wrapped his arms around her, he cried out with grief, as tears streaked down his face.

CHAPTER TWENTY SIX

Detective Inspector Morgan had materialised in his flat after his revenge visit to the home of Clive Brookes.

He had phoned Steven Dukes and had arranged to meet him in the Victoria Hotel for a drink, or as he put it, a celebratory drink!

Consequently, they were both sat at the bar when Morgan's mobile started to ring.

"Ah Sergeant, it's good to hear from you so soon, have you locked up the lesbian bitches?"

"She has what!"

"You are fucking joking."

Morgan stood up from his stool.

"Sergeant, what did I tell you, you fucking idiot!" he shouted.

Morgan then threw his mobile to the ground in a flash of temper. He stood there for a few moments looking at the phone on the floor, and with his head in his hands, sank onto the bar stool, mumbling to himself.

"Fucking idiot, fucking idiot"

All the customers in the immediate area couldn't help but hear Morgan's outburst, and the barmaid, Brenda, asked him to calm down and watch his language.

Steven Dukes put his arm around his friend, trying to console him, and showing real concern, he asked.

"What's happened Peter? Has something happened in Italy?"

Morgan's head was still in his hands, and he was now resting his head on the bar, he just mumbled a reply.

"It's Alice, the WPC who was assisting Sergeant Whitehead, she's been killed."

"Oh Hell" answered Steven.

"I'm very sorry Peter."

Morgan stood up and turned to face his friend.

"Steve, I'm going home, I'll ring you tomorrow."

Morgan picked up his mobile from the floor and walked out of the bar.

As Morgan entered his flat he had calmed down significantly, so much so, that he decided that he should ring Sergeant Whitehead and apologise for his unwarranted outburst.

He removed his mobile from his pocket and tried to use it, unfortunately it wouldn't work.

"Oh bollocks" he shouted, as he deposited the phone back onto the floor!

Morgan removed his jacket, threw it over the sofa and poured a glass of wine.

After a while, once he had calmed down sufficiently, the phone was retrieved from the floor and Morgan began trying to sort out the problem.

He shook the phone, nothing happened, he removed the battery, and then replaced it, nothing.

Not being technically minded, Morgan was at a loss of what to do, so he decided to try connecting the phone to the charger, thinking that an electrical current would sort out the problem. Eureka!

The phone lit up, and, much to Morgan's relief, he was back in action.

He was just about to use the mobile, when his landline started ringing.

"Hello, Peter Morgan" he answered.

"Hello Superintendant, yes I've been talking to Sergeant Whitehead" Morgan confirmed.

Superintendant Jackson then started to speak, leaving Morgan in no doubt, that he was not happy with the manner that Morgan had treated the Sergeant.

"Detective Inspector Morgan, you've already made your opinions known to Sergeant Whitehead, but you should remember that we all regret the demise of WPC Alice Waterman, not least Sergeant Whitehead."

"We all perform our duties to the best of our abilities, and do you honestly believe that Sergeant Whitehead would intentionally put Alice in danger? Of course he wouldn't, he is absolutely devastated, he is inconsolable, and you Detective Inspector, have made it even worse."

"Now stop feeling sorry for yourself, and phone the Sergeant, and treat him in the way that he deserves, in the first part, as a bloody human being, and secondly, and more importantly, as your friend and colleague."

"Finally, I am going to arrange with our colleagues in Italy and Malta, for the two suspects to be brought back to this country, by Sergeant Whitehead. I will also arrange for Alice's body to come home, and in fact, I will be leaving London and travelling to see Mr and Mrs Waterman, sometime soon".

"Commander Kelly will be calling a meeting at the Station tomorrow and I will contact you when I know the time, now Detective Inspector, do yourself a bloody favour and phone your friend. Good night!"

With that final comment, the phone call was abruptly ended.

Morgan just sat there, realising, that he had been a real pillock! Then tentatively he picked up his mobile and phoned the Sergeant.

"Hi Colin, what can I say? I acted like a real dumb pillock, and I am very, very sorry" said Morgan, feeling that regardless of what he said, it would be insufficient.

"Hi Inspector, I don't blame you for the way you acted, I should not have left Alice in such a dangerous situation, It's my fault that she has gone."

Morgan could detect the deep sorrow in Sergeant Whitehead's voice, and tried to console him.

"Listen Colin, we all do our best, sometimes in very difficult circumstances, you have always performed well, regardless of the stresses and strains of the situation, and I'm proud to have you as my Sergeant, Colleague, and most of all as my Friend". Morgan continued, trying to get the conversation back on to the investigation.

"Anyway Sergeant, we have two criminals in our custody, and it won't be long before we have that lesbian Elaine!"

"I'm looking forward to your return to the Station, so we can again work together, and to bring the main culprit to justice."

"Me too Inspector, I'm looking forward to coming home"

"OK Sergeant, have a safe journey, and I'll see you soon, bye"

Morgan placed his phone on the sofa, but although he had apologised to the Sergeant, he still felt like a pillock!

Detective Inspector Morgan entered his office the next morning, still feeling sad over the murder of Alice, and his subsequent treatment of Sergeant Whitehead.

However, he reminded himself that time was of the essence, and he had to move on, especially regarding the whereabouts of Elaine Southern.

He sat at his desk and pondered the recent events;

We know that Elaine has a number of passports in her possession, she seems to be able to change her looks to suit the situation, and she could still have contacts in the criminal fraternity, especially the drugs trade.

But with her nearest and dearest in Police custody, who would she turn to for help? Who could she turn to for help?

Morgan's phone rang.

"Hello PC Dunn, I'd forgotten about you" was Morgan's honest reply.

"Morning Detective Inspector, I've just heard about Alice Waterman, its terrible news, I didn't know her, but it's terrible."

"You said it Constable, bloody terrible."

"Now have you any information regarding our Mr Novak?" asked Morgan.

"Not a lot Detective Inspector, he tends to spend most of his time assisting one of the local Distribution Centres with their agency staff".

"So far, I've not seen him in any of the indicated areas of prostitution, as we had expected."

"Although, there is one thing that could be of interest, he spends most evenings in the old Methodist Chapel, in Vale Park".

"He seems to have changed the building into some sort of living quarters for the agency staff that he provides."

Detective Inspector Morgan's interest was stimulated by this last comment, and he suggested what PC Dunn might do next by remarking

"Now that is interesting Constable, why not now concentrate your efforts in finding out what he is up to in that building?"

"As far as I was concerned, that building had been empty for a couple of years, if he is spending time there it won't be with the agency guys, there will be money involved, you can bet on it."

"OK Detective Inspector, I'll keep you informed". PC Dunn answered.

"Right Constable, speak to you soon."

As Morgan put down the phone, he remembered his damaged windscreen.

"I must get it repaired" he thought.

He phoned the same repairer that had previously informed him of his 'duff' Insurance, and arranged to take his car for inspection at noon, accepting that it would cost near to £500 if the windscreen needed to be replaced.

"If only I had checked the validity of my Insurance Company" he mused

Morgan was just about to visit the canteen, when his phone rang.

"Morning Superintendant, yes I'll be there directly."

Morgan had just been summoned to the Station Superintendant's office.

Morgan entered the office of the Station Superintendant Jackson, expecting a real bollocking, and was pleasantly surprised with the reception he received.

"Ah Detective Inspector Morgan, come and sit down" requested Superintendant Jackson. Commander Kelly was already seated at the meeting table, and he stood and shook the Detective Inspector's hand.

The Superintendant then opened the meeting.

Let me first state that the Commander and I, and of course, everyone within the Police Force and especially the Officers at this Station, regret the death of WPC Alice Waterman in the field of duty."

"But we have to move on, and this meeting is to discuss the details of her demise and to recommend changes, if changes are necessary."

"I can inform all present that Alice died of a broken neck, and that her death was instantaneous."

At this point Commander Kelly interrupted.

"Thank you Superintendant, yes we do need to move on and we need to talk about the investigation that sent WPC Waterman to Italy in the first place."

"I'm sorry Commander, but I had to mention Alice, although I agree, we have to discuss the investigation" answered Jackson.

The Superintendant then signalled to Morgan for him to take the meeting forward.

"OK Detective Inspector. Perhaps you could bring us up to date with the investigation the Commander is so worried about."

"Thank you Superintendant, I'll do my best" answered Morgan.

He updated the Commander and the Superintendant on the progress of the Jeff Thorne investigation, with special attention given to the pending evidence of Tina Woodside.

"So what about Tracy Bingham and Lucy Thorne?" asked the Commander.

"At this moment in time, they have refused to say anything, but that will change when they hear what Tina is prepared to say" assured Morgan.

"Where do you think Elaine Southern will have gone?" asked the Superintendant.

"We are keeping a close watch on her home, and of course the Health Club, but to be perfectly honest, she's like the Scarlet Pimpernel, she could end up anywhere" was Morgan's honest assessment.

"I think you should speak to your mate at the Daily Journal, see if he can bring the case more into the Public domain" continued the Superintendant.

To this suggestion, Detective Inspector Morgan agreed.

The Commander then ended the meeting by stressing a very clear warning.

"I do appreciate your endeavours, but we all stand or fall by our results, and you are no exception Detective Inspector, if this case is not sorted out, and very soon, your head will fall, so to speak."

This statement shook Morgan, he didn't think he should be treated, or his career talked about, in such a matter of fact way, but he accepted it, and left the meeting.

As he walked down the corridor he phoned Judy.

"Hi Honey Bug, are you still OK for tonight?" he asked.

"Very much so, I'm shopping at the moment, looking for a nice piece of Salmon as you requested my Peter Bug" she answered sounding very enthusiastic.

"OK Honey Bug, I'll be round at your place at eight, bye" answered Morgan, every bit as enthusiastically.

"See you later then, my Peter Bug."

Detective Inspector Morgan sat in the windscreen repairers waiting room, while his windscreen was being replaced, cursing the fact that it was going to cost him £525.

His mobile rang.

"Hi Constable Dunn, what can I do for you?"

"Detective Inspector, I am outside the White Swan Public House, our friend Kristopher Novak has just turned up in his car, with a young girl on the back seat."

"From where I'm seated, I can't see the face of the girl in the car, but some young women have turned up, and he seems to be collecting and distributing parcels to these women, from inside the car."

"How old are the women he's giving parcels to?" asked Morgan.

"I would guess, from fifteen to twenty years, there are five of them and they're taking it in turns to enter the front seat of the car to complete the transactions." the Constable confirmed.

"PC Dunn, be very careful, but try and get a photograph of all concerned, especially the girl sat on the back seat of the car." Morgan requested.

"OK Detective Inspector, I'll give it a go, and I'll phone you later tonight".

"Great stuff Constable."

Morgan then hesitated; he didn't want any phone calls after eight.

He continued

"Make sure you phone before err … no, come and see me tomorrow, in my office."

"OK Detective Inspector" the Constable answered, concluding the call.

Morgan rang the doorbell to Judy's home just before eight, and after a few seconds the door opened.

"Hi my Peter Bug" was Judy's greeting.

"Correct, and you are my Honey Bug" answered Morgan.

This brief exchange ended with them embracing and kissing lovingly.

Judy guided Morgan through to her lounge, and sat him down on the sofa.

"Now Peter Bug, don't move, I'll get you a drink, and then I'll finish the meal I'm preparing."

Morgan did as he was told although he had hoped Judy's request would be of a sexual nature.

However, he just sat there until Judy reappeared with his drink.

"Wow, how did you know that I liked Bailey's with Ice?" was Morgan's response.

"Because Peter Bug, you ordered the very same drink when we were on our first date."

"Oh yes, I did" admitted Morgan.

The night progressed more or less as Morgan would have liked, the meal Judy had prepared was very nice, and the desert, well the desert, Judy really did put everything into sex!

Next Morning as Detective Inspector Morgan entered his office his mind was more on Judy's body than on the day's prospectus.

He sat at his desk and pondered over their next meeting.

"Oh sod it" he exclaimed.

"It's time for a coffee."

This was an admission that work was the last thing on his mind.

Morgan walked to the canteen, where he met Ted Draper, who was seated with some of his staff.

"Bloody Hell, Inspector Morgan, just the guy I needed to see" Ted shouted.

"What's up Ted?" asked Morgan.

"It's about that bloody 'K' thing, you remember, the young girl that had the 'K' tattooed behind her left ear?"

"Great, tell me Ted, you've remembered where you last saw it?" answered Morgan expectantly.

"You got it in one" confirmed an excited Draper and continued. "It was a couple of years ago, but I eventually found the file, the name of the girl was Christine, Christine Jones, she was on the streets, but was eventually put with foster parents, Ed and Jane Whalley."

The name Christine didn't ring any bells with Morgan, so he asked.

"What do you know about these Whalley characters?"

"Not a lot, I'll get the guys to check them out, and let you know if anything transpires Inspector"

Morgan thanked Ted and returned to his office with his coffee, his mind was now more into Police Work, putting Judy on the back burner, for the moment.

He sat down at his desk, sipping at his coffee and turning the name Christine over in his mind, he just seemed to think that the name should mean something to him.

There was a knock on the door. "Come in" shouted Morgan.

"Ah Constable Dunn, come in, what do you have for me?" Constable John Dunn entered the office and sat at Sergeant Whitehead's desk.

"Well Inspector, if you remember our last conversation regarding our friend Kristopher Novak, I have some photographs."

PC Dunn provided a couple of photographs that he'd taken with his mobile phone that he had printed through his computer.

They clearly showed the faces of the young women who were in liaison with Novak, and a rather hazy photograph of the young girl seated in the back of Novak's car.

Detective Inspector Morgan checked out the photographs, showing particular interest on the one showing the girl on the back seat of the car.

"Come on Constable" said Morgan "Let's go and see Ted Draper."

They both left the office and walked to the Forensics office.

As they entered the department, Ted Draper was reading the morning paper.

"Now come on Detective Inspector, I said I would check out the Whalley's, but not that quickly" he joked.

"Ted, just have a look at this photograph PC Dunn took, can you 'tweak it', giving us a more defining picture of the girl's face, I need to show it to someone" said Morgan, thinking of the Christine that Judy had mentioned.

"Did you take the photograph with your mobile?" Ted asked PC Dunn.

Constable Dunn confirmed that he had used his mobile, and Ted Draper took the Constable's mobile and disappeared further into his laboratory.

He returned some five minutes later, offering Morgan a copy of the photograph of significantly better quality than before, clearly showing the face of the girl.

"It's the girl that we were talking about in the canteen, Christine Jones" confirmed Draper.

"Magic Ted" exclaimed Detective Inspector Morgan, as he and PC Dunn left Forensics.

As they walked back to Morgan's office and to use the Fax machine, Morgan phoned Judy.

"Hi Judy Babe, where are you at the moment?" he asked.

"What happened to Honey Bug?" Judy replied.

"Oh sorry, Honey Bug, but where are you?"

"I'm at work Peter Bug" answered Judy.

"Can you get to a Fax? If so, give me the number"

"Course I can, but why?"

"Never mind, Honey Bug, just give me the number, stay on the phone, and wait for my Fax" answered Morgan, getting slightly irritated.

Judy complied with his request, and waited for the Fax to come through.

As the Fax started to filter through the printer, Judy looked at the photograph that was appearing.

"Peter Bug, that's Christine Jones, the girl that told me about Katie."

CHAPTER TWENTY SEVEN

Morgan didn't say too much to Judy about the photograph, he just said that he would explain in more detail when they met as arranged in the Victoria Hotel, at six that night.

Judy was going to visit her mother in Birmingham for a few days, and they had arranged to meet for a quiet drink before she set off.

Detective Inspector Morgan phoned Luke Morley.

"Morning Luke, I have a photograph of some young girls, which PC Dunn and I, think may be involved in drugs."

"I'm sending the Constable round to see you, will you take a look at the photograph and give him any information that you and your guys may have on any of the girls?"

"Morning Peter, yes send him round, we'll share anything that we have."

Luke Morley continued with a question for the Detective Inspector.

"While you're on the phone, have you found any new stuff regarding our friend Novak?"

"Not really, but PC Dunn has been shadowing the pillock, so he can give you an update when he comes to see you, thanks again Luke, I'll speak to you later" answered a grateful Morgan, as he ended the call.

"OK Constable, get yourself round to the Drug Squad with the photograph, ring me later and we can discuss our next move."

"OK Detective Inspector, see you later" answered Dunn as he left the office.

Morgan leaned back in his chair with both hands on his head, and again he started to think about Christine Jones.

He posed two questions to himself;

Why was Christine looking for Katie?

And why did Christine go to Judy?

He kept churning these questions over in his mind;

Why look for Katie?

Why go to Judy?

The more Morgan thought, the more obvious it became, especially after seeing the photograph taken by PC Dunn.

Christine Jones was working for Novak.

She needed to find Katie, before Katie blew the whistle on Novak's involvement in child prostitution.

His line of thought was broken by his mobile ringing.

"Hi Sergeant, it's great to hear from you, where are you?"

"Hi Inspector, we are somewhere over France I think, we are due to land at Manchester Airport in about one hour, How are you keeping?"

"I'm good Sergeant, I must say, I'm looking forward to seeing you again, and I don't mind admitting it, I've missed you"

He continued.

"Sergeant, there is only one way to ask."

"Is Alice on the same flight?"

"Yes Inspector, her parents and Commander Kelly are meeting us at the Airport."

"OK Sergeant and our two suspects, are they with you?"

"Yes Inspector, Adelina and I have them, nice and close, they will NOT be disappearing!" stressed the Sergeant.

"Great, have a safe journey, and I'll speak to you sometime tomorrow, bye Sergeant."

"OK Inspector, see you later."

Detective Inspector Morgan thought for a moment, his mind going back to the Christine Jones situation.

"Shit, I promised the Superintendant, I must phone Steven Dukes" he mused, as he made the call.

"Hi Steve, would you like to do me a favour?"

"Hi Pete, firstly, I'm very sorry about your WPC, I could see that you were very upset when you found out."

"Regarding your question, yes, whatever you need, just say what it is" confirmed Dukes.

"Do you remember the Leila case?" asked Morgan.

"I certainly do"

"Well, we need to do something similar, this time it concerns a bird called Elaine Southern."

Detective Inspector Morgan then related the crimes that Elaine was accused of, and the urgency of knowing her whereabouts.

"What about involving the broadcasting media?" Dukes asked.

"That's an option, but we hope that keeping it in the local press may be the best option at the moment" stated Morgan.

Steven Dukes agreed to comply with his request, explaining that with his Editors agreement, he would place an article in tomorrow's morning and evening papers.

Morgan then ended the conversation by thanking his mate.

"OK Steve, thanks again, I'll speak to you later."

"Cheers Pete, speak to you soon"

Morgan was feeling hungry, and he was just about to make his way to the canteen, when there was a knock on the door.

He opened the door, to find Constable Dunn standing there.

"Ah, PC Dunn, you've finished with the Drug Squad, come, you can update me in the canteen, I'm bloody starving."

Detective Inspector Morgan grabbed the Constable by the arm and led him towards the canteen.

Morgan was halfway through a rather large Chicken and Bacon sandwich, when PC Dunn started his update.

"Detective Sergeant Morley and the Drug Squad guys know about Novak's exploits, using teenage and young women as an organised group of pick pockets and to distribute his drugs. They recognised all the women in the photograph, and they would be grateful if we could come up with some kind of evidence, that they could use in a prosecution."

"However, they didn't recognise the photo of Christine."

"As for the Methodist Chapel in Vale Park, they said that Novak is using it to house a number of his agency staff.

Immigration has made regular visits to the site, and all the incumbents have been cleared as being legal."

"Well done Constable" Morgan replied, as he almost choked on his sandwich.

He cleared his throat and continued.

"Keep the Methodist Chapel in your thoughts, but concentrate on the Whalley's."

"If Luke and his Guys don't recognise Christine, she may have just started to be involved, and if that's the case, why?"

"That's what we need to find out, why now?"

The Detective Inspector concluded the meeting, stressing.

"Liaise with Ted Draper regarding the Whalley's, and as always, keep your investigation low key".

"And keep yourself safe" he added.

When Morgan entered the Victoria Hotel, he could see that Judy was already seated, in one of their favourite booths.

He walked over to where she was seated, leaned over her, and started giving her a nice long kiss.

And he just kept on kissing, and kissing, and kissing, and …

"I wish we could continue Peter Bug, but everyone is looking at us, go and get a drink" suggested Judy as she pulled away from his embrace.

"OK, what would you like?" asked a slightly disappointed Morgan.

"I'll just have another Tonic Water, with a dash of Lemon" replied Judy, as she started to readjust her clothing.

Morgan walked to the bar, greeting Julie, as she served another customer.

Julie finished serving the customer and walked over to the area of the bar that Morgan occupied.

"What can I get you Peter? And who is the woman?"

"I'll have a pint of Bitter Shandy, and that woman will have a Tonic Water, with a Dash of Lemon"

Julie started to dispense the drinks.

"Well, come on then, who are you with?" Julie again asked.

"She is the most wonderful woman in the world" was Morgan's surprising, but as far as he was concerned, totally true statement.

"I thought I was that woman?" Julie asked.

"You are the second most wonderful woman" Joked Morgan.

They both ended up laughing until Morgan paid, collected the drinks, and made his way back to Judy.

"You seem to be very friendly with the bar staff Peter Bug?" queried Judy

"Yeah, I used to spend half of my life in this place. That is, until I met you Honey Bug". Morgan answered, as he leaned over, and kissed her on the cheek.

He then sat next to her and changed the conversation completely.

"Judy, what do you know about Christine Jones?"

"I only know what I previously told you, she used to be on the streets, but her life was changed completely when she was adopted by Jane Whalley and her husband Ed."

She continued.

The Whalley's have adopted many young girls, and they seem to be able to educate them into living a useful life."

"Did you handle Katie, during her life in care?" asked Morgan.

"No, her Care Co-ordinator was Tina"

Morgan was just taking a drink, and the mention of Tina, almost caused him to swallow the glass!

"Tina? Tina Who?" he spluttered.

"Tina Woodside, she used to work in Child Care Services, she left about two years ago, but I have to admit, I don't know where she is now"

"Why Peter, is it important?" Judy quizzed.

Morgan had a dilemma, should he tell Judy about Tina?

He decided that, as she doesn't know her whereabouts, and hasn't had contact with her for so long, that he wouldn't.

"Not really, it's just a point, that if we could talk to Tina, she may have some information, which could help to explain the actions of Katie".

This was Morgan's rather hurried, and more to the point a rather untrue answer.

Judy could sense by the expression on Morgan's face that he had struggled with his answer.

"Are you sure Peter? I could make some enquiries at the Centre, if it would help."

"No, don't worry about it, I'll get someone at the Station to find her, and to talk to her".

Judy looked at her watch.

"Peter, it's time for me to go, will you ring me tomorrow?"

Morgan tried to lighten the atmosphere.

"I'll ring you every day Honey Bug, until I have you in my arms again."

They finished their drinks and Morgan walked Judy to her car.

They embraced, and eventually, Morgan allowed her, to actually get into the car!

"I'll ring you around lunch time, Honey Bug."

"OK Peter Bug, I'll speak to you then, take care" answered Judy, as she began to drive the car away from where Morgan stood.

"Bloody Hell I nearly blew it" he cursed inwardly.

He didn't know why he didn't want Judy to know about Tina, he just wouldn't feel comfortable if she knew.

Morgan walked to his car, and as he sat down in the driving seat, he decided to phone Luke Morley.

"Hi Luke, did you know that Tina Woodside used to work in Social Services?"

"Hi Peter, yes, it did come to our attention, why, Do you think it is a problem?"

"I don't know Luke, but I have just found out, that Tina used to be a mentor to Katherine Simpson" Morgan stated.

"So what are you saying Peter, do you think there could be a link to young Katie's murder?" queried Luke.

"I don't know what I think, but we have to be careful, did you take Tina's passport from her before her release?"

"Yes, we released her on Police Bail, and she's agreed to report to the Station every five days and to phone every day, that is, until we can make a decision on her drug charge."

Luke continued.

"On another point, regarding the Jeff Thorne case, when are you going to interview the two suspects?"

"They're both in this country now and the interviews will start tomorrow morning" answered Morgan.

He continued.

"I'll ring you once they are finished, maybe we can meet for a pint tomorrow night?"

"That sounds just about perfect, OK Peter, speak to you tomorrow, bye".

"Yeah, speak to you later Luke".

Morgan placed his mobile in his pocket and drove home still thinking about the death of Katie and her possible relationship with Tina Woodside.

Next Morning as Detective Inspector Morgan entered his office he was greeted by Sergeant Whitehead.

"What time do you call this?" the Sergeant joked.

"Bloody Hell, Sergeant, it's great to see you" said an excited Morgan, as he hugged the Sergeant.

"It's great to be back Inspector, It's just great to see you and all my mates at the Station" answered an equally excited Sergeant. They parted and sat at their desks, both obviously glad to be back together.

"Right Sergeant, bring me up to date on our investigation, Oh, but first, how did the handover of Alice's body to her parents go?" asked Morgan.

"Everything went very well and her parents were very appreciative of our efforts, considering the circumstances."

"Commander Kelly had everything organised, all I had to do was to introduce him to Adelina."

The Sergeant then switched his comments to the case in question.

"As for the Jeff Thorne case, the two suspects Lucy Thorne and Tracy Bingham are in the Station cells, and the interviews can start as soon as you are ready Inspector".

"Have Legal Aid Solicitor's been made available?" asked Morgan.

"Yes Inspector, although Tracy Bingham has hired her own"

"That's good Sergeant, and what are the arrangements regarding Adelina?"

"The Commander has booked her into the Kings Hotel and she is due to return to Italy in a couple of days, but you'll have time to meet her before she returns home" confirmed Whitehead.

"Great Sergeant, now let's get down to business, we need to talk about the procedures we are to adopt at the interviews" said Morgan.

There followed a detailed discussion on all aspects of the forthcoming interviews, with the following decisions:

The first suspect to be questioned would be Lucy Thorne, starting at ten.

Both Whitehead and Morgan thought she would be the most likely to 'spill the beans'.

Tracy Bingham's interview would follow, with Sergeant Whitehead thinking that she was a 'real hard cookie', and it would not be easy to get her to talk.

"Right Sergeant, we're ready, lets have a quick drink, and then we'll give them hell" exclaimed the Morgan.

As Detective Inspector Morgan and Sergeant Whitehead entered the interview room, Tracy Thorne and her legal Aid advisor were already seated, and WPC Morton was also there, sitting on a chair in the far corner of the room.

Commander Kelly and Superintendant Jackson were seated in the adjacent viewing room.

Detective Inspector Morgan opened the proceeding, by introducing Sergeant Whitehead to the advisor, acknowledging that Lucy already knew who they were.

After the introductions Morgan started the questioning.

"Lucy, why did you and Elaine Southern go to Malta?"

"We needed a holiday" Lucy answered.

"If you were going on holiday, why did you dress as a man and use a false passport under the name of Mr Robin Hurst?" asked Morgan.

Lucy Thorne looked at her advisor.

The advisor said nothing, so she turned to the Detective Inspector.

"You must be mistaken Detective Inspector, we travelled using our own passports"

"Lucy, the Maltese Police could not find any passports belonging to you, or Elaine in the 'Villa Les', what did you do with them?" asked Sergeant Whitehead.

Again, Lucy looked at the advisor and again he said nothing.

"Elaine must have taken them when she went shopping Sergeant" she said confidently.

"Lucy, did you kill your husband?" asked Morgan.

Lucy's expression changed instantly, and she shuffled on her seat.

Looking directly at the advisor, she whispered.

"Do I have to answer?"

The advisor nodded.

"No" she answered.

"Did Elaine Southern kill your husband?" asked Morgan.

"No" she again replied.

"Lucy, are you a lesbian?" asked Morgan.

"No" she answered.

"So why do we have a photograph showing you, Elaine and others performing lesbian activities?" asked Morgan, pushing the photograph across the table.

This took Sergeant Whitehead by total surprise, as he had no knowledge of the photograph.

Lucy's reaction was more definite, she started to shake.

Morgan continued, almost shouting.

"And we have a lesbian called Tina, who incidentally is third from the left in the photograph, who has given us a statement;

that you ARE a lesbian and that you DID know that Elaine killed your Husband!"

Morgan continued as he stood up

"And the same Tina has a photograph of Elaine Southern burying your Husband, in her bloody garden!"

That was it.

Lucy's confidence disappeared in an instant.

She burst out crying, covering her face with her hands, and then, after a few moments, she started to mutter.

"Yes, yes, I knew, I knew, I can't go on, I can't" she cried out, before she burst into tears again.

Detective Inspector Morgan asked WPC Morton to attend to Lucy, saying that they would take a break.

After a break of some fifteen minutes, Lucy Thorne made a statement admitting that she knew Elaine Southern had murdered her husband, and that she had tried to escape punishment by using a false passport to travel to Malta.

"One down, one to go" claimed a very happy Detective Inspector Morgan.

Lucy Thorne had now composed herself and signed a printed copy of her confession, and was then returned to the cells.

During the break, before the second interview would start, Sergeant Whitehead took the opportunity to ask Detective Inspector Morgan a question.

"Where did you get that photograph Inspector?"

"Sergeant, from my very reliable source" Morgan replied.

"But when Detective Sergeant Morley told me about Tina Woodside, he never mentioned any such photograph" was Whiteheads next query.

"Sergeant, I took a chance, we had to get a result."

"Anyway, Lucy knew that Tina was there when the photograph was taken, she knew it was genuine, and that is why she gave in, incidentally, without looking at the bloody photograph" and this was Morgan's last comment on the matter.

Morgan then turned to the legal Aid advisor.

"Thanks Jim, I owe you one."

"Anytime Detective Inspector, anytime" answered the advisor, as he left the room.

Sergeant Whitehead just stared in amazement.

"So where did you get Jim from? From your reliable source?" he asked sarcastically.

"No. I've known Jim Western for ages" replied a very happy Morgan.

The Tracy Bingham interview was the exact opposite, of the one with Lucy Thorne.

She was everything the Sergeant had feared; Brash, Confident and as he had said 'a real hard cookie'.

Every time she was asked a question she would consult her brief, and he just advised her to say nothing.

Even the mention of Tina Woodside and her evidence against Elaine Southern didn't loosen her tongue.

This caused Detective Inspector Morgan to lose his temper on a number of occasions, and it was obvious to all concerned, that the interview needed to be suspended.

This they did, allowing Morgan to calm down, and he reluctantly agreed with Sergeant Whitehead, that the evidence against her was a little sketchy.

The end result was to release her on Police Bail, until a more positive case could be prepared.

After this interview, Detective Inspector Morgan and Sergeant Whitehead were summoned to the Superintendant's office.

"Well at least we have Lucy Thorne locked up, but how do you see the investigation, going forward Detective Inspector?" asked the Commander.

"We may have enough to charge Tracy Bingham with assisting an accused criminal, but to take the case forward we have to find Elaine Southern."

"Remember, we have the Tina Woodside evidence, when we finally apprehend Elaine, this evidence, will bring everything together" replied Morgan.

Detective Inspector Morgan continued, trying to be more positive.

"I now have Sergeant Whitehead back in the fold, we have the Daily Journal on board, and with us all in partnership, I'm confident this will be instrumental in a speedy conclusion to the case."

"I've seen the article on Elaine in the morning copy of the Daily Journal, your friend has done us proud, let's hope it stimulates someone's memory" said Superintendant Jackson.

"On a more personal matter, do you know the funeral arrangements concerning WPC Alice Waterman, Commander?" asked Sergeant Whitehead.

"Thank you for asking Sergeant, Alice's parents still have to finalise the arrangements, but they have assured me they will keep us informed" answered the Commander.

The meeting ended with all parties partially happy, all agreed things would only improve when Elaine Southern was finally apprehended.

Detective Inspector Morgan and Sergeant Whitehead returned to their office, and as they sat at their respective desks, Morgan posed a question.

"Sergeant, do you think we should have used Adelina, in the Tracy Bingham interview?"

"On reflection, she could have put some doubt into Tracy's mind, but I'm unsure. After all, Tracy Bingham is as tough as 'old boots'" answered Whitehead.

"Yeah, I tend to agree. While we're talking about Adelina, I'm going to ring Luke about going for a drink tonight."

"I'll suggest to him that we meet at six."

"Why don't you invite her along, it will get her out of the Hotel and give her the opportunity to meet the 'hub' of the Station."

"That could be a really good idea, I've arranged to meet her for lunch so with your permission Inspector I'll go now and talk to her about your invite."

"OK Sergeant, off you go I'll ring you with tonight's meeting details later."

The Sergeant left the office and this gave Morgan the opportunity to ring Judy.

"Hello Honey Bug, come home today, I miss you so much" was Morgan's hopeful request.

"Hi Peter Bug, I miss you too, but good things are worth waiting for" Judy replied suggestively.

"Ah well, I suppose I will have to manage without my Honey Bug for a few more days. How is your mother? I never asked before you left, but do you get on?" asked Morgan.

"Yes, we've always been like two mates, the next time I come down here, you can come too" suggested Judy.

This took Morgan by surprise, and he quickly made up an excuse to ring off.

"Yes I'm coming, sorry Honey Bug, but I have just been called to a meeting" was Morgan's get out clause.

"OK Peter Bug, call me tomorrow, bye"

"You can be sure of that Honey Bug" answered Morgan, as he put away his phone, in preparation of his imaginary meeting. The short conversation with Judy, even with its shock proposal to meet her mother, had really cheered Morgan up. Consequently, he phoned Luke Morley with a smile on his face.

"Hi Luke Baby, are you coming out tonight?" he asked.

"Bloody Hell, you're in a good mood, have you won the Lottery or something?" replied Luke.

"Time is too short to be miserable, let's meet at six, in the Victoria Hotel, Whitehead and his Italian friend Adelina will also be there" suggested Morgan.

"I have one piece of news, which could wipe the smile from your face Peter, Tina Woodside has not phoned in yet"

"Don't worry Luke, she's probably still in bed, I'll see you at six, cheers mate."

"OK Mr Happy. See you then"

Morgan's serious face returned.

He wondered if he should pay Tina a visit. Or should he request that she be given protection? He decided that there was no need to act just yet she had plenty of time to phone today.

Morgan stood at the bar having a laugh with Detective Sergeant Morley, when Sergeant Whitehead and the Italian Police Constable, Adelina Rossi, entered the bar.

Both Morgan and Morley stopped their conversation instantly. They just stared at what Morgan later described as a walking goddess!

Luke was the first to greet Adelina.

"Good evening, you must be Adelina, I'm Detective Sergeant Luke Morley may I buy you a drink?" he asked, as he led her away from the others.

"Bloody Hell Sergeant, you never said she was a walking goddess" stated Morgan, with his eyes firmly fixed on Adelina.

"Careful you don't twist your head off your neck Inspector."

"I didn't mention her beauty, because I didn't think it relevant considering the circumstances we were in when we met" answered a slightly irritated Whitehead.

Morgan sensed the Sergeant's irritation with the response from both him and Luke to Adelina's arrival and her beauty.

"Point taken Sergeant, now come, what's your poison, I'll buy YOU a drink" said Morgan, trying to pacify his Sergeant.

He ordered the drinks and both he and Sergeant Whitehead joined Luke and Adelina, who had sat in the same booth that Morgan and Judy usually used.

As the drinks flowed, all concerned became more relaxed with one another's company, but it became increasingly difficult to detach Luke from Adelina.

So much so, that Morgan began to feel a little uneasy with Luke's actions, so he waited until Adelina took a toilet break before he commented.

"Luke, you're acting like some sort of bloody limpet! Give the bloody girl some space you're becoming a bloody embarrassment."

"What do you mean? I'm only showing our gratitude for her assistance in Italy" replied Luke.

This answer didn't satisfy Morgan, so he stressed even more firmly.

"Well let me put it this way, if you don't calm down your attentions to the girl, Colin and I will be leaving and Adelina will be leaving with us!"

"Now change your bloody attitude, or sit and talk to your bloody self."

This final comment seemed to have the desired effect on Luke, who answered.

"OK Peter, I'll try my best to be more of a gentleman, it's not easy when I'm sitting near to a beauty like Adelina, but I'll try."

It was just after 0800 hours when Detective Inspector Morgan entered the Station canteen, in great need, of a large and very strong cup of coffee.

He used the self serve machine to fulfil his need, and then he made his way to his office.

Once in his office, he sat at his desk feeling like 'death warmed up'.

"Morning Inspector" said Sergeant Whitehead, as he entered the office.

Detective Inspector Morgan just mumbled "morning."

The Sergeant could see that Detective Inspector Morgan was suffering from 'alcoholic poisoning', so he went for the jugular! He then raised the tone of his voice significantly.

"How are you feeling today Inspector, could the bottle of Baileys you consumed last night have any bearing on this?"

"Quiet Sergeant, we're not at a football match" ordered Morgan. He then asked

"How did Adelina get back to her Hotel last night?"

"Well, once I managed to detach Detective Sergeant Morley from her, I ushered her into a Taxi, ensuring that she left for the Hotel, safely and alone!"

"Good work, Sergeant, the only thing I can remember of last night was Morley, making a bloody nuisance of himself."

The phone rang.

"Hello, Detective Inspector Morgan".

"Well, talk of the devil, how are you feeling today? Crap I hope."

It was Detective Sergeant Morley on the phone, he confirmed, that he did feel 'crap, but the reason for the call was serious, Tina Woodside had not phoned in yesterday.

"What about her phone, have you tried to contact her?" asked Morgan.

"Course I have Inspector, but to no avail, I've sent a couple of my guys to her flat, they should ring shortly, hopefully with some positive news."

"Bloody Hell Luke, I don't like the sound of things, if your guys find her, they should bring her back to the Station until we can set up some kind of protection do you agree?"

"Yes, on reflection I think we should have done that before we gave her bail."

"OK Luke, keep me informed, speak to you later."

Morgan relayed to Sergeant Whitehead, the content of the phone call from Luke Morley, and then started to update the Sergeant on the ongoing investigations.

This discussion continued for some fifteen minutes when the phone rang.

"Detective Inspector Morgan"

"You are fucking joking, how was she killed? She had what!"

"Bloody hell, Luke, we have to find the twat"

"Right Luke, once Forensics have finished, get your guys to turn the bloody flat over, apart from finding the pillock who has murdered Tina, we need to find that bloody photograph."

"OK Luke, ring me soon, hopefully to say you've found it, bye" was Morgan's final, rather hopeful comment.

He turned to face Sergeant Whitehead, who was still sat at his desk.

"Sergeant, the woman that we were just discussing, Tina Woodside, she's been found dead, and not content with killing her, some lowlife has cut out her bloody tongue!"

CHAPTER TWENTY EIGHT

Detective Sergeant Morley's team, did search Tina's flat extensively, but the much wanted photograph wasn't found. So when the Drug Squad members returned to the Station, Luke Morley's phone discussion with Morgan didn't contain many words of comfort.

"We did find a couple of floorboards that had obviously been disturbed, and maybe that is where the photographs were stored" suggested Morley.

He continued.

"However, the building opposite houses some more expensive dwellings, with CCTV cameras, and my team are to study the tapes."

"Maybe we should call for Constable Dunn, if that bird Elaine turns up, he is the one to recognise her arse" joked Morgan, trying to maintain his sense of humour when all he wanted to do was strangle the said Elaine.

"What did Ted and his Forensic team, say about the death?" asked Morgan.

"Apart from the cause of death being a broken neck, and the time of death around lunch time, he hasn't found any other evidence that would be useful" Morley answered.

"OK Luke, thanks for the update, maybe you should call and update the Superintendant."

"If your guys see anyone that looks anything like our friend Elaine on the tapes, give me a shout" requested Morgan.

"You got it. See you soon Detective Inspector"

Morgan sat back in his chair, and with both hands on the back of his head, turned to Sergeant Whitehead.

"Well Sergeant, what do we do now?"

"I have a sneaky feeling that Elaine Southern is still involved with drugs and still in contact with Novak."

"Maybe we should concentrate on Novak and his illegal activities, and with a little luck, we catch two birds, so to speak" answered Whitehead.

"You're exactly right Sergeant, we need a team meeting"

Morgan picked up his mobile and phoned PC Dunn.

"Hi Constable, where are you?"

"You're in bloody bed!"

"Oh, sorry Constable, can you make a meeting in my office at noon?"

"Right Constable, I'll see you then, bye."

Dunn had informed Morgan that he was in bed when he phoned having been on his covert activities most of the night.

"Right Sergeant, PC Dunn will be here at lunch time, and we'll decide on our next move at that meeting."

Morgan's phone rang.

"Hello, Detective Inspector Morgan."

"You have? We're on our way."

"Come on Sergeant, we have some tapes to view."

They left the office and made their way to Forensics.

As they entered the office, Ted Draper was in discussion with Detective Sergeant Morley.

"Ah Detective Inspector, come, have a look at this" said Ted, as he waved the Inspector and Whitehead towards the large screen he had erected.

"Bloody Hell Ted, you really have got things organised." complemented Morgan, as he, Whitehead, Morley and some of Morley's team, took their places in front of the screen.

Ted had already wound the tape to the pertinent position, before he turned it on.

When the tape started, they could see a figure wearing a long overcoat, loitering close to the entrance to the flat where Tina lived.

When someone walked up to the flat entrance, entered the appropriate code, and entered the building, the figure quickly followed.

"Well I can't see the arse!"

"And I would assume a wig is being worn, but I'll bet my annual salary that Elaine Southern is back" stated Morgan.

"What time was that taken?" asked Morley.

"Just thirty minutes before noon" answered Ted.

"What do you think Sergeant Whitehead?" asked Morgan.

"I agree with you Inspector, that person, although wearing an overcoat has the same stature as our suspect, but, isn't Elaine's neck a little longer?"

"But you can't see the neck, because of the bloody overcoat!" claimed Morgan.

"Maybe so, maybe so," conceded Whitehead, although he was still unsure, that the figure in the overcoat was the elusive Elaine

The Detective Inspector then changed the subject.

"What about the Tina situation Ted, found anything?" he asked, hopefully.

"There is one thing Inspector, behind the left ear, yes you guessed, a large K."

"We'll soon have to check behind the left ear of all the Station staff" Morgan joked.

Ted Draper then continued.

"As for evidence, unfortunately, nothing, whoever the perpetrator's are, they are well organised."

There followed a general discussion regarding the Tina murder, until Morgan ushered Sergeant Whitehead towards the office door, asking Luke before they departed.

"Luke, have you updated the Superintendant?"

"I've arranged a meeting at two, Inspector" he answered.

"OK, if you need any information from me, give me a ring" he answered, as he left the office.

As they walked down the corridor, Morgan asked Sergeant Whitehead if he would call in to the canteen and get him a Chicken and Bacon sandwich, and a cup of coffee.

Whitehead agreed and made his way to the canteen, Morgan carried on to his office and a call to his dream woman.

"Hi Honey Bug, are you missing me" said Morgan, trying to sound sexy, but failing.

"Hello, my Peter Bug, I am always missing you" purred Judy.

"When are you coming home, I need you?" yearned Morgan.

"I'll be back tomorrow night, around seven, if you come over to my place, we can catch up, Peter Bug" was Judy's sexy invitation.

"I will …"

Sergeant Whitehead entered the room.

"I will be there" was Morgan's stunted reply, as he ended the conversation.

"Who was on the phone?" asked Whitehead.

"Oh nobody" replied a slightly uncomfortable Morgan.

"It was your bird, Inspector, it was your secret woman!" the Sergeant joked, as he pointed to the Inspector.

"Oh shut up. Give me my sandwich, I'm bloody starving."
End of conversation as far as the Detective Inspector was concerned.

Morgan was halfway through his sandwich, when his mobile rang.

"Hi Steve, how are you today?" he answered.

"Hi Peter, what's the latest on this Tina Woodside murder?" asked Steven Dukes.

Detective Inspector Morgan explained in detail all the facts surrounding the murder to his friend from the Daily Journal. He ended by asking Dukes.

"Have you had any contact from the public, regarding sightings of our lost friend, Elaine?"

"No Peter, we have had a few crank calls, but nothing positive."

"OK Pete, speak to you later" answered Morgan.

He had just returned to eating his sandwich, when PC John Dunn, knocked on the door and entered the office.

"Come in Constable, talk to Sergeant Whitehead, while I finish this bloody sandwich!" complained Morgan.

After a couple of minutes the Detective Inspector was ready again.

"Right Constable, bring Sergeant Whitehead and me up to date with your investigation."

"Yes Inspector, you told me to concentrate on the Whalley family's activities."

"Well, this I did, but I found it particularly difficult, owing to the fact, that they always seemed to go out at different times and in different directions."

"However, on one occasion, I observed Jane Whalley and the girl called Christine visit the Methodist chapel in Vale Park."

Detective Inspector Morgan's eyes widened.

"Great stuff Constable" he exclaimed.

Constable Dunn interrupted Morgan.

"It gets better Detective Inspector; they were welcomed at the door, by no other, than Mr Kristopher Novak."

PC Dunn then produced his mobile and showed the hazy photograph that he had taken of Novak, Whalley and Christine at the door of the Chapel.

Detective Inspector Morgan jumped up from his chair.

"Bloody Great, This could be the break we have been looking for. But we need to be more professional, we can't be offering this type of photograph, as evidence, we need to provide something more concrete."

He continued offering his perception of their next move.

"We also need to be 24/7; all of us need to be consistently involved, covering the Whalley's and Novak."

"What do you think Sergeant?"

"I agree Inspector, PC Dunn has done a good job, but it's like he said, working alone, he couldn't cover all the suspects."

There followed a lively discussion on the additional staff they could need, in order to move the investigation forward to a 24/7 activity.

Morgan knew that Sergeant Morley didn't have anyone he could spare, and, more importantly, Superintendant Jackson, at this stage of the investigation, would be reluctant to authorise the release of other Officers from their respective duties.

With this knowledge, Morgan summed up their possibilities.

"Well chaps, it looks like we have to go it alone, at least until we have some concrete information that would turn the Superintendant's head."

"With this in mind, I suggest that you Sergeant, concentrate on Novak, you Constable, will continue with the Whalley's, and I will concentrate my attention on the Methodist Chapel."

"What about overtime Inspector, I have quite a lot already?" asked PC Dunn.

"You just work the hours that are necessary, I'll make sure that you're paid accordingly, as for the Sergeant and I, well, we will have to see maybe a few days leave when the investigation is concluded."

They started to discuss the Detective Inspector's plan, when the phone rang.

"Detective Inspector Morgan"

"Yes Superintendant, OK, see you soon".

Detective Inspector Morgan had been summoned to a meeting with Detective Sergeant Morley and Superintendant Jackson.

"Well Guys, I have to go, keep me informed with your progress, and I'll speak to you both on a daily basis" said Morgan to his team as he left his office on his way to see the Superintendant.

The meeting with Superintendant Jackson went as expected, the Superintendant talked about what was needed, and Detective Sergeant Morley and Detective Inspector Morgan told him how it was.

When Morgan returned to his office, both Sergeant Whitehead and Constable Dunn had already left to prepare for their covert duties.

Morgan sat at his desk and pondered his next move.

He decided that he would start his part of the investigation, by checking out the Methodist Chapel.

To this end, he left his office and headed for his flat, intending to get some sleep, before he ventured out into the night.

Morgan entered his car at ten minutes past midnight. As he encouraged the engine into life he began to wonder why the hell he was out at that time of the night.

Consequently, he hesitated for a while, but he knew what he had to do.

He drove to the Methodist Chapel in Vale Park, parking his car a couple of streets from the Chapel.

As he approached the Chapel, he could see that the building and the surrounding area's were in total darkness.

Initially, Morgan just walked around the perimeter of the Chapel from a distance, ensuring that he had not been seen by anyone within, or anyone passing the building.

Once happy that he had not been observed, he moved significantly closer to the Chapel building. He then wandered to the rear of the Chapel where there was an outside yard surrounded by a fence of possibly two metres in height.

Morgan peered through a gap in the fence where he could see a black Mercedes parked adjacent to what looked like a rear entrance to the Chapel.

"How many agency guys could afford to run that car?" he mused.

Morgan continued to walk the perimeter of the Chapel, often wondering if he should go into Transit Mode.

He decided that he needed more information about the layout of the building, before he could use his special powers.

With this in mind, Morgan returned to his flat with the intention of returning to the Chapel, in Transit Mode once he had checked over the building layout.

Next morning Morgan arrived at the Station just before nine, calling as usual into the canteen for a coffee on his way to his office.

Once he was at his desk, he used the internet to investigate the Methodist Chapel building in Vale Park.

The layout was as he would expect any place of worship, a central aisle with pews on either side. This led to a central pulpit with an organ at one side, and seating for the choir at the other. Just behind the organ, was a door that led to some kind of meeting room, and to another door that led to a cellar area.

His mobile phone rang.

"Morning Ted, what can I do for Forensics today?"

"Morning, Detective Inspector, I have some very interesting news for you, last evening, my team and I attended to a call regarding a body that was found in Pitts Woods."

"After a thorough examination of the body and various Forensic tests, it became clear that it was your missing friend, Elaine Southern!"

CHAPTER TWENTY NINE

Detective Inspector Morgan made his way to Forensics, to talk to Ted Draper about the discovery of Elaine Southern's body. "Now Ted, give me the sordid details, how did the bitch meet her maker?" asked Morgan, as he entered the Forensics department.

"Morning again Detective Inspector, our friend had meted out to her, what she used to do to others, namely, a broken neck."

"Oh dear" said Morgan sarcastically.

He continued.

"How was she found?"

"She was discovered by a woman walking her dogs through the woods, and it was the dogs that started to uncover the body from a shallow grave."

"How long had she been dead?"

"I would estimate three days, which means, if you're thinking what I think you're thinking, that rules her out of the Tina Woodside murder" answered Ted, having anticipated Morgan's next question.

"Exactly Ted, so Sergeant Whitehead was right, the person on the CCTV tape, wasn't our friend Elaine, which means that we have to readjust our thinking on Tina's murder."

"One last thing Ted, was she a member of the K club?"

"No Detective Inspector, it looks like she never had the pleasure" Ted joked.

"OK Ted. I'm going for a late breakfast, fancy it?"

"No breakfast for me Inspector, I've eaten already, but I'll come with you, and you can buy me a cup of tea."

With that comment from Ted, Morgan and Ted Draper left for the canteen.

After satisfying his hunger, Detective Inspector Morgan returned to his office, and once again started to study the layout of the Methodist Chapel.

He decided that when he performed the Body Transit, that he would materialise on the cellar stairs.

He knew that Novak had altered the ground floor of the Chapel, incorporating rooms to accommodate his agency staff, and with this in mind Morgan's thinking was that the cellar would be the safe option, where he expected the layout would have remained much the same.

He picked up his mobile and phoned Judy.

"Hi Honey Bug, I'm still missing you, can't you come home now?" was Morgan's plea.

"Hi Peter Bug, I wish I could, unfortunately, my mother has twisted her ankle, and I have to stay for a couple more days" Morgan's world seemed to collapse, as he heard the words 'a couple more days'.

"Oh Honey Bug, I'm very sorry about your mother, but do you have to stay so long?" he pleaded.

"I'm afraid so, I have to stay until she's confident with her ankle, I'm sorry Honey Bug" was Judy's genuine response.

When his call to Judy ended Morgan was distraught, it was the thought of having to wait a few more days before he could get to grips with Judy's body again.

He consoled himself by kicking the waste bin against the office door!

Shortly after, there was a knock on his door and Superintendant Jackson entered the office.

"Morning Detective Inspector, I have just heard about the demise of Elaine Southern, and as I was passing your office, so I thought I would get an update".

Morgan was shocked.

He'd never known the Superintendant venture from his own office!

"Morning Superintendant, sit yourself down and we can go over the latest details" answered Morgan, and then proceeded to outline the progress of the investigation;

"As you know, our main suspect on the Jeff Thorne, WPC Waterman and Tina Woodside murders, Elaine Southern, has parted this world."

"Her real life partner, Tracy Bingham has returned to her job at the Health Spa, and at this moment in time, we do not think that she is involved with any of the murders."

"We do however still think that our Mr Novak, and possibly Ed and Jane Whalley, are involved in child prostitution, and could be involved with the said murders."

"With this in mind, Sergeant Whitehead, Constable Dunn and I are involved in a covert exercise that we hope will provide the necessary evidence against Novak and his associates."

"When do you expect to obtain this evidence?" asked Jackson.

"If we don't get something within the next five day's or so, I will be very disappointed" admitted Morgan.

"OK Detective Inspector, I'll expect something in five day's time" said Jackson as he stood and walked towards the door.

"Oh, by the way, the funeral of WPC Waterman has been arranged for tomorrow at two, you'll get a confirmation email, make sure you and the rest of your staff attends."

After that comment, the Superintendant, rather abruptly left the office.

It was obvious to Morgan that the Superintendant was not entirely happy with the progress being made, and he might regret his statement that evidence may be forthcoming.

He rang Sergeant Whitehead.

"Sergeant, how are you getting on with our friend Novak?"

"Hi Inspector, at the moment I've only been able to confirm what PC Dunn has already told us, he spends a lot of time in the Methodist Chapel in Vale Park" answered Whitehead, disappointed at not adding to Dunn's findings.

"OK Sergeant, keep at it, oh by the way, it's Alice's funeral at two tomorrow, don't be late"

"I'll be there Inspector" answered Whitehead sadly.

The Sergeant then asked.

"Are you coming to see Adelina, before she takes her flight home tonight?"

"I'd like to Sergeant, but I'm too busy. Give her my best wishes and thank her for all she has done for us."

Morgan had forgotten that Adelina was leaving tonight, but he was more concerned with his visit to the Chapel.

"OK Sergeant, speak to you tomorrow."

Morgan then rang PC Dunn.

"Constable, how are you? Tell me that you've found out something exciting" he asked, feeling a little desperate.

"You could say that Detective Inspector, early last night, just after nine, I observed Ed Whalley with another guy in the passenger seat, drive two teenage girls from the Chapel in a black Mercedes".

"He drove to a private house on the Grange Estate on the East side of town."

"The other guy escorted the girls inside the property, and it was a couple of hours, before he returned to the car with the girls, and then they all drove back to the Chapel."

"Which entrance did he use?" asked Morgan.

"He drove into the yard at the rear of the building, by the time I reached a viewing position, they had already gone inside, I assume he used the door close to the bins" answered PC Dunn.

"Bloody fantastic Constable, that's just what I wanted to hear."

"Constable, I will be observing the chapel tonight, so you keep concentrating on the Whalley house."

Morgan continued.

"It's the funeral of Alice Waterman at two tomorrow, so we'll catch up when that has concluded, see you then. Great work Constable"

Detective Inspector Morgan sat back in his chair, with his hands in their usual 'thinking' position on the back of his head, and a smile as wide as the English Channel.

His mood having changed since the Superintendant had left his office.

There was a light shower of rain falling as Morgan parked his car. It was just after midnight, and he was just one hundred metres from The Methodist Chapel.

He wanted to make one last observation on any activities that may be ongoing before he made his entrance.

The Chapel was in total darkness as expected when Morgan made his approach, and as he peered through the same gap in the fence he could plainly see that the black Mercedes car.

The car was parked in the yard, just as he and PC Dunn had previously observed.

Once he was satisfied he started the transit;

Think PETER, Visualise; Top of Cellar steps, Methodist Chapel.

As he materialised, he stumbled on the cellar stairs banging his head against the wall, he wiped away the blood, and quickly looked around his surroundings.

He was standing at the top of a well-lit flight of twenty or so stairs, which led to a door at their base.

Morgan slowly and quietly descended the stairs, listening for any noise from beyond the door.

All was quiet he noticed a light switch to the right of the closed door, which he used to switch off the light to the stairs, before he slowly opened the door.

He stood at the beginning of a dimly lit corridor with four 'prison like' cells to his right and what was obviously a toilet and shower facility to his left.

As he walked slowly along the corridor looking inside the cells he could hardly believe what he was observing, in each locked cell slept one teenage girl, they were all very much asleep, so much so, that he had to assume they had all been drugged.

Morgan wanted to shout out loud to show his feelings against such a situation, but common sense prevailed and he continued to the end of the corridor, where there was another door with a small central window, through which he could see Novak, drinking what looked like Vodka and playing cards with another two men.

The room where they played was obviously used as the sleeping quarters of the two men, who were probably employed as guards on the girls he had seen in the locked cells.

Morgan hesitated.

He could see that behind where Novak was seated at the far end of the room, there was another door, and he had to find out where it led.

Think PETER, Visualise; yard next to Mercedes Car.

"Perfect" he thought, as he materialised a metre from the car.

Morgan walked over to the building, looking for an entrance to the cellar.

Apart from the ground floor entrance close to the waste bins, no other entrance was visible.

"There must be an entrance to the cellar somewhere" he mused.

As he stood, there was a noise from the building, and Morgan quickly crouched down behind the waste bins.

A section of the wall just slid to one side, and one of the card players entered the yard.

The player entered the Mercedes car, removed a packet of cigarettes and returned to the Chapel, closing the walled section behind, as he descended a flight of stairs.

"So that's how the buggers get in" whispered Morgan.

Now that Morgan knew how to get into the Chapel from the yard, he had to find the entrance to the cellar, from inside the Chapel building, but how?

After a few moments of thought, he decided that he had to take a chance he had to enter the living quarters of the Agency Staff.

As far as he was concerned, he had to materialise no more than a metre from the top of the cellar stairs.

"OK then Morgan" he whispered to himself.

Think PETER, Visualise; Top of Cellar stairs, Methodist Chapel.

Morgan materialised in the location he had arrived at earlier.

Think PETER, Visualise; one metre to the right.

When he materialised, Morgan was in a store room, but unfortunately, one foot was on the floor, and the other foot was on some racking.

This caused him to fall, hitting his head on the racking as he fell.

The recent wound he experienced at the top of the cellar stairs reopened, which resulted in more blood to wipe from his face.

"At this rate, I'll need a bloody blood transfusion before I can go home!" he muttered.

He began to observe his surroundings.

"This must have been the meeting room, on the original layout" he muttered.

He looked at the wall; he knew that the cellar stairs were just behind the wall.

"Maybe it slides open like the yard", he thought.

After a few pulls and tugs, a section of the wall slid to one side, exposing the cellar stairs.

"You have to push against the wall slightly, before it disconnects and will slide open, very clever" he thought.

Think PETER, Visualise; one metre from my parked car in the street.

As he materialised, the rain was really pelting down and he quickly jumped into his car.

Morgan drove home feeling very proud of himself he had materialised exactly where he intended every time, and his only minor mishap, was a cut just above his left eye.

Next Morning It was just after 0700 hours, when Detective Inspector Morgan entered his office and prepared for his meeting with Sergeant Whitehead and Constable Dunn.

Morgan had already phoned them both from his flat, arranging a meeting in his office for eight.

He printed a copy of the Methodist chapel layout from the internet, marking on it the secret entrances to and from the cellar.

Morgan then rang Luke Morley and Superintendant Jackson, arranging a meeting in the Superintendant's office for nine.

Constable Dunn was the first to arrive, his first comment being.

"What have you done to your eye Detective Inspector?"

"Oh nothing, I walked into the bathroom door" he lied.

Morgan and Dunn were talking about the Methodist Chapel, when Sergeant Whitehead entered the office.

"What have you been up to Inspector, has that bird of yours given you a smack?" he smirked.

"Never mind my bloody eye did you see Adelina on her way?"

"Yes Inspector" answered Whitehead.

"Well cast your eyes over this" Morgan demanded.

Morgan then explained the alterations to the layout concerning the cellar doors, and the layout with the cells that contained the girls.

"How did you find out about the cellar?" asked Whitehead.

"My source Sergeant"

"And did your source tell you about the girls Inspector?" asked PC Dunn.

"Exactly" answered Morgan.

"Have you been in the cellar?" asked Whitehead.

"No" answered Morgan.

"Who is this source Inspector? He seems to know bloody everything, about everything" stated Sergeant Whitehead suspiciously.

Morgan raised his voice, stressing to the Sergeant.

"I've told you before Sergeant, my special source does know what he's talking about, and you can rest assure that the cellar layout is as I say, and it does contain the poor bloody child prostitutes."

"So what's our next move?" asked Dunn.

"I've arranged a meeting with the Superintendant and Luke Morley, for this morning at nine; we need to plan a raid on the Chapel premises tonight"

He continued.

"As I see it, it is important that we catch Novak in the cellar, and my source tells me that he is always in the cellar once the girls have returned from satisfying their clients. So, we wait until the anticipated visit the girls will make to their clients is over and they have been returned to the Chapel."

"You, Constable will lead a team on a raid at the Whalley's home, and you Sergeant will lead a team at Tracy Bingham's apartment."

"Sergeant Morley and I will accompany the rest of the team, we will enter the Chapel premises dressed as Immigration Officers, and will give the occupants the belief, that we only checking the validity of their passports etc."

"There will also be a unit of Special Firearms Officers on call in one of the side streets adjacent to the Chapel."

"Will there be a Special Firearms Officer with me?" asked Sergeant Whitehead.

"Sergeant, if you can't handle Tracy Bingham without armed support, you're in the wrong job" answered Morgan scathingly.

"Any more questions?" he asked.

"What if Tracy Bingham isn't at home" asked Whitehead.

"Well to start with Sergeant, she is supposed to inform us, if she is leaving the City, or living anywhere other than her apartment, the second thing, Sergeant, if she doesn't answer the door, break the bloody thing down!"

He then ended the meeting, with the comment,

"Right, let's go and talk to the Superintendant."

They left the Detective Inspector's office and made their way to the meeting with Superintendant Jackson and Detective Sergeant Morley.

"Ah come in Detective Inspector" said Jackson, as he greeted the Detective Inspector and his team and ushered them into his office.

"What's happened to your eye Detective Inspector?

"Oh nothing Superintendant, just a small accident" answered Morgan.

"It's his bird Superintendant, he can't control her in the bedroom" joked Luke Morley.

Luke was already sat at the meeting table, and when all the others had stopped having a good laugh at Morgan's expense, they all settled down into their seats, and the Superintendant opened the meeting.

"Detective Inspector Morgan requested this meeting it concerns a request to carry out various raids within the City tonight. So without further ado, I'll hand over to Detective Inspector Morgan, so that he can put his request to the meeting."

Morgan updated them all regarding the ongoing investigation into Kristopher Novak and his associates, specifically regarding child prostitution, and outlined the plan of action he had already explained to Sergeant Whitehead and PC Dunn.

"So you expect me to authorise warrants on three properties, on the information from one of your informers, who by the way, is a total unknown to anyone but you Detective Inspector?" asked a very serious looking Jackson.

"Superintendant, both Constable Dunn and I have witnessed the use of young girls as child prostitutes, by Novak and his cronies."

"We know that Novak deals in drugs, but as Detective Sergeant Morley will tell you, we don't have the evidence to prosecute."

"We know they operate from the Methodist Chapel in Vale Park, specifically with the child prostitutes, why wouldn't we want to put them out of business?" asked an exasperated Morgan.

Superintendant Jackson thought for a moment then turned to Luke Morley.

"What do you think Detective Sergeant?"

"Well Superintendant, I agree that we are taking a chance, especially when using the Special Firearms Unit, but if we can prosecute the scumbag Novak and his gang, then I think it's a risk worth taking."

Another pause from the Superintendant, obviously churning over in his mind the relevant facts as presented.

"OK, I'll arrange for the warrants, I'll also inform Sergeant Thompson of the Firearms Unit, and you can go ahead as planned.

But one thing Detective Inspector Morgan, if you make 'a balls' of this your career could be over."

He then continued.

"You can all return to my office after we have put WPC Alice Waterman to rest."

"What time, Detective Inspector?" he asked Morgan.

"Between seven and half past should be OK" answered Morgan.

Jackson continued.

"Detective Inspector Morgan can finalise the members of each raid team, and my secretary will have the appropriate warrant paperwork."

The Superintendant then closed the meeting and ushered them out of his office.

They all made their way to the canteen, and, as Morgan put it, a well-earned chicken and bacon sandwich.

Once he had disposed of the sandwich in double quick time, Detective Inspector Morgan left the others in the canteen for he had someone to ring.

With this in mind, he made his way to his office sat in his chair and phoned his perfect woman.

There was no answer.

"Bloody hell", he moaned.
"Where has she gone now?"
"Typical woman" he thought,
"Never around when you need them"
He then decided to go home and get himself dressed and ready
for the funeral of Alice.
He would ring Judy again, after the funeral.

WPC Alice Waterman's funeral was very well attended; a
sombre occasion, and according to the wishes of her parents, it
was a celebration of a lovely human being.

As Detective Inspector Morgan left the activities to return to his
flat, he was more aware what a wonderful person Alice really
was, and he would surely miss her.

CHAPTER THIRTY

It was just after 1900 hours, when Morgan returned to his office, with one thing on his mind, to ring Judy.

He sat down at his desk and dialled her number.

No answer.

Morgan began to wonder if anything had happened to Judy, he didn't know the address of her mother, or her mother's telephone number.

He was beginning to wonder if he should phone the Care Centre to ask the Manager if she knew Judy's mother's details.

Sergeant Whitehead entered the office.

"You're looking rather pensive Inspector, worrying about tonight?"

Morgan looked up and his expression changed.

"Nothing worries me Sergeant, come, let's go and meet the others."

They walked to the Superintendant's office where most of the others had already gathered, including Sergeant Thompson from the Firearms Unit, and two WPCs.

Detective Inspector Morgan collected the warrants from Superintendant Jackson's secretary, and passed Sergeant Whitehead and Constable Dunn their copies.

Detective Sergeant Morley soon entered the office, carrying varying sizes of Immigration Officer outer coats, which he just threw on the floor.

Detective Inspector Morgan then undertook a visual roll call on those in attendance, and when he was satisfied, he opened the session.

"Right gentlemen and ladies, listen up, I will now outline the expected flow of activities in chronological order.

Morgan then talked through the plan he had devised, stressing to all, that nothing was likely to happen until the child prostitutes had been returned to the Chapel, and this was expected to be between eleven and midnight.

He also stated that he wanted all personnel in place by ten thirty, stressing that they should split into small groups and park in different places, as this would be less noticeable to the general public and others.

Once everything was in place, Morgan would then give the go ahead to all concerned and the raids would begin simultaneously.

He then asked for any questions.

"Will my Officers be staying outside the Chapel until required?" asked Sergeant Thompson.

"Yes Sergeant, Detective Sergeant Morley, six of his staff, the two WPCs and I, posing as Immigration Officers, will secure the ground floor of the premises."

"Your first team will be called into the Chapel when we are ready to enter the cellar from within the Chapel."

"Your second team will position themselves at the rear of the Chapel, within the yard, and adjacent to the secret door to the cellar."

"And as already stated they will only act if and when someone from the cellar tries to use the hidden entrance as their route of escape."

"Any more questions" asked Morgan.

None were forthcoming.

"Right, gentlemen and ladies, thank you for your attendance, take this opportunity to prepare, and to all those in the Immigration team, you can select your coat from the ones on the floor."

It was just before 2200 hours when Detective Inspector Morgan rang Constable Dunn.

"Where is the Mercedes?"

"It's parked outside No. 3 Gable End Road, Inspector, Ed Whalley is still sat inside the car, and the other guy and three of the girls have been inside the premises for the last thirty minutes" answered the Constable.

"Right, phone me back when they leave Constable."

Morgan then phoned Sergeant Whitehead.

"Any sign of Tracy Bingham Sergeant?"

"There's been no sign of her at all Inspector I arrived here just after eight thirty, so she must have arrived home before that time."

"OK Sergeant, as you say, we have to assume that she is in her apartment, ring you later."

Morgan turned to Detective Sergeant Morley and Sergeant Thompson.

"Gentlemen, everything seems to be as we expected, so I suggest that we take up our respective positions."

They all agreed and left the Station to organise their teams, and to travel to the predetermined waiting areas.

It was 2255 hours, when Detective Inspector Morgan received the call from Constable Dunn; the black Mercedes was on its way back to the Chapel.

He turned to Luke Morley.

"Another ten minutes and the car will be here."

Luke Morley just nodded, impatient to get his hands on Novak.

Morgan was standing some twenty metres from the premises as he watched the Mercedes pull up outside the Chapel yard.

He moved closer to the fence so he could observe the car being parked, and the occupants enter the Chapel.

Once he was satisfied, Detective Inspector Morgan walked back to where Detective Sergeant Luke Morley and the rest of the team were parked.

He then phoned Sergeant Whitehead and then, Constable Dunn."

"OK guys, GO!" was the message.

Morgan then phoned Sergeant Thompson.

"OK Sergeant, time for your guys to get into position, and wait for my call."

THE RAID HAD STARTED.

Detective Inspector Morgan, Detective Sergeant Morley and their team quickly made their way to the front entrance of the Methodist Chapel.

They knocked on the door and were greeted by one of Novak's so called Agency Staff.

The relevant introductions were made, the warrant was served, and with all the formalities concluded, Morgan and his team marched inside the Chapel.

The search began within the rooms that were occupied by the incumbents, but it was only a casual search and Morgan and the team moved swiftly from room to room.

Searching in this casual way brought some strange looks from the occupants, some twenty in all.

The main complaint emanating from them was why they had to put up with these continual checks when, as the authorities already knew, they were not connected to an Agency, and anyway they were the same group of people that had been checked many times before.

Once the initial searches were over, all the Chapel occupants were ushered into one of the living quarters, along with four members of Luke Morley's team, who would supervise the passport checks.

This of course was just a ploy, keeping them all occupied whilst Detective Inspector Morgan organised the introduction of the Special Firearms Unit.

The Detective Inspector had by then, phoned Sergeant Thompson, inviting him and his unit into the Chapel.

As soon as the Firearms Unit arrived, Morgan directed them all to the storeroom, where he quietly, opened the door to the cellar.

As soon as the secret door was opened and they all had assembled at the top of the stairs, they could hear that 'All Hell' seemed to have broken loose, in the room below.

Detective Inspector Morgan and his team just stood to one side, and allowed the Firearms Unit members to descend the cellar stairs and into action.

Morgan, Luke Morley and their team just waited at the top of the stairs, until they heard Sergeant Thompson shout.

"OK Detective Inspector, it's safe to come down."

Apparently, Novak, Ed Whalley and two of Novak's men, had tried to make their getaway, through the rear entrance of the cellar, but had been apprehended by the second Special Firearms Unit.

Detective Sergeant Luke Morley was in heaven. He and his Drug Squad had been trying to catch and prosecute Novak for years, and the success of the operation showed in his face.

Detective Inspector Morgan concentrated on the cells, and the release of the unfortunate girls.

Once the cell doors had been unlocked, he allowed the two WPCs to usher the unfortunate girls, now six in total, into the toilet and shower facility to tend to their needs in private.

Once Morgan was satisfied that the girls were being looked after, he walked into the yard and phoned Constable Dunn.

"Now Constable, tell me you have executed the warrant, and that you have arrested Jane Whalley and Christine?"

"You have? Great stuff Constable, now turn the bloody place over."

"I'll see you back at the Station."

He then rang Sergeant Whitehead.

"Sergeant, did you arrest our friend?"

"No!"

"She wasn't there" answered the Sergeant.

This news really deflated Morgan.

"OK Sergeant, check out the bloody place and return to the Station"

Detective Inspector Morgan rather disappointedly returned to the cellar, where there was an air of real excitement.

"Detective Inspector Morgan, or should I say Superman" exclaimed an excited Luke Morley.

"It has been a total pleasure observing your organisational abilities and control during this raid, you were bloody well fantastic" he continued, as he shook Morgan by the hand. Morgan just answered.

"Thanks Luke"

Luke noticed the lack of excitement in Morgan's voice.

What's wrong Peter?"

"That bloody Tracy Bingham, pillock. She's bloody well disappeared again."

Back at the Station, it was just after 0330 hours and all of those arrested had been charged and booked in, and then locked up in the cells for the night.

Detective Inspector Morgan, Sergeant Whitehead, Detective Sergeant Morley and Constable Dunn all met in the Detective Inspector's office.

The Detective Inspector was still seething over the disappearance of Tracy Bingham, but the 'Copper' in him had come to the fore, and he was acting like the professional that he was.

He'd called the meeting to discuss the relevant facts of the raid and to plan the necessary activities for later in the day.

His intention was to keep the meeting as short as possible, bearing in mind that they all had a very busy day and everyone needed some sleep.

Detective Sergeant Luke Morley, on the other hand, was still on 'cloud nine', he was continually talking and cracking jokes, it was very unlikely that he would be able to sleep for a considerable time.

"Calm down Luke, we have to decide on the interviews and who will conduct them" pleaded Morgan.

"Sorry Peter, but I've waited so long to get that bastard!" Luke replied, with reference to Novak.

"OK, well that's sorted, Detective Sergeant Morley will interview Novak" stated Morgan.

Morgan then continued.

"Detective Sergeant, cast your mind away from Novak for a moment, what evidence did we get from the raid at the Methodist Chapel?"

"Well, apart from catching the bastard with his hands in the till, so to speak, we recovered a vast amount of Class A drugs and maybe up to twenty thousand pounds of obvious drug money" answered a still excited, but decidedly calmer Morley.

Morgan then turned to Sergeant Whitehead.

"Now Sergeant, did our friend Tracy, leave anything of interest to us in her apartment?"

"There wasn't anything that we could use to bring charges Inspector, most of her personal items had gone, so I would say that her departure is most likely to be permanent" answered Whitehead glumly.

"OK Sergeant, your next move is to instigate the usual checks at the Airports etc. and check her bank account, check on money transfers and the like."

"OK Inspector, I'll get on it first thing tomorrow, or I mean later today" confirmed the Sergeant.

"Now for the Whalley's, we'll have to interview them separately, how did Jane take to her arrest Constable?" Morgan asked PC Dunn.

"Initially she didn't say much, but once in the wagon, and on our way to the Station, she became very forthright, muttering about some woman from the Care Services."

Morgan interrupted Constable Dunn.

"What woman? Did she mention a name?"

"She said that a woman called Judith had been, as she put it, poking into their affairs for a couple of days, asking lots of questions, about Tina Woodside."

"Were these recent days?" asked Morgan.

"It appeared so, Detective Inspector, she also mentioned that the Judith woman had asked how Christine was being treated and what contact, if any, she had with Kristopher Novak."

"Did she ever mention Tracy Bingham?" asked Morgan

"Jane Whalley just muttered that

"Tracy would stop the interfering bitch and…"

Morgan stood up from his chair, interrupting the Constable in mid sentence.

"I'm sorry Gentlemen, but I have to go."

He then sped from the room, quickly followed by Constable Dunn.

"Detective Inspector, Inspector" shouted the Constable, as Morgan rushed down the corridor.

"Go back Constable, go back to the office, I have to go somewhere, tell Sergeant Whitehead that I'll ring him shortly" answered Morgan, as he disappeared round the bend in the corridor.

Constable Dunn returned to the office, saying to the others as he entered.

"What did I say, what did I say?"

"Never mind what you said, what did the Detective Inspector say to you?" asked Luke Morley.

"He just said to tell Sergeant Whitehead that he would ring him shortly."

"Shortly, what the Bloody Hell does that mean?"

"And where did he go Constable?" asked a dumbfounded Sergeant Whitehead.

"I don't know Sergeant, he just said that he had to go somewhere" answered an equally puzzled Constable.

Detective Sergeant Morley then made his intentions clear.

"Well it's nearly fifteen minutes before four, I don't know about you two, but I'm bloody tired, I'll give the Detective Inspector until half past four and if he hasn't rung by then, I'm off to my bed!"

After a brief discussion, they all agreed to wait until half past four for the call, and if there wasn't a call by then, it was bed time for them all.

Morgan didn't bother with his car, he ran into the Gents toilet, made sure that he was alone, and then;

Think PETER, Visualise; Lounge, Flat 34, Vickers Road.

Morgan materialised in the lounge as he had expected, and his worse fears were immediately realised.

There had obviously been a fight, because the room was in total disarray.

Many of the ornaments were broken and lying on the floor, the television was on its side, and its screen was smashed.

Morgan was putting his gloves on, when he looked towards the bedroom, and it was then, that his world fell apart!

Someone's foot was clearly visible on the floor in the doorway, as he moved towards the foot more of the prone body became exposed, and for some unexplainable reason tears were already appearing in his eyes.

The tears were soon flowing freely, as Morgan recognised the body of his beloved Honey Bug, lying on the floor, with her head turned at a very acute and abnormal angle.

Morgan sank to his knees, now crying uncontrollably, he tenderly caressed the body of his beloved Judy, pulling her close to him.

He began to talk to her lifeless torso as if she would be able to hear what he was saying;

"Why, oh why did you not tell me?"

"Why did you not tell me?"

"My Love, My Love."

CHAPTER THIRTY ONE

It must have been five minutes, before Morgan composed himself.

He lifted his Judy from the floor and carried her into the bedroom, where he placed her on her bed, arranging her clothing as if to make her more comfortable.

HE NOW KNEW WHAT HE HAD TO DO!

But first, he had to get Judy moved to a more appropriate place. He walked to the door to the flat and checked that it wasn't locked then he removed his mobile phone from his pocket and phoned Sergeant Whitehead.

"Hello Sergeant, I have something that I need you to do."

"Bloody Hell Inspector, where are you?" asked Whitehead.

"I'm at Flat 34 Vickers Road, the Body of a Miss Judy Armitage can be found in the bedroom, organise for her to be taken to the Station Morgue, or, and inform Ted Draper."

"What about you Inspector, are you waiting there, or are you coming back to the Station?"

"Never mind about me Sergeant, just do as I ask" replied Morgan, as he ended the call.

"Was that the Detective Inspector?" asked Luke Morley.

"Yes, but something's wrong, he sounded very strange" answered Sergeant Whitehead, he then continued.

"I have to go, Constable Dunn, can you contact Ted Draper and organise the Morgue Guys to attend at Flat 34 Vickers Road? I'll meet them there."

"OK Sergeant, but what about Detective Inspector Morgan?" asked PC Dunn.

"Never mind the Inspector for now, we will have to do as he has asked" answered Whitehead.

They all then left the office, with Luke Morley stressing.

"I'm coming with you Sergeant Whitehead."

As Whitehead and Morley entered the Station car park, they could see that Detective Inspector Morgan's car was still parked in its designated parking space.

"That's the Inspector's car, how the bloody hell did he get to Vickers Road?"

Exclaimed a very surprised and worried, Sergeant Whitehead.

Morgan materialised in the empty apartment of Tracy Bingham, he couldn't help but notice Sergeant Whitehead's handy work on the door.

"Sergeant Whitehead must have used a bloody bomb" he mused appreciatively.

He hopefully searched the drawers of the computer desk, but there was no photograph of the yacht.

His continued his search for any documents concerning the yacht in the rest of the apartment, but this proved fruitless.

He just stood there for a while in the centre of the lounge, thinking of his next move, he then muttered to himself.

"OK I'll just have to go to the place where the photograph was taken."

He had decided to take a chance, he was so confident that he would find his 'prey' on the yacht that he decided he would "Just have to bloody find it!"

Morgan materialised in his flat, changed into jeans, casual shirt, trainers and a hooded jacket, and placed a change of clothes and another pair of trainers into a shoulder bag.

He pocketed a couple of hundred Euros from his holiday fund, and then to the internet, to interrogate the area of his destination, Almeria, Spain.

Detective Sergeant Morley and Sergeant Whitehead arrived at Judy's flat, and once Sergeant Whitehead had put his gloves on, he tried the door and was pleasantly surprised, to find it unlocked.

"That's good, I'm fed up with smashing doors down" he muttered.

"Never mind Sergeant, I'm sure we could have handled the door together" Morley assured him.

Whitehead cautiously entered the flat closely followed by Luke Morley and they made their way to the bedroom, and, just as Detective Inspector Morgan had told them, they found the body of Judy Armitage on the bed.

As they looked at Judy's body, Luke Morley commented.

"She looks so peaceful, what was Peter's relationship with her?"

"I don't know Luke, maybe she was the bird he's been seeing" answered a totally rattled and confused Sergeant Whitehead.

"Do you think the Inspector has a good idea who is responsible for Judy's demise?" asked Morley.

Sergeant Whitehead thought for a moment, and then answered.

"Bearing in mind that the Inspector made his disappearing act as soon as Constable Dunn relayed to the meeting what Jane Whalley had said;

'Tracy would stop the interfering bitch', I have to conclude that if we find Tracy Bingham, we will find Inspector Morgan."

This they were both agreed upon, but taking into account the seeming ease and speed of movement that the Detective Inspector seemed to enjoy, his mode of transport was also of concern.

There followed a brief period of relative quiet as they both conducted a quick search of the premises, which was interrupted by the appearance of Ted Draper in the apartment.

"Bloody hell Sergeant Whitehead, do you always have to call on me in the early hours of the bloody morning?" was his grumpy entrance.

"I'm sorry Ted, but I wish that we all were excused this situation" answered Sergeant Whitehead, as he led Ted into the bedroom.

"Who am I looking at Sergeant?"

"Her name is Judy Armitage, and we think that she was in a relationship with our Inspector" confirmed Whitehead.

"You mean Detective Inspector Peter Morgan? So where is he?" asked Ted.

"He has been here, Ted, but he's gone….."

Sergeant Whitehead hesitated.

"Well to be honest Ted, we haven't a bloody clue on his whereabouts."

Ted Draper then stated

"Oh that's a real pity Sergeant, because I've just learned of something very interesting regarding Mr Ed Whalley, something that the Detective Inspector needs to know."

Their conversation was interrupted by Detective Sergeant Luke Morley's mobile;

It was the Desk Sergeant back at the Station.

"Hello, Detective Sergeant Morley"

"Yes Sergeant"

"You are fucking kidding!"

"When did you say? Twenty minutes ago?"

"Sergeant, How the bloody hell did he get out of the bloody cell?"

Luke Morley started to pace impatiently about the flat as he listened to the rest of the call, he then shouted to Sergeant Whitehead.

"Sergeant, come on, we have to go that 'Bastard' Novak has escaped!"

Morgan materialised on the Envia Hotel golf course, the sun had risen just an hour ago, and he was surprised to see so many golfers already using the course.

"Fore" he heard, as a golf ball flew no more than a metre from his head.

Morgan ducked, but well after the ball had landed!

"Bloody golfers" he muttered, as he walked off the fairway and onto the adjoining road.

He was heading towards the Marina, and his search for Tracy Bingham's yacht.

As he walked along the Calle Formigal that wandered along the perimeter of the Marina, he couldn't help observing the very expensive looking boats and yachts moored there.

This left him feeling a little jealous of the money that some people had at their disposal.

It was a few minutes later, as he watched a couple of young girls preparing to lie in the sun, that the name 'Sunseeker' entered his mind.

Morgan instantly knew that he had seen that name on the photograph of the yacht, which he had studied in Tracy Bingham's apartment.

Assuming that this name could be a make of yacht, he centralised the name Sunseeker into his search.

After about twenty minutes he reached the Beach Front Spa Hotel, so with his search producing nothing and feeling a little parched, he walked into a café for a cool drink, and perhaps a rethink.

Sitting in the sun, and peering over all the boats moored in the Marina, he started to think about his Honey Bug, and tears started to form in his eyes.

Morgan finished his drink, wiped his eyes and walked into a small shop adjacent to the café, where, he purchased a tin of lighter fuel and a hunting knife.

The search continued for a further twenty to thirty minutes, until the name on the side of one of the yachts caught his eye.

The name was 'Yacht Les'.

Morgan knew that he had also seen that name somewhere before, so he moved a little closer.

"Yes!" he shouted, he could see the yacht makers name quite clearly on the bow, 'Sunseeker'.

Walking away from the yacht, Morgan began to think of his next move, especially how to react when, as he hoped, he came face to face with his target.

He decided to observe the scene from a discreet distance, while focusing his mind.

He looked around noticing that there was another café only fifty metres away from where the yacht was moored, so that's where he headed.

Once at the café, he located a suitable table outside on the veranda from where he could plainly see any movements to and from the 'Yacht Les'.

Once seated in this observation position, Morgan practiced in his mind the move that he intended to employ, when, as expected, Tracy Bingham would try and immobilise him, and possibly worse. Putting to use the Karate skills that Morgan was convinced she had at her disposal.

Time passed and Morgan was feeling a little agitated that nothing had stirred.

Just as he was wondering if he should get a little closer, there was movement.

A figure appeared on the deck of the yacht, stretched, had a quick look around the Marina, and then disappeared below deck again.

Morgan's heart started to race, his prey had surfaced!

He quickly moved towards the yacht, deliberately slowing his pace as he got closer, and, peering through one of the open portholes he could plainly see the partly dressed figure of Tracy Bingham.

Not even thinking if anyone else could have been aboard, he quickly jumped on to the yacht and down into the living area below deck, where Tracy was standing.

She obviously had heard his entrance and turned quickly to face him.

"Jesus, Detective Inspector Morgan!" she shrieked.

"Yes, Detective Inspector Morgan" was Morgan's initial answer.

He continued.

"Are you surprised Tracy Bingham!"

Morgan had practised his next move, so he wasn't surprised when he observed Tracy's body tense in preparation for a forward surge.

When her movement became imminent, Morgan made his move first.

He lunged forward fending off her anticipated Karate forward strike with her right fist, with his left arm, and with his right hand, he thrust the hunting knife under her rib cage and deep into her heart.

This he followed by grabbing hold of her body in a vice tight grip.

Her body started to shudder, but he held her tightly and looked directly into her face as the blood pumped from her wound.

After what felt like an eternity to Morgan, but was only a matter of minutes, he saw her eyes close and simultaneously, he felt her grip on him relax.

He hesitated slightly, and then with blood still oozing from her body, he allowed her to drop to the floor.

His emotions for what he had just done were Nil!

As far as he was concerned, he had avenged the death of his loved one, his lovely, lovely Judy.

Morgan quickly retrieved the shoulder bag he had left on the upper deck, and changed his clothes and trainers.

The bloodied items and the shoulder bag were then purposely placed on to Tracy Bingham's prone body and sprayed with lighter fuel.

Morgan then sprayed the surrounding area with the fuel until the container was emptied.

He made a quick check outside of the yacht, ensuring that the area was clear, before he lit the fuel and made his exit, throwing the hunting knife into the harbour as he left.

Morgan swiftly made his way towards the café from where he had initially observed the yacht, once at the café, he hesitated slightly and turned to check the scene, he was surprised how quickly the fire had spread.

He could clearly see flames licking through the open porthole. Satisfied that he was done, he casually walked away, taking one last look at the burning yacht as he turned and headed up the Calle Formigal on his way back to the Hotel Envia.

Once at the Hotel he decided to enjoy a drink before he journeyed back home, so he took a seat adjacent to the Hotel pool and ordered an Amstel Beer.

When his drink arrived, he just sat there in the sun, relaxing and enjoying the pleasant surroundings, he was now acting just like any other tourist, what he had just done was conveniently erased from his mind.

Only when half the beer had been drunk, and when Morgan had started to feel a little light headed, did he decide that he should make his way to the golf course, where he could transit back to the UK.

Once on the course, he entered a small secluded area of bushes close to the eighteenth green.

By now Morgan was feeling very tired, so he prepared himself quickly for his entry into Transit Mode.

Think PETER, Visualise; My bathroom UK.

Nothing happened!

Morgan took a deep breath, and tried again.

Think PETER, Visualise; My bathroom UK.

Again nothing happened!

Morgan was now feeling really dizzy, so much so, that he was finding it very difficult to breathe, never mind to concentrate, but concentrate he must.

Think PETER, Visualise; My bathroom UK.

DETECTIVE INSPECTOR PETER MORGAN just collapsed sideways to the floor, life slowly leaving his exhausted body.